SUSIE NEWMAN

This is a work of fiction. The events and characters described herein are imaginary and are not intended to refer to specific places or living persons. The opinions expressed in this manuscript are solely the opinions of the author and do not represent the opinions or thoughts of the publisher. The author has represented and warranted full ownership and/or legal right to publish all the materials in this book.

Diaries
A Collection of Short Stories

v5.0

Outskirts Press, Inc.
http://www.outskirtspress.com

ISBN: 978-1-4787-1479-8

Library of Congress Control Number: 2012922367

PRINTED IN THE UNITED STATES OF AMERICA

RUTHIE

waste not these few,
precious earth years.
The bird of life
has but a short arc
of time to fly
Soon - —ah,
how sadly soon!-!—
It will slip its earthly form
and vanish
into the infinite.

Moments of Truth
Excerpts from the Rubiayat of Omar Khayyam
Explained
by Paramhansa Yogananda

January 1, 1999

Today is a good day. The sun is shining brightly through my bedroom window and a large beam of sunlight sits in the middle of the room. I've been watching dust particles dance in the spotlight, and it's been pretty. I bet nobody ever thought that they would hear me say dust is pretty. I don't think it's pretty when I look over at my bureau and see it all laid out like a dirt blanket resting on top of my beautiful cherry wood. But swirling around in circles, caught in a beam of light, that's pretty. And not just pretty, but peaceful and poetic.

Maureen and the boys have been here all morning. Maureen has put a large roast and sauerkraut in the slow cooker. The smell of the roast has drifted and filled my room. It's mixed with the smell of lilac pillow spray that Donnell buys and sprays profusely when she comes to visit me. She was here last night for my New Year's Eve party, so my room got plenty drenched with the smell of lilacs. I believe these may be my two favorite smells: lilacs and a slow-cooking roast filling my home with warmth, a smell that reminds me of family and gives me a sense of calm. Everyone knows I've always loved lilacs, for their scent as well as their beauty. It's quite a shame the flower comes and goes so quickly. Lilacs are the reason Earl and I had a spring wedding, it was so I could carry a bouquet plum full of lilacs.

Maureen's boys, as hyper as they are, have been quite good today. Troy was pretty revved up earlier and kept shouting at Maureen that he needed to be somewhere, but Maureen stood her ground this time and hasn't let him leave. The boys have learned if their mom says no, all they have to do is ask her three more times, and she will say yes; however, today Maureen is set on keeping the boys here, at least for now. I even told her when she came in to check on me that it is probably very hard for a sixteen-year-old boy to spend a day with his sick grandma and grouchy granddad. I said, "It is so boring here, Maureen; it's fine if Troy wants to go see a friend."

But she said, "No, Mama, that boy is in and out socializing all the time, and it will not hurt him to spend New Year's Day at home with family. Besides, I'll cut him loose tonight for his friends."

Earl got out the playing cards and poker chips and started teaching the boys different types of poker games. That calmed Troy down a bit. I think he may even be enjoying himself. Maureen gave me my pills about an hour ago, and like always, they have knocked me for a loop.

Maybe I'm just tired from all the partying we did last night. Yeah, boy, did we have a party. Everyone I love and I have ever known came through my door last night. The kids and Earl really did go out of their way. I saw cousins I hadn't seen in a while, and all my neighbors were here. The wonderful ladies from church brought food and drinks and stayed late into the night. I believe they even helped clean up. Thanks to this new Internet and e-mail stuff, those kids of mine were even able to get a hold of my oldest high school friends. I saw people I hadn't seen in years. There were even a couple people here that at one time, I had difference with, but I can't remember why, and I suppose they don't recall either, 'cause they too came to my party, and I welcomed them in, just the same, and it felt good to be surrounded by all. Each one of those individuals has touched my life in one way or another, and we all came together for just one night in time. My night.

The invitations that Beverly sent out were beautiful. She used pretty poinsettia paper and had one of my favorite Bible verses scripted at the top. *"The Lord is my rock, my fortress, and my deliverer: my God, my strength in whom I will trust; my buckler, and the horn of my salvation and my high tower." Psalm 18*

Beverly also wrote that my party was an open house from the hours of 6:00 p.m. to 1:00 a.m., so people kept coming and going all night long. That way, it didn't get overcrowded. The spread of food was impressive and beautiful. It must have cost a fortune, but for once in my life, I am not going to worry about it or ask. There was every type of casserole you could think up. A large spiral-sliced ham sat in the center of my table, with its plate covered in pineapple rings. There were baskets full of dinner rolls and my prettiest crystal butter dish filled with soft butter. There were baked beans, green beans, lima beans, and bean soup. I was truly worried that my whole house was going to get gassed up, but I guess the bean eaters took off before they started farting, because I didn't smell anything foul going on. We had scalloped potatoes, baked potatoes, potato wedges for the kids, and potatoes au-gratin. We had cakes and pies and cookies and brownies. Beverly made sure the table had a shrimp plate (that she refilled probably four times) and a gigantic fruit bowl heaping with three different colors of melons and strawberries.

Michael was in charge of picking out the music for my party, and he put Troy in charge of playing it; they both did a wonderful job. Folks sang and danced to tunes from Elvis Presley, Johnny Cash, Frank Sinatra, Tony Bennett, and Roy Orbison. Once Donnell set up the karaoke machine, it was Donnell's picks and country the rest of the night—not true country, just new country. That is, except for when Michael sang "*They can't take that away from me.*" Oh, my beautiful Michael; there was not a dry eye in my house when he sang to me. His smooth voice and silly smile as he danced around my chair with jazzy steps, "*The way you wear your hat, the way you sip your tea, the memory of all that, no, no! They can't take that away from me.*" It was the highlight of my evening. Donnell singing the whole Shania Twain CD was nice too. Good job, honey. I loved watching you have so much fun.

Thank you, Michael, Beverly, Maureen, and Donnell. I have such good kids, but now I'm so tired, I think I'm beginning to slur my words and my eyes refuse to stay open. I'm going to sing myself to sleep with memories of last night and dedicate it to my four beautiful children.

"*The way your smile beams, the way you sing off key (not you, Michael), the way you haunt my dreams, no, no they can't take that away from me! We may never, never, meet again, on the bumpy road to love, still I'll always, always keep the memory of...*"

Michael woke me at 7:30 p.m. with a kiss and a plate of dinner. I slept the day away, and the world went on spinning without me. It's such a hard realization to come to, but I must. I just have to accept my fate. Michael, my boy, is so in tune with me. He read my mind and then he held my hand, and said, "Mama, it is because of you that we are able to be so okay. You grew us strong."

My Michael, the youngest of my four children and my only boy, he is such a lady's man. He always has the right words to say, the right presents to give. This tape recorder that he gave me for Christmas is absolutely the best present I could have been given. How did he know that my journaling had become so very painstaking? My hands were constantly shaking. It was taking hours, sometimes days, to put one thought or prayer down on paper. Now I just talk, which is what I've always been best at doing anyhow. I lay my new tape recorder on top of all my new Christmas bedding and pillows that Beverly gave me, and I talk. I suppose what I'm intending to do is leave my mark. I was here! See my handwriting, hear my voice; this is what I thought and felt and left behind. I want to give my children a glimpse of me, all of me. Not just me as Mama or me as Mrs. Snodgrass. I was someone before I was your daddy's wife, and I was someone before I was your mother, and I was someone before cancer. I still am that special someone. As any mother and any wife, most of my life was spent behind the scenes of our life's drama.

"Dear God, let people remember me, the true me."

January 2, 1999

I am Ruth Anne Carroll-Snodgrass, but I insist my friends just call me Ruthie. My favorite color is purple and my favorite meal is Thanksgiving dinner with all the trimmings. My favorite holiday has always been Easter, and it is also my favorite time of year. I simply love the spring and the waking of a new season. I love the yellow and purple crocus poking through the soft new grass. I even love how the rain washes the snow into the earth and everything smells and looks wet, like it just had a bath. I love the howling of the wind, perfect kite flying weather, spring. I love the children's new spring clothes, little girls in daffodil-yellow dresses and little boys in knickers and ties on Easter Sunday morning. I love Easter egg hunts and Easter lilies, chocolate rabbits, and baskets filled with green plastic grass and hidden treats. I believe I will miss it this year.

Dying is so damn hard. The hardest thing I've ever done. Cancer itself has been no picnic. First it took my left breast and then later it took my right. Oh, how terrible I thought it was to lose my breasts. I felt cut and robbed, degraded and then cast aside, or at least my boobs were.

I know it sounds silly, especially after forty-eight years of marriage, but I worried about Earl. I mean he is such a boob man. I think they, meaning my boobs, may have been how I caught him in the first place. He liked my tight pink sweater, the way it stretched across my size 36 C chest. He liked going up my shirt when we were dating, cupping my breast as he kissed me. He liked my boobs when we were naked; he would stare at them, and then he would begin kissing them, and it felt good. I had such nice boobs. I nursed all four children; Michael, the longest. He was hard to wean 'cause I knew he was my last baby. By the time Michael came along, I was so worn out from the girls at night, I needed all my rest, so I would simply lay the baby down between me and Earl and unbutton my nightie to my navel. Michael would climb into my clothes and form into the crevices of my body. Nice and cozy and warm, he would latch on. When he fell asleep, he would let go, and when he woke, he would blindly root around for a nipple, as if he were a puppy, latch on, and go back to sleep. He cried and cried, when I finally began to refuse him, except it was time. The boy was more than two and had begun to lift up my shirt in public; or just whenever he wanted a little nip. He called it titty milk. Earl taught him that term, and it infuriated me. I wanted him to just call it milk or num-nums or something cute like that. I didn't like to hear my baby calling for titties.

Losing your boobs to cancer is one thing, but losing your life is entirely another. It's not that I'm afraid to die. My life has been full; I believe deeply in God, my maker, and look forward to greeting him. I just worry so about Earl and the kids and our grandkids. Maybe I'm just selfish. I not only wanted to live to be a grandmother, but also a great-grandmother, and I don't feel my children are fully grown. Sure, in age they're old, but their minds and spirits are still not fully developed. Each one of them lives with a void. Each child different, each empty space different from the other, something they need to figure out, and I must start convincing myself that my job on Earth is done.

I also don't want to die because of Earl. I always thought that I would be the widow, not that I want Earl to meet our maker first; it's just that I don't want to be the one to leave. I feel like I am a deserter, like I am skipping out on him to go rest and leaving him here all alone to deal with life. I'm so sorry, Earl; you have been wonderful through all this sickness. You have handled things I would have never given you credit for.

Dying makes you truly think about living, and I am so sorry, Earl, for the ways I treated you at times. It's hard to believe, in our younger days, I complained because I felt I had to do it all alone, take care of the kids and the house and the pets. I'd be mad as hell standing at the sink up to my elbows in sudsy water, while you sat in the next room watching *Barney Miller.* Now I would give anything to be able to do my own dishes, to watch the world out my kitchen window as my hands worked in the warm water and soap, and to be able to hear your laughter mixed among the dialogue of Detective Miller and Detective Fish, floating in my background. This is a good memory. I shall fall asleep.

January 4, 1999

I slept all day yesterday and did not journal at all. I could barely lift my head. I know Earl was worried; but I think I was just recovering from my big party. I'm feeling much better now.

Maureen's been here all morning, going about her daily routine. She spends the first few minutes talking to her father over coffee and the newspaper. Earl and Maureen have been getting along great. Out of all four children, Maureen is the one who understands her daddy. She accepts him as he is—a quiet and cantankerous old man. Earl truly enjoys Maureen. He gets a kick out of her. She's simple, she's real, and she's damn funny. Every morning Maureen fixes all three of us breakfast. This morning we had pancakes and sausage. All I need to do for complete and total satisfaction is to smell it. A few bites here, a few bites there—I savor the aroma and taste, eating slowly, complete and total satisfaction. I now realize the sin in rushing through a meal; gulping down food that you don't even taste, not thinking to give thanks, eating junk out of greasy bags passed to you through an open window; just plain sinful.

After breakfast, Maureen clears away my breakfast tray and we watch The View, just Maureen and me, propped up on my bed, pillows behind our heads, arguing back at those big-mouthed ladies. We talk to them just like they're right here in my very own living room, sitting around my own coffee table. Thank goodness they're not; I could not stand to have people that obnoxious and opinionated in my home. It's funny, though, when you think about it, how life just keeps repeating itself. Now it's Earl who stands at the kitchen sink washing our breakfast dishes, up to his elbows in warm, sudsy water, peering at the world out our kitchen window and listening to Maureen and me and the five ladies on *The View* argue and laugh.

This morning Maureen was not laughing or arguing. In fact, she was quiet, and Maureen is never quiet. I patted her hand, and that's all it took. The tears started to roll. I asked her what was wrong, and Maureen began sobbing about her miserable morning. Turns out all three of Maureen's boys had gotten suspended from school that morning for fist fighting each other on the school bus. Imagine all three of your children suspended at once!

Maureen said the fighting had started at home over T-shirts and CDs. Lee was angry at Dwayne for wearing his shirt and refusing to take it off. Troy was angry at Lee for taking his CD and leaving it at a friend's house. The boys' arguing escalated at the bus stop. By the time the bus arrived, a few punches had already been thrown, but the worst of it occurred when they got on the bus and started to take a seat. Troy punched Dwayne, who then lay in the aisle of the bus and laughed, mocking his big brother. At that time, Lee, the youngest, snapped. He took a flying leap and landed on Troy's back. Well, you can imagine, Troy just flipped out, and with Lee clinging to his back, he thrashed his body around, trying to flip him off. Dwayne, still on the bus floor, kicked at Troy. The bus driver had to get out of his seat and pull Lee from Troy's back. Some of the kids on the bus were hurt by Lee's legs being whipped around as he rode on his brother.

Honestly, a crowded school bus has no room for Maureen's rowdy boys to get into a fight. Maureen is extremely embarrassed by their behavior. Not only have the boys been suspended for three days, but they have also been kicked off the bus for good. Maureen will have to drive them every day for the rest of the year, as if she needs something else to do.

Maureen cried buckets as she told me what happened, but Earl thought it was the funniest damn thing he had ever heard. He thinks all of Maureen's boys are a little bit crazy, but they crack him up. Earl said it was damn stupid for those boys to get suspended for fighting each other. "Hell, that's what brothers do." he said. "So now what?" asked Earl. "The boys, get to spend three days at home kicking each other's ass when they should be in school getting an education?"

"I guess," responded Maureen. That's when Earl got on his political high horse, exclaiming that he pays too much money in taxes for his grandsons to be sitting at home for fighting each other. Earl picked up the phone to call the principal, and Maureen wiped her tears and cheered, "Go get um Daddy!"

January 5, 1999

Well, leave it to Earl! The boys are back in school and back on the bus. He spent all day yesterday fighting for those boys, and I think he was truly enjoying himself—the phone calls back and forth from school and the transportation people, the letters he sent off with copies to the school board president and superintendent. After Earl's personal visit to the principal's office, Earl's battle was won. Maureen was so relieved that she woke me to tell me what happened, and Maureen never wakes me, unless she has to give me my medicine. It was nice to be woken by Earl and Maureen, Maureen bouncing around the room and Earl standing in the doorway gloating. That's when Beverly came by, and Earl got to gloat to Beverly.

That scenario happens to be the whole highlight of each experience. Earl feels there is an injustice done to him, or in this case, his grandsons. He laces his boxing gloves, and the fight is on. Afterwards, he gets to gloat to Beverly, and in return she gets to compliment her daddy on a job well done. That truly is the common link between Beverly and Earl, fighting for what they believe is right, Beverly for her livelihood, and Earl for fun.

Beverly is a lawyer. She is a prosecuting attorney for Common Pleas Court. Her husband, Timothy, is also a prosecutor. I do believe Earl's proudest day was the day Beverly graduated from law school. She was the first member of the family to get a formal education.

Earl never went to college. He began working for the post office in his early twenties and retired forty years later. I took care of the kids and worked occasionally; when we needed the money. I could usually find work in retail and did it when I had to, but I was always content to stay home with my children. I never had the feeling that I was missing out on anything, like other housewives claim. I never dreamed of being anything else. Acceptance makes living a happy life easier.

Maureen got pregnant before she was even college age, a senior in high school. She married her boyfriend, also a senior in high school. They went on to have two more children right after graduation, but they're still together, and I think for the most part, they're happy; however, there is that void.

Donnell tried schooling but flunked out. She decided she preferred bar life and works as a bartender after years of being a cocktail waitress. Michael got his real estate license and does quite well.

Beverly though, was always the perfectionist: straight A's in high school. She was senior class president and got a scholarship to Bowling Green University for her bachelor's degree. She majored in political science, always knowing that she would go to law school, and she did. On the day Beverly found out she was accepted into the Ohio State University law program, she and her daddy went crazy, insane with happiness, both of them beaming; Beverly because her hard work and dreams were going to form a reality, and Earl because his beloved oldest child was going to the college of the great Woody Hayes and The Ohio State Buckeyes.

Beverly, I do worry about her so. You would think that she would be happy and content, having exceeded all her major goals, but that's not so. I believe she may be the saddest of my four children. With Beverly it's never enough; she can never, ever live up to her expectations, and as soon as she reaches one goal, she raises the bar on the others, always working toward things and never just living in the moment. That's what dying teaches you, to live in the moments. I want to pass that insight onto Beverly. I want Beverly to look back and see all that she has done, and then I want her to exhale.

Beverly and Timothy live in a mansion. They both claim that it is not a mansion, but we all disagree, even Michael, who sells houses for a living. They have one child, my only granddaughter, Madeline. We all call her Maddy. She is six years old and the most precocious child I have ever come by, except maybe her mother when she was little.

Maddy loves to come spend time with Grandma and Grandpap. She loves to eat my fried chicken. Maureen will make it for her now, when she comes to visit. Beverly and Timothy don't prepare or eat fried foods, so Maddy has to come here for her grease intake, and I will tell you this, we are more than happy to oblige.

Maddy likes her cousins. She calls them "the boys," and is quite content just to sit around watching them. Maddy will stay for their farting contests (that is, until she begins to gag). She will try to listen to music with them or watch their shows (until her mom briskly removes her). Maddy will even be the towel girl for their homemade wrestling tournaments. Maddy also enjoys playing checkers with her Grandpap, because he doesn't let her win; he truly challenges the child. Earl started to teach Maddy chess, and you know what she said? That smart child said; "Grandpap, chess is interesting, but I'm happy just to play checkers with you." See what I mean? It's the moments. All Beverly has to do is to watch her child in life or me in death, and the picture should be clear.

"Dear God, help Beverly see how easy life can be."

January 5, 1999, much later in the day. Sleep, sleep.

I take pills to ease my suffering, and I sleep. I know it's dark outside, but that doesn't mean it's late, not in January. I'll have to tell Earl I want a clock in here. He threw out our alarm clock on the first day of his retirement, and we haven't had a clock in here since. I don't think the clock made a bit of difference anyway. After forty years of waking at 5:00 a.m., Earl is still up before the birds.

I lie here, and our house is quiet. Earl must be downstairs in the basement watching television. That was a good project, finishing the basement. Earl did it after his retirement and after our children were already grown, but we just didn't have the money or the time to finish it before that.

Maureen must have gone home, because if she were here, I would hear her. I can usually hear Maureen; her laughter and spirit carry. I have a silver bell I can ring if I need someone. I had always thought, *Wouldn't it be nice to have an eye pillow and breakfast tray and a little silver bell to ring for your servants?* Well, I now have an eye pillow (thanks, Donnell) and a breakfast tray and a silver bell, and it is not so nice.

My body has already died. It has been a slow death, full of hurt and slow deterioration. In October I could still make it down the hall slowly and with help. I was able to sit outside on Halloween and pass out treats to the beggars, the little princesses and young Draculas. How much fun Halloween is! That was the last time I was outside in the fresh air. In reflection, I say if there is to be a last time, that was a good one. I now need help to get into the bathroom. I was using a walker and attempting it on my own. That was months ago. I now am practically carried to the potty or put on a bedpan, which I deeply hate. I do not want to shit in my own bed; shit where I live.

Earl helps me in a shower every other day; I have one of those chairs in there. Last month I could still get myself in and out of the tub. I'm fading fast. Maureen or Earl rubs lotion on my body every day. I smell of lilac lotion. I also smell of cancer. Did you know cancer has a smell? Well, it does. Nobody says anything—they just rub me with lotion and light serenity candles. It's all said to be my "aroma therapy." I think they're just trying to cover up the smell of my cancer.

My hair is very short, gray, and thin. Before chemo, I had long silver hair, which I liked to keep up in pretty combs or braided down my back. My hair was so much a part of me; a representation, a piece of my persona. Losing my hair was worse than losing my breasts. I got through it by saying, "It's just hair, and isn't it nice not to worry about hair?" Inside I was devastated.

I am also thin. For the first time in my life, I am thin, deathly thin. I grew up a big-boned girl and grew into a plump woman. I didn't mind my fatness; it suited me, just like my hair. I was comfortable with my weight. I don't believe I was ever what you would call obese, but always rather plump; nice big boobs; nice big, round bottom; and a middle to match.

I am overwhelmed with sadness, but not only because my hair and boobs are gone. I am sickly thin and all alone. I think that's the worst part of dying; you do it alone. I've never done much alone. I went from living in the full house of my parents to living in a full house of my own. Now I must learn, like an old dog, to do a new trick.

"Dear God, I don't want to be afraid. I am sorry that I fear death, that I fear the loneliness. I know in my heart that when I do let go, I will not be alone, that I will be in your embrace and that you will carry me through."

January 6, 1999

Shannon, Michael's girlfriend, came by today. She is such a sweet girl. She did my hair. She brought me gifts and talked of Michael. Shannon owns a small beauty shop that she named after herself- *Shannon's*. It's a cute little brick building with pink awnings in downtown suburbia. Shannon's shop is on the first floor, and her apartment is on the second. I worry that someone will rob her. It doesn't take long to figure out that a young attractive woman works and lives in that building. Shannon tells me not to worry, but what's an old mother of four to do?

Shannon and Earl got me into a wheelchair and then wheeled me right into the bathroom. She wrapped some plastic capes around me and then wet my hair with a wash rag. Shannon gently squeezed a very warm wash cloth over my head, letting the water drip down, liked a cracked egg, over my short, soft hair. She used her hand to keep it off my forehead. It reminded me of how I washed my newborn babies. I felt a mixed bag of emotions. It felt good to have shampoo gently massaged through my hair, and the scent of honeysuckle filled me up, but my own neediness kills me.

After a rinse, the plastic came off, and then my shirt. Shannon took hold of the bottom of my top and began to lift up. At that moment, I froze. Not meaning to, I had panicked. I looked up at Shannon, and to her and my own surprise, I was crying.

But Shannon was so sweet, she just simply whispered, "Ruthie, your shirt is all wet, and you seem cold. There is a pretty blue fleece hanging right here on the bathroom door. We are just going to put that on." She added, "Ruthie, I think you're brave and beautiful."

That girl sure did choke me up. I let her undress me and see my flat, flat, chest. I let her see the thinness of my body, sunken, wrinkled, and old. It's a dead body still holding my spirit and mind.

"Dear God, you have taken my body; please let me keep my mind until death."

Shannon dressed me in the light blue fleece and combed and blow dried my hair. The dryer felt nice blowing on the back of my neck, and the stuff she put in my hair to style it smelled good. I actually felt pretty. Surprisingly, my hair looked decent when she was finished. I was stylish. Shannon had spiked my short gray hair up and combed the sides back. As if that were not enough, Shannon then pulled a gift from her pocket, a small silver box that held beautiful blue topaz earrings, the most beautiful earrings I have ever seen. I have never worn earrings before. My ears are not pierced. The blue topaz earrings are clip-ons and actually, they are quite comfortable. Shannon said she found them in a vintage store and had to get them for me. She said they matched my eyes. True, my eyes are a very pretty blue. They used to hold a sparkle.

Shannon clipped the perfectly blue stones to my lobes and then added lip gloss to my lips. I faced the mirror and met the woman who was staring back at me, Ruthie, in her parting chapter.

It was such an emotional experience, having my hair done; a makeover, as some would say. The only reason I didn't cry the entire time was because Shannon talked all the way through it. You know how beauticians do, here you are having a cleansing and uplifting experience, and they are just going on and on about themselves. Well, Shannon talked nonstop the entire time about my Michael. I know it's been hard for Shannon. I admit Michael is such a skunk when it comes to women. There you go—Michael's void. He has been dating Shannon for five years now, and he has cheated on her, always playing the field. Michael takes Shannon for granted, just like she said. He won't commit.

Michael can't commit. He fears relationships. I believe he fears being in love, staying in love. He fears the giving of himself. He fears all it takes in making it work, the compromising and giving in. He fears loving only one, having his last and only sex partner. He fears leaning on someone, and he fears having someone lean on him. He fears sharing his money, sharing his home, and sharing his life.

Shannon said she is done. I cannot really blame her. I don't understand why she has held on this long.

Shannon has always been my favorite of Michael's, and I know she has always been Michael's favorite. If Michael is ever to commit to one, I know, and have always known, it will be Shannon.

I am proud of her. I like her strategy; though, I know she is not playing a game. Michael needs this wake-up call. He needs her to walk away; he needs to miss her and to realize she is the only woman he has ever truly loved. He needs to want her back, to realize that he wants to be with only her. He needs to feel miserable without her, and he will.

I didn't say that to Shannon; I didn't want to bring her hopes up. She was there to tell me good-bye, to tell me that she loves me, but that she can no longer chase after my son. I let her tell me those things because I needed to say the same. I need to start saying good-bye and I love you.

"*God, I know that I need to start making closure; you have given me so much time already. Maybe that is the beauty in knowing the time of your death. It is the chance to make amends, count blessings, kiss your loved ones, and leave your mark. Thank you, God, for that chance.*

January 7, 1999

Hospice sent a bed over, a hospital bed, a single with a cheap mattress, cold side rails, and wheels. Nobody even told me that Hospice was going to send over a bed. It was Maureen and Earl's idea; they thought it would be nice to have me out in the family area during the day, so I could visit with all the company that comes by and be a part of everyday living. They said they miss my being part of their daily conversations. I responded angrily, and I am still feeling angry.

"I am not lying in a hospital bed in the middle of my living room," I shouted at Earl. He tried to explain, but I cut him off. Maureen tried to explain, and I cut her off too, and then I laid into both of them.

I asked them if they realize that I sleep half the day. My eyes are shut, my short hair is stuck to one side of my face, my mouth is hanging open, and I snore. I do not want to be laid out in a drugged sleep for presentation. I told them I couldn't bear to turn my home into a sick house.

I then started to cry. I said, " I don't want people walking into my home and seeing a hospital bed in my living room and a sleeping, dying woman lying inside its cold rails. I feel more dignity in my own room, and dignity is a hard thing to come by when you're terminal." By that time, Earl and Maureen were crying, so I had to add how much I love my bedroom.

I love my new green and purple floral bedspread and my big soft pillows and featherbed mattress cover. I told them that my bed is so elegant and soft that I feel like the princess and the pea. I love my new television and DVD player, a gift from Maureen and Ben. I like my candles burning. Donnell is good about bringing me scented candles, and I like to hear the serenity fountain that she got me. The chairs that Beverly put in my bedroom are simply gorgeous, and they look comfortable. My guests have never complained while sitting in them. And Michael set me up a nice small CD player and brought me an entire collection of CDs in a cute little basket, and they are both small enough to sit right on my nightstand within my reach. And then I have my tape recorder, and I journal. I journal at all different hours of the day and night, anytime I'm awake and alone. I like to do it in private. I don't mind my guests seeing me sitting up in all my pretty pillows when I am ready for them to enter, but I can't lie out in my living room exposed and sick.

Earl got down on his knees and kissed my hands. He said he should have known. He got up and called Hospice and told them to come and pick up the bed.

"Thank you, God, for Earl."

I felt bad for Maureen. She has this thing. It's like an obsession or maybe a sickness, but she makes herself everyone's savior. She has always felt my pain, but now she feels my sadness.

To make Maureen feel better and give her something to do for me, I told her I would like my bed moved so it faces the window. Right now, my bed faces the wall with a TV. I'd rather turn sideways to see the TV and face the window, and I would truly love to have some birdfeeders out my bedroom window.

Earl just chuckled. "You know I don't want bird shit all over my deck." He said it just like he said it when I wasn't sick and suggested some birdfeeders, except this time he was joking.

January 7, 1999—later that day

Well, my bed faces the window and my curtains are pulled back and I'm watching the neighbor's dog poop in our yard. I know it's hard for everybody to have me hidden away in the back bedroom when I used to be the centerpiece of this home. Now I'm its ghost before I'm even dead.

I wonder if I will be a ghost; maybe that's a weird thing to think when you're dying. I guess I believe in ghosts or spirits, but God, I don't want to be one.

"Dear God, please do not make me a ghost. I would much rather just sit up in heaven in all its beauty and eat chocolate."

Okay, I've gotten off track here. What I wish to say is that I understand how hard it is for my family to see me bedridden. I have been confined to my bed for only the past few months. This summer I spent so much of my time outdoors. Earl, Maureen, and I had a whole little schedule arranged between breakfast, lunch, dinner, and naps. I would sit outside in a wheelchair and give pointers as Maureen and Earl gardened.

Gardening—that was my passion in life. If I was anything besides a mother and a wife, I was a gardener. This summer I gave my gardens over to others, as well as lessons on how to care for them. I taught them from a wheelchair when to plant the vegetables, how to weed and keep the bugs away, how to prune the roses, and how to cover them when it gets cold. I taught them how to snap the heads off of some flowers that will reseed themselves and how to tie up certain flowers and plants that need it. I taught them how to make a sunflower fort, growing the long flowers in a large square, leaving an opening for a door.

The sunflower fort was gorgeous, and Maddy spent her summer days playing in our back yard. Mostly she ran through the sprinkler or sat inside her fort with Barbie dolls, crayons, and coloring books. She suffered a few bee stings, and I did feel bad for that. The boys were here a lot, too. They rode their bikes through the neighborhood, hanging out with other kids and checking in about every two hours.

I wish I could have died at the end of summer, when I had a tan from the sun and I felt warm and satisfied, when I could still get myself on the pot with just a little help, and when I hadn't yet lost all my dignity.

"Dear God, I wish to be dignified in death. I wish to make a graceful exit."

January 8, 1999

Well, I got birdfeeders. I guess everybody heard of my rant and then heard of my request for birdfeeders, and now I got birdfeeders. I got a long and tall birdfeeder ,and I got a small birdfeeder. I have a feeder that looks like a house and one that looks like a barn and another feeder that just looks like a feeder. I got six altogether, two from Maureen, one from Beverly, one from Michael, one from Donnell, and my favorite of all, the one from Earl. Earl made his birdfeeder.

After my little monologue, he went down to his workshop—a small room he created in a section of our basement—and he went to work. The birdfeeder Earl made sits on a post, like a bird bath. On top of the post sits a beautiful wooden platform. The sides of the platform are the most beautiful, well- rounded, shaved and sanded wooden rods, perfect for bird perching. Earl cemented his birdfeeder into the ground and centered it in my bedroom window. The other birdfeeders hang beside or behind Earl's feeder. Earl hung them on shepherd hooks. The birds love it, and not just the birds; the squirrels are happy too. They get up there and sit on the big feeder and eat and stare in at me, and I'm having a grand time. I feel like St. Francis.

"Thank you, God, for the birds that sing. Thank you, God, for everything."

January 9, 1999

Well, yesterday I watched the birds and I slept. I was much too tired to do anything else. Donnell came by. She looked pretty in her tiny little skirt and tiny little top, but she's too thin. I wonder how she stays warm, although she was warm, because she gave me a foot message with her hot hands.

Donnell is my spirited child. I suppose others call her my wild one. Donnell can out-drink, out-smoke, and out-swear a sailor, but such a heart that child has! Donnell's void will be the hardest to fill; because she has already filled it up with alcohol. Her work lies ahead of her. She's gonna have to dry herself out and then find out what it is that is truly missing—could be love, could be self-respect. I don't know what it is that drives some to drink. Could just be heredity; my daddy drank too much and too often, and two of my brothers fight with the bottle. How was I to know that my tiny baby Donnell was going to pick her genes out of the pool of alcohol?

I believe Donnell began drinking in high school, and then it just got worse, that one year of college. Donnell didn't just drink when she was young; she also did drugs. I don't believe she does drugs anymore. When she was just a teen, I was cleaning in her room, and I found a marijuana cigarette and all its little seeds. Well, I confronted Donnell; Earl and I grounded her for damn near the whole year and wouldn't let her see her friends. She would climb out her bedroom window and take off. Oh, it was just hell, one of those things you thought would never end.

"*This too shall pass*," my favorite verse.

Well, anyway, I flushed all that marijuana—except some of the seeds. I guess the gardener in me just took over, along with curiosity. I wanted to see what that plant looked like, so I planted those seeds. I planted them right there in my garden, with all my other greenery and flowers. Well, I'll tell you, that marijuana plant was the prettiest thing I have ever grown. In no time at all I started seeing little green tufts, and then it just kept getting larger and larger, almost fern-like, with the cutest little leaves. Well, I grew that marijuana all summer, and nobody knew. Made me believe my children were not all that hip after all, because we had marijuana growing in our own back yard, and they didn't even know it. I finally cut it down near the end of summer, harvesting time, I guess. It had gotten big and pretty, and I was afraid that somebody would notice and tell the authorities.

Nobody knows that I grew pot, but I did. I have always had passion for growing things from the earth. I guess it was stupid, but it sure was fun having a little secret garden, watching how a forbidden plant can grow so pretty under my care. It's a shame people use it to get high.

January 9, later that day

Maureen came in after my marijuana story and drugged me; I then took two bites of soup and fell asleep. I sleep longer now, and I know I'm hard to wake. Most sadly, I cannot talk as long to journal. Sometimes I have to replay, to see what I was saying, and then try to finish. I know it will not be long, and Earl and Maureen know this also. They have talked to all the kids. It must have been the birdfeeder talk, or maybe they knew before, and that's why they got the bed. For whatever reason, they have asked people to start stopping over daily. Donnell comes before work every day now, and Michael comes every day and brings me my dinner. Beverly, I know, tries, but she is tied up on a big case, so if she can't swing by, she sends Timothy, her husband. Maddy's here all the time, because she practically lives with Maureen. Maureen picks her up from kindergarten every afternoon and brings her to me. It's been nice to see the kids.

Michael, I can tell, is sad. He hasn't mentioned Shannon, but something is on his mind, and I'm not too conceited to know it's more than his dying mother. Donnell is going to be a mess when I die. She's a mess now, but such a sweet mess she is. Today she must have been tired, because she climbed right up into bed with me, right under the covers, snuggled up against my body, and then promptly fell asleep. It was so nice to feel a body up against mine that I cried.

Earl mostly falls asleep in the La-Z-Boy. When he does come to bed, he stays on his side. I believe he fears he will hurt me. He lays stiff as a board on his back, looking uncomfortable, but then reaches over and takes my hand, and we sleep holding hands. The poor man has gone without sex for so long. I love you, Earl, and I'm sorry I got sick.

I'm sorry I stopped making love to you. I'm sorry my boobs were cut off and my beautiful hair fell out. I'm tired and in pain, and I lie in bed. Thank you, Earl; you stuck to your vows "for better or for worse, in sickness and in health," and they may be the hardest vows to endure. I know it sure ain't easy.

January 10, 1999

I was up before anyone else. It was still dark outside when I opened my eyes. I watched the sun rise out of my window. I got lost in its red and orange glow. The leafless trees of our neighborhood, barren and black, stood tall and strong within the orange light. There was snow on the ground, and I could see a long, sharp sparkling crystal-like dagger hanging from the gutter above my bedroom window. As night faded and light settled in, a male cardinal, the most vibrant red, came and sat on the edge of Earl's birdfeeder. Within a minute, the female came. Not as pretty as the male, plain and placid, yet familiar and reliable, she sat next to him.

I've been dreaming lots lately, long story dreams of my past. I've been reliving my life while I sleep. I have told no one of my dreams; I have just been enjoying them. It's nice to be healthy again. I am healthy and young in my sleep. I have dreamed back as far as I can remember, and I am moving forward. Sometimes my dreams are scattered. Sometimes I will be a young mother with a toddler, believing it is one of my own children and then realizing I am also the toddler. I have dreamed of my father and mother, and I have seen them young and happy and alive.

Mostly when I dream of my siblings, we are young. That's when we made all our memories, before I got pregnant and then married. Before my brother Joe was killed in Vietnam (damnable war), before Esther died, little Esther. She died when she was six, of pneumonia. My poor parents buried two of their five children. Everybody was so sad after Joe died. They had mourned and grieved Esther for years and maybe had grown to acceptance or solace, but then we lost Joe, and my other two brothers, Paul and John, were still over there fighting. Well, they did their tours and then got the hell out. When they came home, they took factory jobs and drank away their pain. Both of them eventually moved away, two different directions, both far from home. Damn near killed my parents, again. My father stopped talking, never really said much after that.

I stayed close. Earl and I and the kids tried hard to be their family, but their pain was too great. Eventually they got sick and died within six months of each other, Daddy from emphysema, and Mommy from a broken heart; doctors called it cardiac arrest.

In my dreams Joe is alive and handsome, and so are John and Paul. All three boys—young and ornery—getting into trouble like they did. The three amigos, they were always laughing and talking a little too loud, acting a little too ornery, and having a little too much fun.

In my dreams Esther is a sweet little girl who carries around a rabbit, a white rabbit with red eyes. I remember Daddy saying, "A rabbit is no pet; rabbits need to run, and they need space," but that rabbit of Esther's followed her around at a child's pace and allowed her to carry him without kicking fiercely like he did when anyone else tried to pick him up. Esther called him Snowball. After Esther died, one of the boys, I think it was Paul, let Snowball go. It pissed Mommy off something bad. Just as Mommy had her spiritual reasons for wanting to keep Snowball, Paul had his spiritual reasons for letting him run.

So much pain has been endured; so much loss has been witnessed. With all those who have gone before me, why am I still frightened to die? It will be good to see Mommy and Daddy, Joe, and Esther; it is something positive to look forward to in death.

"Dear God, help to ease my fear of dying."

I suppose when I think about it, I don't know what I fear. I honestly believe that dying is as easy as taking your last breath. The hard part is trying to stay alive while you die. I assume eventually my eyes will be too tired to open, my heart will be too tired to beat, my blood too tired to flow, and I too tired to breathe.

I imagine death to be like lying out in the sun during my schoolgirl days; lazy, warm, effortless, and soothing; the sun burning my eyes that hide behind my lids; the taste and smell of sunshine, warm and thick; the rays absorbing into my skin, warming my nakedness.

"Dear God, it might not be so bad. In fact, I think I will embrace death in order to make it go more smoothly. When the time comes, I will fear not!"

January 10, 1999, much later that day

Earl's quiet. It was a hard day for him. My good friends Betty and Martha have been here all afternoon. I called them and told them they got the task of cleaning out my closet and deciding what to do with my clothes. I no longer wear any of them; I now live in soft fleece sweats and warm pajamas. Shoes and jackets, pants and dresses, skirts and blouses hang untouched in my closet, waiting for someone to go through and discard them, a job usually left to the surviving children and spouse. It's an uncomfortable job that nobody wants to do, so your things hang around for too long, unembodied, and collect dust.

I called Betty and Martha and asked for their help. They stood at my closet and went through my drawers, whipping item after item out as I directed them to which pile it should go. Almost everything will go to the church; the people there will take it to the shelter. A few things got set aside for the girls. Not much, though; they don't want to wear old lady clothes. I left instruction with Martha and Betty that my sick clothes are to be thrown away when I'm gone.

Martha wanted to know what I wanted to be buried in. Earl knows; we have already had this discussion. Just put me in something soft, comfortable, and light, maybe some of my new pajamas. I have a few pairs that I have not even had the chance to wear; the kids are always buying me something soft and pretty. Nothing I had before fits, I have lost so much weight. It doesn't matter anyway, because my casket is not to be open. I absolutely do not want my loved ones viewing my dead, cold corpse. Shut the damn lid and cover it with flowers, place my best picture beside it, and tell stories about me, ones that give my life meaning.

Along with asking both Betty and Martha to clean out my closet, I asked Betty to buy me four special boxes or containers for holding items that I have already set aside for my children. Of course I planned to pay her back. Betty has such fine taste that I knew she would do a great job; however, she far exceeded my expectations and then wouldn't accept payment.

I had figured she would buy the type of storage boxes the stores sell for holding photographs, pretty ones, neat and square. She surprised and enlightened me with the most beautiful hat boxes. All four boxes are different from one another, yet each has been selected with great taste and perfection. There is a deep burgundy box with navy blue striping that will be Michael's; a shimmering gold box trimmed with a glittery fringe and tassels for Donnell; an ivory lace box, clean, simple, and elegant, that's Beverly's; and a floral box with flowers of pink, peach, lavender, and cream for Maureen.

When I received the news "terminal," I began my collection. I set aside small mementoes for each child, placing them only in gallon-sized Ziploc bags and then into a Rubbermaid tub. I looked for a special container. At first I thought maybe for Michael something crafted from wood and for Beverly something with an antique flare. Time slipped away from me. I never found my special boxes. When I requested the favor from Betty, I did not go into great detail. I just simply stated I need a container for each of my children. She had read my mind. Better yet, she was able to carry out what I had created in thought.

In Beverly's box are a few photographs of her and me, the day of her birth and the day of her first sibling's birth, all three of us sitting on my hospital bed. The first day of kindergarten—this is my favorite photograph of me. I am in a pretty dress, young and happy. My hair is down, and I am bending over, kissing a pigtailed girl before she gets on a school bus. I look prettier in this photograph than I ever did in actual life. The other photos are the two of us on her wedding day, me with her and Maddy, although she probably already has that same picture, and then one of just Maddy and me.

I also placed in her box the rhinestone combs that I wore in my hair on her wedding day, an old hand mirror that Beverly used to play with when she was young, two antique perfume bottles, my pearls, my favorite pen—the one I did most of my last journaling with—and a copy of *Gone with the Wind*. Beverly needs to read just for sport. I made her some lace doilies. I wrapped the doilies around gladiola bulbs and wrote instructions for planting them and tips on keeping the squirrels away. I placed in her box one of my journals. I left a note about where she could find the others, and I wrote her a letter.

I wrote a letter to each child. Beverly's letter is about living in the moment. I tried to pass on some sort of insightful knowledge; however, they may just giggle at my attempt.

Maureen's box contains a photo of the two of us when she was about a year old, one of us on her thirteenth birthday, and a photo of her big and pregnant with Troy. She is just seventeen years old, wearing a man's white T-shirt stretched to the max, belly button poking through, and a pair of sweat pants. My hands and face are pressed to her stomach, a reaction on my face to feeling the baby kick. There is also a photo of all three boys and me with shaven heads, taken when I did chemo and lost all my hair. Maureen shaved the boy's heads at their pleading, and we all did a little photo shoot. It stopped my crying. Lastly, there's a photo of her and me laying on my bed that Earl took just last month.

Also in the box is my "mother's ring," each child's birthstone set in gold. It's really pretty, because all four kids have good stones. First Beverly, a diamond, born in April, wouldn't you know it? Maureen came in September—a sapphire, Donnell in July—a ruby—and Michael in May—an emerald. It's a gorgeous ring. I also gave to Maureen my recipe book, my gold cross necklace, my straw gardening hat (it fits perfectly into the box: everything else must lie inside or around the hat), and a scarf and mittens that I knitted this summer. They're aqua, you know, that blue, green, turquoise shade, the color of Maureen's eyes. I also gave to Maureen my favorite book of poems that's titled *When I am an Old Woman I shall wear Purple.*

Inside it I inscribed, "We are the purple ladies. Love, Mom." As a bookmark I placed a packet of tomato seeds at my favorite poem. "Post Humus" by Patti Tana. The poem goes like this:

Scatter my ashes in my garden
join hands in a circle of flesh.
so I can be near my love.
Say a few honest words, sing a gentle song,
Please tell some stories about me
making you laugh. I love to make you laugh.
When I've had time to settle, and green
gathers into buds, remember I love blossoms
bursting into spring. As the season ripens
remember my persistent passion.
And if you come in my garden
on an August Afternoon
pluck a bright red globe,
let juice run down your chin and the seeds
stick to your cheek. When I'm dead
I want folks to smile and say That Patti (I crossed out Patti and wrote Ruthie)
she sure is some tomato!

The first time I read that poem I couldn't believe my eyes. This is me; this is what I should have or could have written. Here it is, like a Bible verse leaping out at me. I leave it to Maureen; she will know what to do and make sure it is done. Maureen's letter is filled with thank-yous. Maureen is my giving child, and along with the thank-yous, I gave her some small advice. Please, I begged her, be careful with your giving. Leave something for yourself. I fear Maureen will give all of herself away. I fear that with each favor done, she will fade, like she is slowly being erased.

January 11, 1999

Too tired yesterday to finish, I'll start where I left off.

In Donnell's box is my Bible. Placed throughout the Bible on different highlighted pages, mostly in Psalms, I gave Donnell photographs. In three of the photographs she is nude. That child was forever taking her clothes off. Go figure. The first photo is of her in the bath happily seated between her two sisters, and me sitting on the edge of the tub with a wet shirt, washing down babies. There is also a photo of a naked Donnell eating berries off the back yard bush, her summer clothes lying beside a basket. I am at the clothesline hanging up wet towels. Next photo, again naked, Donnell is about seven years old. She has stripped off her summer dress to run through my sprinkler as I sit in the garden planting. That child always has been a free spirit. In the last two pictures, Donnell is grown. There is a photo of us outside, near my gardens, sitting in lawn chairs. Donnell has a beer, and I'm smiling. Finally, there's a photo of Donnell kissing my cheek at the New Year's Eve party (my going-away party).

In Donnell's box is also the serenity prayer I scripted before my handwriting died. I framed the words along with pressed flowers in a shining sterling silver frame. I also gave to Donnell my sterling silver and turquoise rings, a total of three, and my silver cross necklace. Donnell gets my silk scarves, eight of them, bright purples and pinks and orange. I tied these scarves around my head during my bald seasons. I want Donnell to have them. In each scarf I placed a tulip bulb. Tulips are the flowers of happiness. Again I gave instruction for planting and tips. I then gave to Donnell my favorite book, *Lonesome Dove,* which I have read so many times that the binding is cracked, and my favorite Mary Chapin Carpenter CD. I inscribed both of them with words of love. Donnell also gets a baby blue and white poncho that I knitted for her. It's just like the one she wore as a child and loved. The poncho will not fit in the hat box, so Earl will have to give it to her. In Donnell's letter, I tried not to be too preachy. I wrote of family and soul searching, life's journey, and the completion of self, or at least my definitions of these things.

Michael's box contains a breast-feeding photo. I know they do that lots now, but when Earl photographed Michael and me, it was almost taboo—like I was a child molester or something. There is a photo of Michael and me at the beach posing in our swimsuits near the water's edge. Michael and me sitting in church the day of his confirmation. Michael and me at the kitchen table drinking coffee (now he is a man), and Michael kissing me under the mistletoe, two Christmas Eves ago. I also gave to Michael the topaz earrings from Shannon, my Frank Sinatra CD collection, and my first wedding band (Earl traded up on our twenty-fifth anniversary). I also gave to him a copy of *101 Best Loved Poems,* which I inscribed, and a brown hat and scarf that I knitted. Inside the hat are cone flower seeds. Easiest damn plants to grow; don't need much of a committed person, don't need good soil or certain amounts of sun and shade. Just plant the seeds in the ground, and they will grow and spread and grow. Michael should be able to handle at least that much.

I also left to Michael the most sacred of my collections, the only one I have worked hard at. It is my collection of stones. Not just any stones, heart-shaped stones. I found the first one while planting my first garden during the first summer I was married. I dug up a smooth stone perfectly heart shaped, and I believed it to be a sign from God. I washed the stone and put it in my jewelry box. Over the years I have dug up many heart-shaped stones, enough to fill a marble bag. I give these stones to my only boy, Michael James. The letter I wrote to Michael was more or less a story. It is the story of love between a man and woman. It is a story of compromise, of hope, of faith, and of endurance. It is the story of Earl and me.

I realize these boxes don't contain much. The kids will actually receive so much more when I have been turned to ash and they will have it all after Earl dies, but right now, I wanted to give them special pieces of me that they can relate to and pieces of me that bind. I want to share traces of things, to give them memories that are precise yet ordinary.

"Dear God, help my children understand my meager assortment of items. These are not just beloved belongings of mine but rather things of

mine that will be individually understood by each child. Each child's treasure chest is separate, apart, and different, yet connected to me with an understanding shared."

January 12, 1999

I'm tired today; simply cannot shake my extreme fatigue. I think the whole closet and box drama has worn me out. Sometimes I'm too tired to journal, yet I feel that if I don't, I will miss recording the last days of my life. I don't know why this is such an obsession for me, and I don't know what it means. It's just something I feel compelled to do. I have decided if conversation between the kids, Earl and me is going to be good, I will just simply hit record, so I don't have to go back and retell the story. Earl is not going to like this; he is such a private man. It is the reason I didn't choose videotaping my last months. That and because I do not want to be forever captured on video as a thin, short-haired, sick old woman. It is truly not who I am. For most of my life I was plump with long hair a hearty laugh and was never sick.

"Please, dear God, let people remember that."

January 13, 1999

Maureen was late this morning, so Earl made our breakfast, and it was delicious. We had oatmeal, toast, and orange juice. Earl sat on the edge of the bed, and we had a nice talk. He told me it was hard for him to see my clothes being discarded and my closet empty, but then he admitted it was probably easier this way, to have that task already taken care of and done the way I wanted. And he thanked me. He thanked me for thinking of everything; he thanked me for forty-eight years of marriage; and he thanked me for being the wife and mother that I was. He told me that he was the luckiest man that lived, and through me, he got everything he ever wanted in life. I didn't push the record button, even though I wanted to so badly, but I do respect

Earl's privacy or need for it. I think his short and tender monologue this morning was filled with more terms of endearment than I have ever heard him speak. The most I ever got was "I love you, too," "You look real nice," and "Want to fool around?"

He made up for all that this morning. We cried together too. Cried and held each other. Earl kissed my mouth, and then he said, "Come on, beautiful, let's get our shower." It took us longer than usual to get me into the shower. It is getting much harder just to do the simplest of things. This shower was the best of all showers, when I did finally get in. Earl, that devil, climbed right in there with me. Usually I take my showers alone, while Earl or Maureen waits outside the shower door making sure I'm okay. I have a chair in there and a plastic basket of everything I need. This morning as I was sitting in my shower chair looking in my basket for soap, Earl opened the shower door stark nude and came on in. He found my soap and lathered me up real good. We were laughing and having the best time when Maureen came into the bathroom and asked, "Mama, you okay in there?" Well, she flung open that door and saw her daddy and me naked as two jay birds. I was sitting in that chair soaped up like a bubble bath, and Earl was standing in front of me, his nakedness just dangling. Well, she about had a cardiac arrest. She screamed, "Oh, my God!" shut the door, and then burst into laughter.

Earl and I laughed inside the shower, and finally Earl said in his stern Daddy voice, "Go ahead and get out of here, Maureen. Can't you see me and your mama are busy?" Well, that made me laugh even harder, and if I had died right there in that shower, I would have been all the more closer to heaven.

[Record] "Well, Mama, it's nice to see you dressed."

"Thank you, Maureen, now how are you doing?"

"Here, take these, Mama; here's your water. I swear, my boys—well, I think they are crazy. I mean it. They don't seem to have the sense God gave a goose. Are you taping me?"

"Oh, never mind that."

"The reason I am late is because of those crazy children, not that you and Daddy needed me here, obviously. It's mostly Dwayne's fault, oh that boy. You would not believe the night I had. Ben called me around six o'clock as I was preparing dinner to tell me he had a hard day at work, and if I didn't mind, he would be stopping off at the VFW for a few drinks before coming home. Well, hell yes, I minded. That man's bad days hold no comparison to mine. So I fed Maddy and the boys.

"I tell you, Mama, Beverly just has not been around lately. Guess she is tied up on some murder case—but anyway, I've been having Maddy past seven o'clock every night. Not that I mind, but her father needs to do a better job of picking her up if her mother is not going to. You know we all love Maddy; I just feel bad for her. I think she misses her parents.

"Anyway, Tim got Maddy around seven o'clock, so I spruced myself up a bit and went over to the VFW to get me a drink too. I think Ben was surprised to see me, but we ended up having a blast. We had a few drinks. You know I'm not much of a drinker, so around eight or eight-thirty, I realized I hadn't eaten any dinner, so Ben and I went over to Damon's. They was having a special on ribs, and we about ate our weight in baby backs. We were having a grand time laughing and talking. It's been so long since we have just been together. We left close to ten.

"Well, Mama, as we pulled down our street, one of my worst fears came to be. There were sirens blaring in front of my house. Paramedics, a squad car, fire trucks, you name it; neighbors out on the lawn. Ben didn't even have the car stopped when I jumped from the passenger side and went tearing up the front lawn. Paramedics tried to calm me down. I thought someone was dead in there. I saw Troy and Lee sitting on the couch when I came through the front door. I frantically looked around for Dwayne. I turned the corner, and there he was, lying on a gurney. Oh, Mama, I about started to have a panic attack, but he was just a laughing and joking with the paramedics. So then I thought I would have to kill him for scaring me half to death, but then I saw his arm.

"Oh, Mama, he broke his arm so bad. You could actually see the bone pierced through the flesh. I think he was talking and laughing just to appear brave. Ben and I had to talk to an officer and explain who we were and then got the full story. Well, it turns out that Dwayne, the dumbass, had been skateboarding down our staircase. He crashed and broke his arm. Troy called 911, and they dispatched everything imaginable to my house. Ben and I comforted Dwayne, who was very scared but trying hard to fake it, and then we went over to the couch to talk to Troy and Lee. Ben started first with, "Where in the hell were you two, while your brother was doing dumbass stunts in our house?"

"'We were videotaping it, Daddy,'" Lee shot back. I thought Ben was going to choke that child. The officer must have thought so too, because he guided Ben and me right out the door. We had to follow the ambulance to the hospital, lights blaring and flashing, racing at top speed. Troy and Lee really would have loved the ride, but Ben said that was their punishment.

"We were at the hospital all night. In fact, Ben is still there. I just left to come and check on you and pick up Maddy in an hour."

"Oh, God, Maureen, is Dwayne all right?"

"Well, Mama, they had to do surgery on his arm. He has pins now holding it together."

"Oh, dear God."

"I know, crazy-ass kids."

"You still have to get Maddy? Can't Beverly do that?"

"Mama, she is in the middle of a murder trial. Tim is going to try to get out of court today at a reasonable hour. I'll just pick her up from school and take her up to the hospital with me."

"Maureen, you could leave her here with Earl."

"But Mama, you look so tired today, I couldn't do that."

"I'm not going to die today, Maureen. Earl can play with Maddy while I sleep."

"Are you sure?"

"Maureen, for heaven's sakes, let people help you. Lord knows you help everybody else."

"Oh, those damn boys, and Daddy, what are you laughing about? We kids never gave you the headaches that my boys give to me. If so you, would have killed us."

"Oh, bullshit, Maureen. Raising three girls wasn't no picnic; it's just a different type of headache. Now ain't nothing wrong with them boys except they're just a little bit crazy."

"Thanks, Daddy, that's really reassuring."

January 14, 1999

Thank God. Dwayne is okay. In fact, I believe he is leaving the hospital today to go home. They just treat them and street them. However, it will be easier on Maureen to have him home. Yesterday was hard. Maddy stayed here and played with Earl.

That child is such a precocious thing. She came into my room as I was waking, her arms overflowing with drawings for me. I was thanking her and was looking at each piece of art and giving her praise when she said, "Grandma are you dying?"

"Yes, I am," I simply answered. I didn't know how Maddy was going to do. She looked up at me and held back any tears that were about to fall.

"When you die, you gonna go live in heaven?"

"That's my plan." I answered.

"Then you're not gonna be sick no more?"

I told her, "That's right; I'm going to be out of this bed." And then I said "Maddy, you know what I'm going do when I get to heaven?"

"What?"

"I'm going to dance and twirl."

Maddy seemed pleased with that, and then she asked, "Except Grandma, we won't be able to see you, right?"

"That's right," I told Maddy again, but then added, "Unless you close your eyes and think of me, and then I'll bet you could see me, and you know I'll be watching you from heaven."

Maddy closed her eyes as if she was testing my theory.

"See me yet?" I asked.

That beautiful child stood motionless and quiet for about thirty seconds and then a grin broke across her face. "Yeah, I see you." she said.

"Well, what am I doing?"

"You're dancing and twirling," Maddy said with a smile.

When Tim came to pick Maddy up, I heard him and Earl talking. Earl told Tim that he needed to tell Beverly to get her ass over here to see me. Tim tried to explain that Beverly is working on a murder case right now that is draining her.

"Family comes first!" Earl snapped at Tim, "and that is something Beverly is damn well supposed to know."

I felt bad for the scolding Earl had given Tim. It isn't his fault, and I'm not angry at Beverly. If she is in the middle of a trial, especially such a big one, I know she will do her best to get the job done right and see that justice is served. It is who she is and it is what makes us so proud of her.

January 15, 1999

Michael has shown up every day this week with a different hairstyle. I believe he must be trying everything in his power to talk to Shannon, so he goes into her shop every day as an excuse and has something done. First he got a small trim, and it looked real nice. Well then, he went back and had it colored, and if that wasn't enough, he went the very next day and got highlights. He has had his mustached trimmed, gotten a manicure and a pedicure and had his eyebrows waxed. When he came today, Earl asked, "Is she talking to you yet?"

Michael just slowly turned his head and looked down.

"Well, I know why," Earl stated, "She probably thinks you've turned into a queer."

I gasped. "Oh, Earl."

He asked Michael, "What's next, a bikini waxing?"

Michael did his best to ignore his father, but Earl chuckled in spite of himself. Michael pulled a chair up beside my bed. He eased himself down, rested his hand in mine, lowered his head, and began to cry.

"Cry," I whispered. "Go ahead and let it all out."

"Oh, Mama," Michael said, "What the hell is wrong with me?

How could I have let her get away from me? How could I have treated her so badly for so long? Now it's too late." Michael cried that he has only ever loved two ladies, and now both of them are leaving him.

Oh, my sweet boy, Michael. I stroked his hair as he laid his head upon my bed. "Quite pretty," I said "The twirls of blond and brown, and the smell is delicious." Michael laughed through his tears, and sometimes that's the best we can hope for.

January 16, 1999

Everything hurts. The pain I feel no longer subsides. I believe it could lessen with more medication, which is what the hospice nurse wants Maureen to do, but I have held her off. I know what they are doing to me; they are not just easing the pain, they are helping me die.

I have now worked my way up through my childhood in my dreams. I am at the point of being a newlywed. I dream of being pregnant. I dream of giving birth. I can feel the pain of labor as I sleep. I practice my breathing, and Earl thinks I am flipping out, that maybe the cancer has traveled to my brain.

January 16, 1999 still

Just when you think you can close your eyes and die, one of your children interrupts you with life. Donnell has gone out and gotten herself arrested for drunk driving. I'm not supposed to know this. They have been keeping it a secret. But Dwayne, sweet little can't-keep-a-secret Dwayne, was visiting me with his broken arm and told me everything.

Actually, Dwayne and I had a very nice visit. He brought the video of his skateboarding accident. That child really is a good little skateboarder. He must have gone down that steep staircase six times before he crashed. I will tell you, though, that child is ornery. He just about had a laughing fit when it came to his brother's reactions to his crash. Troy just flipped out, screaming and swinging that camera from side to side, all the while he was asking his brother, "You all right? You all right?"

And little Lee, well, he just stood there in shock, repeating over and over, "We're in trouble for sure."

The whole video made me grimace, and I think Dwayne was enjoying that too.

After we watched the video, Dwayne told me all about Donnell. He said she was leaving work last night and got pulled over. He also told me that Maureen and Beverly are fighting because Donnell called Beverly while she was being arrested. Beverly and Timothy both know the arresting officer, and not only did they tell him to go ahead and take Donnell downtown, but they also told him to impound her car. Maureen thinks they should have gone and gotten Donnell. She thinks the car thing was a little much and just an additional headache that we don't need. I guess Maureen would think that way, since she will probably be the one driving Donnell around. Beverly said she was acting on tough love.

Now I ask, how am I supposed to die? I have one child that doesn't come home from work, one that does the work for everybody else, one that is brokenhearted, and one that is just broken.

"Dear God, please help us fix what has been broken, mend what can be mended, and learn what we are being taught."

January 17, 1999

I lie here and I hurt. I have sores, because it is so hard to move. My showers have become sponge baths. My last shower was the one I took with Earl; a good ending. I sleep all day, and I sleep most nights, a drugged sleep. I cough and I have coughing fits. At times I feel I will drown in my own mucus. I also smell bad. I mostly smell of death.

January 18, 1999

[Record] "Hi, Mama, you okay? I guess you heard that I have gotten myself into a little trouble, but I don't want you to worry, because I think that maybe this is a good thing. Maybe it is even a blessing. I spent a night in jail, Mama, and it was horrible. Maureen and Beverly both showed up to my arraignment, and Beverly had already talked to the judge as well as the prosecutor, the police officer, and my public defender. With Beverly's insight, work, and guidance I just pled guilty right there in arraignment court. I guess there was no need to drag it on with everything that we are all going through. I don't need court dates looming over my head. Beverly had already worked out the minimum sentence for me, and that's what they gave me. I have to do three days in a drug and alcohol program. I'm on one-year probation, and part of that is to attend daily AA meetings. I got a bunch of points on my license, and it cost me over a hundred dollars to get my car out of the impound lot. I still can't drive it, because my driver's license has been suspended. I guess I can get driving privileges to and from work, but I don't have a job now, because I quit."

"That's good, baby."

"I think so too, Mama. I mean I can get any old job. It's time for me to get out of the bar. Maureen said I can come and stay with her if I need to, and maybe I will. I haven't yet decided if it's needed, and today I think I am just going to sit here with you. And tomorrow, well maybe I'll do the same thing tomorrow."

January 19, 1999

Michael was here. He has a black eye and bruises on his cheek. "Good heavens, what happened to you?"

Donnell, who was lying in bed with me asked the same thing at the same time, and then comically, Maureen walked in and said it. Michael rubbed his newly permed hair.

"To be honest, Mama, I ran into the fist of a very angry and jealous husband."

"What in the world, Michael, were you doing with someone's wife?" I asked.

Michael smirked. "Like you said, Mama, just trying to fill a void."

"Yours or hers?" This must have been my parting joke, because the next thing I remember was falling asleep listening to the giggles of Maureen and Donnell.

January 20, 1999

Earl is worried. The kids come daily. Beverly's trial is over; it was an acquittal. She's down, but she's strong and will be okay. "Win some, lose some," is all she said when I asked her about it. We all let it drop at that.

January 21, 1999

[RECORD]

"Hey, Mama, how ya doing?"

"Fine, Donnell, just fine. How you doing?"

"I feel good. Just came from an AA meeting. I'm meeting a lot of good people. Ben brought me home an application from his work and said they are looking for a new receptionist. It would be ideal, because I could just catch a ride with him to and from. He and Maureen have been real good to me. Maureen is taking me to all my meetings, and I may take her up on that offer to stay with them. That way, if I do get a job working with Ben, he won't have to come pick me up. I know I won't be able to stay long in that married-with-children house. You know me, Mama, your free spirit, but maybe just till I get a few paychecks and have my feet on stable ground. I want you to know that I plan on helping Daddy some too. He sure is gonna miss you, Mama."

"I love you, Donnell. You're a good girl. Now don't cry. There isn't anything to cry about. Things are looking good. Everybody is going to be okay. I am finally figuring this out, Donnell. Now listen to me, the secret is not in the busy parts of the experience. It is not in the excitement, and it is not in the resolve. The secret is hidden in the quiet and calm part that lies halfway between the beginning and the end."

January 22, 1999

[RECORD]

"Hey, Mama, you got some pretty birds out there. I do believe birds are coming from all over this damn state to eat at your feeders."

"Sit down, Michael."

"I don't know, Mama, how did you and Daddy do it? How in the hell did you know that Daddy was the one? Why weren't you scared shitless? Why wasn't Maureen scared, for Christ's sake, she was what, about sixteen years old? Tell me if it's that damn elementary, why in the hell can't I see a love that is staring me in the face?"

"Because, Michael, you look past its face. You see the long road to success, but then you also see its torturous journey. There are not just hills on this journey, but there are mountains to climb. Then there are the sharp and dangerous curves, the endless vast bridges, the speed at which you sometimes travel, just frightening; other times it is nothing but a slow, boring poke. We haven't even mentioned the construction, the traffic jams, red lights, honking horns, stopping and going, getting lost, having to detour, and asking for directions. It truly is a never-ending, unpredictable journey. And Michael, I think you focus on this whole impossible process. You have to ignore it, son. The happiness lies in the journey. You have only a short time to travel Michael, stop at as many viewing points as you can."

"Goodnight, Mama."

"Goodnight, Michael."

January 23, 1999

[RECORD]

"Hi, Mama. Okay, Maddy, climb up there and give Grandma a kiss. Gentle now, good job. Go see Grandpap now. I think he has a surprise for you."

"Hey, Mama, how ya feeling?"

"Tired."

"Everybody told me you were recording our conversations. I see they were right. Well, I owe you a lot of talking anyhow. First, Mama, I'm really sorry about being away so much. Damn trial, I gave it everything. Seventeen, Mama, the girl who was killed was only seventeen. Her name was Tiffany. I guess it's not supposed to matter, because she was a bad girl. She did drugs, she danced in a strip club, lied about her age. Her thirty-six-year-old boyfriend pimped her out. He eventually killed her, accidentally, I guess.

"Her death consisted of an overdose on the bad drugs he had been feeding her and then really rough sex. The combined two caused her asphyxiation. Involuntary manslaughter is the least he is guilty of. He was found guilty of nothing.

"The defense stated that Tiffany didn't die during the act of sex (regardless of the choke marks), but shortly after. She choked on her own vomit from a drug overdose. They further stated that she took these drugs of her own free will. The same free will that liked rough sex. They went on to parade scuzzball after scuzzball into that courtroom to testify how she liked sex rough, including being choked while she climaxed. It was of her own free will, right, Mama? Except I know that this child had no such thing as free will. For crying out loud, I couldn't even get her mother to come to court for her dead child. The crazy mother referred to her own daughter as a "little slut." The truth is Tiffany was being sexually abused by her mother's boyfriend. The mother blamed Tiffany and kicked her out.

"What meaning does that have, Mama? What was the meaning of that child's life? A sexually abused and tossed-away kid that went on to more sexual abuse, numbing her pain with drugs and eventually dying. And nobody is held responsible. What am I supposed to learn from that, to take from that? I don't get it. To say that a seventeen-year-old child is to be blamed for her own death is the same as saying she is blamed for her own birth.

"I don't know, Mama, I think I'm burned out. It wasn't supposed to be like this. I was supposed to make a difference with my life. Instead I have neglected my child, basically given her to my sister. I have neglected my husband, and I think there have been times when I have given him away too, if you know what I mean.

"I wish you weren't recording me, Mama. Honesty is hard. I have led everyone to believe that I have it all figured out, and in the process I have deceived myself and everyone else."

"Beverly, I don't know the reason for your seventeen-year-old-murder victim. It certainly is unfair. Maybe she was an angel, the kind sent to expose pain, to sharpen our senses, to awaken our compassion, and maybe she was just a seventeen-year-old girl who had a hard life. I do not understand man's inhumanities to man; it is one of the things I have been praying for, to understand suffering. I do believe there was meaning in that child's life, and I do believe there was meaning in her death, even if it was just to put an end to her suffering. As far as your life goes, your happiness does not come from things or accomplishments. Honey, you can get happiness only from the triumphs that you win inside your soul, not outside."

"But Mom, what about Maddy? I have already failed her."

"Beverly, she is six years old. You have failed at nothing. On the contrary, you have shown her what strong women can accomplish."

January 24, 1999

[RECORD]

"Hi, Ruthie."

"Hi, Shannon, come on in."

"I brought by some nail polish. I thought you could pick a color, and I would paint your fingers and toes."

"Oh, Shannon, you are such a treat. I think I like that pink."

"I thought that's what you would pick. I'll do your toes first, but I'm going to start by giving them a little massage and soft scraping.

"Mmmm."

"Ruthie?"

"Yes"

"I need to talk to you about Michael. I want to apologize that he is dealing with me and our problems during a time when he should just be focused on you. I am so sorry. I never meant to intrude into your family like this. I feel like such a selfish person, to go change things up on him at this particular time in his life. I should have just waited."

"You mean until after I died, Shannon?"

"Oh Ruthie, I didn't mean…"

"It's okay, Shannon. It is perfectly all right to live within reality. I guess you could have waited, but then you would have to break it off with a man who just lost his mother, so then you would wait even longer. Then who knows what would come up. Life does seem to be unpredictable. No, Shannon, I think you did the right thing. I believe all my children are being tested right now, and all of it seems to be happening while they watch their mother die. Now don't cry, Shannon. It's not your fault. No, honey, you did nothing wrong. It's bigger than both of us. We have no control of our situation at this time. It is clear to me that it is all being guided by a stronger hand, and whatever is meant to be, will be."

"Ruthie, I'm going to miss you. You may be the best person I have ever known."

"Well, thank you. That certainly is a nice thing to be remembered by."

"Ruthie?"

"Yes."

"I do love Michael. I love him more than any man I have ever known. He is so bad, but he is also so good, and I can't help but love him forever, whether we are together or not. So it's not that I don't want Michael. On the contrary, I want him more than I want anything. I just don't want to go through life loving a man more than he loves me. My mother did that, and it wasn't good. Maybe no love is equal, but I don't want to be so in love that I appear needy or pathetic. I need to know Michael's love is equal to mine. I need to be respected and desired. I want to be the one that is the beloved."

"Makes sense, honey; that's what all women want."

"Well, your toes are done; now let me get to those beautiful hands."

"Shannon is gone, my feet and hands are soft, and my toes and fingers are a pretty pink. I do believe everything is going to be fine with Michael and Shannon. They don't realize it yet, but I see clearly that they will be the happiest of married couples."

January 25, 1999

I haven't eaten in days. I can no longer swallow. Hospice came, and I signed papers. No feeding tubes, no nothing; just drugs, more and more drugs. I am in a fog. In my dreams we have just bought the home that we have lived in for the past forty years. My birthday is February 2, and I will be sixty-nine. I don't believe I will be here to celebrate.

[RECORD]

"Do you have to hit that God damn recorder every time someone tries to talk to you?"

"Well, Earl, of course I do. It is my last project; my last little bit of doing something."

"You always did have to be doing something. Foolish to try and stop ya now."

"Earl, I don't know what this obsession is. You know how Beverly was during her pregnancy, recording everything, keeping calendars and journals, photographs and video tape. She was into recording a miracle. I think that's maybe what I'm doing."

"Well then, you go ahead, baby, because you are a miracle. You are my miracle."

"Oh, Earl."

"Shh, now, Ruthie, I just came in here to nap with you."

"That would be nice...Earl, I have been dreaming of my life, and I'm almost to its end."

"Ruthie, shh, I want to nap."

"No, Earl, let me say this. Thank you for making my dreams so nice."

"No. Thank you, Ruthie. Thank you."

"Earl, it's going to happen soon. I know it will be hard, but please don't take me over to the hospice house. I want to die here. If I can no longer move or talk, please push Record for me while the kids say their good-byes. I don't want this project to go unfinished."

"Ruthie, let's just take a nap. You are wearing me out."

January 27, 1999

[RECORD]

"Hey, Mama, how ya doing?"

"Tired."

"Your fingers look pretty."

"Shannon did that. She did my toes too."

"Shannon, she's a good girl. You know she and Michael are going to be just fine."

"I do know that, Maureen."

"Mama, I know you are worried about Daddy and everybody, but I want you to know that Ben and I will make sure everybody is okay, especially Daddy. We'll have him over and help him out."

"Now Maureen, honey, I want you to promise me something."

"Yes, Mama."

"I know you are here to take care of everybody, but I don't want you to leave yourself out. Sometimes people have to heal themselves, Maureen. Sometimes it works out better that way. Maureen, you have the gift of healing, the gift of understanding people, of knowing and not judging, the gift of acceptance and compassion, the gift of bringing out the beauty of others. People come to you to be healed, and you do a fine job. But honey, don't lose yourself in the process. Somehow, Maureen, you're going to have to create a balance."

"I understand what you are saying, Mama, and I know you are right. It is already happening, and I don't know how to stop it."

"Well, Maureen, all talents must be fine tuned. You surely are practicing, but what are you learning? You're like the little girl who practices her violin daily until her fingers bleed, yet she never gets to play in the concert. Focus your gifts, Maureen."

January 28, 1999

I have never been so weak. I can no longer lift my head; my body is a weight. I barely have enough energy to talk. Mostly I live inside myself now.

January 28 (later that day)

[RECORD]

"It's just me, Mama, Maureen. We are all hitting Record on your player, just as you requested. You have been sleeping all day. You look comfortable in your sleep; sometimes you smile, and sometimes you laugh. I wish I knew what you were thinking. I've been giving a lot of thought to what you said yesterday, and I know you are right. I'm just gonna have to ponder it so much more to figure out how to change things, but right now, I'm too busy to even ponder. I have to run and get the boys and taxi them to every activity there is. I'm still getting Maddy from school, even though Beverly has been better at picking her up. Most days she is there by five o'clock, which is a good thing, 'cause AA meetings usually start around seven, and I take Donnell. And then there is this sadness, Mama, my overwhelming sadness at seeing you sick and Daddy scared. We are all going to lose you, Mama, and you are the one that makes this family work. You are the touchstone."

"Maureen?"

"Did I wake you? Mama, I'm sorry."

"Maureen, I'm not dying."

"What?"

"I'm not dying."

"Mama, you're dreaming. It's okay, you can go back to sleep."

"I saw them, Maureen."

"Who, Mama?"

"I saw both paths. They're both so serene and beautiful. The smell of pine fills you up. The path itself is soft earth blanketed by pine needles. The trees are enormous and green, and the sky blue. One path does lead to death, Maureen, but here's the catch: it's your choice. The other path leads to an eternal life in God's center. I assume that may be where the light is. I didn't see the light, just the two most beautiful nature trails that exist."

"Mama?"

"It's okay, Maureen, I'm going to walk the path of eternal life, and it will be so good to be out of this bed."

January 29, 1999

[RECORD]

"Hey, Mama, it's just me, Donnell. Maureen said that you have been tired lately, so I will not wake you. I just wanted to talk. Don't you worry, though, because I'm recording. Actually, Mama, I wanted you to know that I am now fourteen days sober. That's right, Mama. I haven't had a drink in two weeks. It is hard, extremely hard, and from looks around here, it's just going to get harder. Could I have picked a worse time to give up drinking? I mean, good heavens, Mama, the odds on me getting caught now, it all just seems ridiculous. I've been a drunk for so long and hadn't had any trouble with it at all, well, except for the occasional sex with someone you wouldn't have had sex with if you had been sober. But even that seemed fun, Mama. Then wham, all of a sudden, here you are sick and getting ready to leave us, and I'm trying to get my head around all of it and then slam, alcohol has the nerve to start fucking with me. It just starts screwing my life up, and all that seemed fun is now nothing but embarrassing moments, and all that seemed to be in my control, is no longer.

"Donnell?"

"Hey, Mama, sorry I woke you."

"Donnell, did you bring Maddy in here?"

"Maddy? Mama, Maddy's not here; she's at school."

"No, Donnell, Maddy, she is right beside you."

"Mama, what are you talking about? You're scaring me."

"Oh, I see now. Oh, honey, I'm sorry I scared you. You're right; she's not Maddy."

"Mama, do you see a little girl?"

"It's okay, Donnell, it's just Esther; little Esther is here."

"Daddy! Daddy come quick!"

January 29, 1999 later that day.

[RECORD] (Earl)

"Ruthie, all four kids are here. We are going to stay with you honey, we are not going to leave."

[RECORD] (Beverly)

"Hey, Mama, it's three o'clock in the morning, and I can't sleep. Nobody really has had much sleep. We are supposed to get our rest in turns and wake each other when it's time. Except I'm terrified that we won't know the time and we will miss it. Daddy is scared of this too, so he has propped his recliner chair right up next to your bed, and he is holding your hand. He has nodded off for a minute, so I thought I would talk.

"I want to thank you for the insights you have given to me. After years of thinking I was smarter than everybody else, years of only listening to professors or highly degreed professionals for my meaning in life, as if they have a clue. I now realize that all the understanding I needed was right inside the head of my very own mama—housewife, gardener, church lady extraordinaire, all that seemed unimportant to me.

"Please forgive me, Mama. Please forgive me for not realizing until now how truly brilliant and talented and amazing you are. Please forgive me for not wanting to be more like you. I do now.

"I tried like hell, Mama, to run from this place; to rise above it and to have more than you and Daddy. I felt so damn superior. I thought education was my ticket to a better way of life. But it's not better, it's just different, and most of the time it's not as good. You are right, Mama. It is not our outward appearance. It is our middle. Thank you for my final and most inspiring lesson. You are and have always been my greatest teacher. I love you."

January 30, 1999 – morning

[RECORD] (Maureen)

"Well, Mama, it's morning, and you're still with us. I scrambled some eggs this morning and made some coffee, and everybody is out in the kitchen trying to choke down some food. I don't think any of us has the stomach for food right now. Daddy didn't want to leave his chair, but I told him I wanted a few minutes alone.

"Mama, I need to know, what do I do now? Oh God, what am I to do now? How do I fill my time? I've just been thinking how you and I have made a life out of being each other's caretaker, first your being mine, of course, up to and even after the acceptance of my early pregnancies. I was so young, Mama. I know now, being the mother of a teen, how difficult it must have been on you and Daddy. How shocked and disappointed you must have been. But you, Mama, you always made me feel accepted. My teen pregnancy and then my teen marriage and then two more pregnancies right after that—the whole time you believed in Ben and me. Through it all, you were my rock. When others criticized us, you congratulated us. You taught me to be a mommy before I was ready. You taught me how to be a wife before

I was ready. Then when you got sick, we were able to bind our souls even tighter. I thought we would flip positions and that I would be able to give a little of what I got. Little did I know that I would still be on the receiving end.

"You're amazing, Mama. Nothing ever has brought you down. Even in sickness—good Lord, even in death—you continue to be our nurturer, our mentor, our teacher, our leader. What are we going to do without you, Mama, and how am I supposed to fill my days? My best friend is dying, and I'm going to miss her so much. I love you, Mama. Thank you for everything.

January 30 (10:00 a.m.)

[RECORD] (Donnell)

"This is so hard, Mama. There has never been anything so hard. I need to tell you how sorry I am, so sorry, if I made things harder on you in life. I can't bear to think of the pain I caused you. I do apologize for being such a fuck- up. I guess that was my role, or at least I thought it was. I didn't have the tools to be anyone else. Beverly had cornered the market on brains. She got to be the smart one, and she sure did let us all know that she was smarter than we were. But hey, that's all right. We are all glad she is smart. She wouldn't be Beverly if she weren't. Then there's Maureen. I couldn't have played that role either. Maureen was born good-natured, mature, and responsible. She is the caring one. Michael got to be the only boy and your baby. So that left me, "The Wild Card." Oh, and I did play it so well, didn't I, Mama? I was so ornery, Mama; but fun. You have to admit I was fun. Now I am sorry. Now I'm tired, and I've been sitting here in this sick room with my siblings and my father (needing a drink) and watching my mother take her final breaths. There is nothing in the world harder than watching you die.

"I love you, Mama. You are my light."

January 30, 1999

[RECORD] (Michael)

"It's high noon, Mama. I guess this is what you wanted, a recording. We are trying to do our best, but you have asked a difficult and morbid task. I guess I shouldn't complain; you have never really asked us all to do that much before. You mothered us by letting us be ourselves, by accepting our sometimes-flawed behaviors, and always having good advice. For that, we all thank you.

"Daddy sits beside you, holding your hand. Maureen and Beverly are to your right. Donnell is at your feet, and I am on your left, next to Daddy. Your curtains are open, and the sunlight is pouring in on you. You almost appear to be glowing, Mama. The animals must have a feel for what's going on, because your back yard, Mama, is full of birds and chipmunks and squirrels, and they are eating the generous amount of food there. They also seem to be watching and listening, and to tell you the truth, Mama, it is quite an eerie feeling.

"We have been playing Frank Sinatra real low on your little CD player all night and day. Daddy says you would want to die listening to "I Did It My Way," or at least the man who sings it. We have been burning tea-rose candles, and we put fresh flowers in your vase. Your room is pleasant, Mama; it smells real nice, and feels warm and cozy, just the way you like it.

"The hardest part is that your chest is rattling, and you struggle with your breaths. You haven't talked in over twenty-four hours, and I don't believe Daddy has either. You are both sharing this kind of godly silence. You drift in and out of consciousness, and you still smile. I guess your request for taping this is to create some little piece of heritage we are supposed to preserve or to just have tangible evidence of your existence that lasts beyond our lives. I think we are all starting to understand all this, Mama; you always did think ahead of us. I think that Maddy will grow up to take on the responsibility of these recordings properly.

"Being your only son, I am honored to record your last minutes on this earth. You have always been an earthly angel, Mama, with a spirit beyond our mere grasp. We have been honored to live in your presence, in your light, under your care. There has never been a better Mama.

"Mama, you just opened your eyes and looked at me, so I do know that you hear what I am saying. I love you too, Mama. You are now looking around the room, and we are all crying, trying hard to contain ourselves, but we are pouring over. You are leaving us, Mama, aren't you? I guess that smirk means yes. You are now gazing at Daddy, and he at you. You squeeze his hand, and you are gone."

End:

LIBBY

The stars go waltzing out in blue and red,
and arbitrary blackness gallops in:
I shut my eyes and all the world drops dead.

God topples from the sky, hell's fires fade:
exit seraphim and Satan's men:
I shut my eyes and all the world drops dead

"Mad Girl's Love Song" by Sylvia Plath

Feb 2, 1999

I'm waiting to hear about the groundhog. If winter lasts any longer, I think I may die. The darkness is slowly killing me. I haven't been warm since October. My hands are always cold. I can't stand my own touch. Why is it that the shortest month of the year feels like the longest? A cruel trick of Mother Nature. I guess she can be a bitch too. Honestly, March isn't much better. That "in like a lion out like a lamb" is just bullshit. I have never seen a lamb in March.

FEBRUARY

The wind howls in my ear
Darkness rolls in before dinnertime
The sun is so fickle this time of year
Only the coldness can I call mine.

Feb 2, 1999 – 6:00 p.m.

The stupid-ass groundhog saw his shadow, and like the dumb, wimp-ass animal that he is, he crawled back into his hole to sleep, leaving us bigger, stronger animals to fend for ourselves. Move over, groundhog, share your dark hole with me. I want to cuddle around your fur and sleep winter away with you.

Instead I am forced to endure six more weeks of cold and dark, of suffering, of starving deer and gray, slushy streets. It all makes me so sad—I cannot even function. Like the groundhog, I will sleep.

Feb 3, 1999 3:00 a.m.

Cannot sleep any longer. I am now up and wanting something to do. I have already eaten three bowls of cereal. Will watch MTV.

Feb 3, 1999 second-period math class

I am sitting here in this fucking math class about to go out of my mind. I am not doing this F-ING test sitting on the desk in front of me. I can't even force myself to look at the paper. All those numbers, rows and rows of equations and signs. One runs into the next, which runs into the next. I can't concentrate on the first problem, because all I see are the numbers that come after—two fucking pages of numbers. Numbers are swirling in my head. Formula after formula, they are on a hamster wheel twirling inside my brain.

I AM SO FUCKING OVERWHELMED! I can't do it. I will die if I try. My brain will explode, my head cracking apart, spilling bloody numbers onto the floor. Ms. Faulkner is just going to have to make another phone call to my mother. Tell her I am unmotivated, tell her I am oppositional. I guess you are right, Ms. Faulkner, but fuck you anyway.

Still Feb 3 Lunchtime

EAT NOTHING. I feel bad. I blew math big time. My grade about sucks in there. I need my mind to stop spinning. I am getting worse. Maybe I am retarded.

Feb 3, 7:00 p.m.

School was terrible today. I could do nothing. I can't believe I handed in an empty math test. I wrote nothing. I ended up having to leave school, I cut out sixth period. Shit, it will be another call home.

Feb 3, 9:00 p.m.

I can no longer keep the wolf caged. He now paces back and forth inside of me, prowling around all night, keeping me from sleep. He is so strong and aggressive. He is feral, always prepared to attack. He keeps me safe; he empowers me; he scares me.

I think I hate myself most when the wolf is awake. My mother just came into my room a little bit ago, and the wolf snarled. The wolf caused me to scream, "Get the fuck out!" which caused my mother to cringe in horror as she laid a neat pile of folded laundry on my dresser. She can be so lame. She swore last week she would no longer do my laundry, and then here she comes, in all her weakness, with a stack of Downy-smelling T-shirts and panties. Thanks, Mom, you wuss.

God, see how mean I am when the wolf is out? I HATE ME! I HATE ME!

I try to beat the wolf back by scratching my long and sharp nails down my arms, but it feels too good. I need something sharper, something that cuts open the flesh and bleeds all the anger out. I use a straight razor. I hide it under the red felt of my jewelry box. I cut my arms in short parallel lines across my forearm. I never go as far as the wrist. It is not about death; it is about the turning of pain. If it ever gets too hard, I am not afraid to use the razor for my death. My arms look like a patchwork quilt. I have plenty of cocoa butter lotion to soften my scars. I wear long sleeves. When my arms are too sore, I cut my upper thigh. When I'm cutting, I think I just want my pain on the outside. It is so hard to deal with the wolf alone. If I could just show what the pain looks like, I could get better. But when I'm done cutting, I don't want anyone to see it. My horrid flesh—I'm a monster—what would they think of me?

I can usually keep the wolf chained while I'm at school, but the frustration that he causes by the end of the day is unbearable. I have held him off so long that by 3:00, when the door shuts behind me, I release my grip on his chain, and the wolf tears back and forth inside me, hyper and wild from being chained up all day.

I guess I started calling my out-of-control anger "the wolf" when I was about twelve. Before that, I didn't know what to call it. What was it that caused me to shake on the grocery store floor because I couldn't have both peanut butter and chocolate chip cookies? What was it that always kept me awake, never getting a full night's sleep, never being able to nap?

It was the wolf who knocked Jimmy Safco off his bike, causing him to chip his front tooth. Jimmy shouldn't have been taunting me. It pissed the wolf off. It was the wolf who told Ms. Evans, my ninth grade home-ec teacher to fuck off! That was after she turned her nose up at my corn soufflé, which by the way tasted fine. The wolf is my protector, my guard dog from within. Yet I wish he would disappear. I wish he would die.

THE WOLF

A snarling dog lives inside my brain.
The snarling dog causes my pain.
He growls, bites, barks, and drools.
He's always frightened—yet he's always cool.
This beast prowls ravishingly in my head.
I wish I could live with the beast dead,
But we're one and the same, him and I;
for the beast to go, I must die

February 4

I am wearing my favorite soft blue sweater, with my hair pulled back in a French twist. I think I may look a little pretty today. I didn't get much sleep last night. Wolfie prowled around until about 2:00 a.m. He finally found a place to curl up inside my brain and go to sleep. My mom woke me at 6:00 a.m., and I am so proud of myself for actually being able to get up and out of bed, which I did quite easily.

I have decided to do better. Who cares that it is f-ing cold and dark all the time? I am not going to let it affect me. First thing to do is make math right. I will go to Mrs. Faulkner and ask her if I can retake the math test. I think I can do it now. I'll tell her I was sick yesterday.

Feb 4, third-period class

I can't stand Ms. Faulkner. I went to her and basically begged that I get another chance, and she stared me straight in the face and mockingly said "No" and then went on to lecture me on my attitude and personality. I didn't listen. I couldn't hear her, the voice and words were not audible. I had checked out after hearing "No." I wanted to scratch her eyes out. I can't stand her. I did not scratch her. I just glared back. What the fuck would it hurt her, if I retake a math test? What's the worst thing that could happen, I actually accomplish something? Stupid bitch, she wants me to fail.

Feb 4 – Lunch

Not eating today, not after all the crap I ate in the middle of the night. I've had a Slimfast bar for breakfast. I'll smoke my cigarettes for lunch, and then I'll eat a sensible dinner. How's that for a Slimfast commercial?

Feb 4, 11:00 p.m.

Shit hit the fan tonight, and now I feel like shit. Ms. Faulkner called my mom to let her know that I refused to take a math test. Mr. Phillips called my mom to let her know I cut my last two classes. I tried like hell to explain to her that I was sick on the day of the test, so I didn't take it and then came home to sleep. I told her I had asked if I could retake the test, and Ms. Faulkner wouldn't let me.

My mom didn't listen, or if she did, she didn't truly hear me. Ms. Faulkner and Mr. Philips had gotten to her first and had filled her mind with crazy notions about me. I'm a worthless student who is disrespectful and defiant. I cannot fight them all. Not without the wolf tearing through my brain, causing me to say too many horrible things.

My mother ended up grounding me, for things I couldn't even control, things I had already tried to make right. It's a conspiracy to make me lose control. I wasn't going to go anywhere. I was tired and mentally worn out, but just the word "grounded" caused me to climb out my bedroom window after my mom had gone to bed.

I was walking down the road bundled up to my nose but enjoying the night, and then here comes Jimmy Safco in his new little Mazda, and I end up getting in. First we just drove around, but then Jimmy found someone who would buy us beer. We ended up drinking inside his car with the windows rolled up, heat cranked on, and stereo blaring.

Next thing I know, I'm giving Jimmy Safco head, which is one thing I want to stop doing. At the time I felt powerful and sexy; now I feel like a slut. The worst part is Jimmy doesn't even talk to me at school, yet here he comes every time I'm alone and vulnerable, searching me out and taking advantage of me. What's worse is I have always secretly loved Jimmy Safco. I wish I could hate him too.

Feb 5, 1999

I am a seventeen-year-old grounded teenager. You would think the phone would ring off the hook for me. Sadly, no one has called. I have no friends; not real friends, anyway, just a few guys who like to pal around with me and then expect something in return. Girls don't like me, probably because the guys do. I could hang out with the popular girls if I wanted to. I'm thin with a nice complexion and long, dark hair. I could have any wardrobe I want, because I am the only child of divorced parents who both try and buy my love (or at least Daddy does). But the popular girls don't like me. I'm too quiet, too standoffish, and I have slept with their boyfriends. The bad girls don't like me for the same reason.

February 6, 1999

It's one hell of a boring weekend. Oh well, I like things being quiet. I think I like being grounded. It is an excuse to stay in my room. I read, I write, I listen to music. Nobody opens the door and tells me to do something.

For breakfast, or rather brunch, I cooked with my mom, just the two of us filling up our small kitchen. We made scrambled eggs with vegetables and cheeses covering the skillet, which is basically a scrambled omelet, and we had bread with butter and hot tea.

This is what can be cool about just a mom and a kid living together. We talked and got along great, neither of us bringing up any bad stuff I have done recently. I am now in my room and my mom is in hers. I am writing, and she probably is too.

I hope I can sleep. I will have to get more pot from Jimmy tomorrow. I will probably have to put out for it this time, but I don't care. If it makes all my days go this smoothly, it is well worth it. Girls sleep with guys for a lot less.

February 6, 4:00 p.m.

Dad just called and asked me for dinner. It would be nice if it was just him and me. I love dinner with Daddy; he has really expensive taste. He likes to wine and dine his ladies, and I'm one of them, his favorite. But it's not that, tonight. Oh, tonight we will go someplace nice and beautiful, but not just the two of us. No, tonight I get to meet his new princess bitch. It will be great fun. It's not like I haven't been through all this before. Dad treats his women the same way he treats his cars. He takes such pride in picking them out, purchasing them, washing, waxing, and driving them, and then when they get more mileage than he finds attractive, he trades them in for a younger and more improved model.

Mom got to be Dad's first wife, and I got to be his only child. Since my mom, there have been two more wives and a slew of girlfriends.

I'm still the only child. Stepsisters and brothers come and go. I make relationships, and then I get to break them. Sometimes I even get to babysit for some younger girlfriend's spoiled brat. Dad pays me well, but the whole ordeal isn't good for either the child or me.

I guess at least Dad does something. He tries to have relationships, unlike Mom, who would prefer to stay home and hate all men. Oh well, better get ready. I wonder what shocking outfit I could come up with to make the bitch's hair curl.

February 6, 9:00 p.m.

Well, it's Saturday night, and I'm back home. Couldn't spend the night with my Dad, thanks to the princess bitch. This totally sucks, 'cause I really need to get away, and I like Dad's pad, which is exactly what it is, "a pad." He lives in a freaking condominium for the fucking rich and privileged, F-ing pools, indoor and out, a racquetball court, tennis court, and weight room.

I like to play racquetball just by myself. I shut myself into the room, four walls, can't even tell where the door is, and everything echoes. Nothing but me, a small, blue ball, and a racquet. I pound the hell out of that ball. The speed and the sweat, the violence of the sport, the solitude, I love it all. I love smashing that small ball into the wall and the momentum with which it tries to strike back at me, and I smash it again. Racquetball works like my mind, and for a short while, I get to act it out and not look so crazy.

Dad said maybe I could come over tomorrow night. He's an ass to pick that princess bitch over me. Now I know how my mom feels. I must admit the princess is pretty, and she tried very hard to be nice. The Lord knows I didn't make it easy on her. The thing I like most about her is she has no kids, no one for me to watch, no one for my father to spoil, and no one else to get tangled up in his monstrous web.

I mean it's okay for me; I'm used to my father's web. I was born into it and fit nicely in its strings. They cradled me as a baby, and now

I use them for my personal hammock, but if you don't have to experience the magical strings, it's probably best if you don't.

Maybe tomorrow afternoon I will go shopping with my mother, a ritual that takes place after I meet a new princess. Mom says it's to make me feel better, make sure I'm all right. Yeah, f-ing right, Mom. You just want to know who she is.

February 7, 1999

Mom tried like hell to get me to go to church this morning. I'm like, What the fuck? If I want to go to church, I will, and it won't be with her. She doesn't even go to a real church. She goes to some unity house 'cause she doesn't even know what fucking religion she is. She says she has no one prescribed religion; she is a "spiritualist" and does not believe in organized religion. Well, guess the fuck what, Mom. A Sunday morning spent in a unity house is a fucking organized religion!

I swear I hate hypocrites. Besides, I'm supposed to go to Dad's, remember? When I said this, she gave me one of those pity looks. She can be such a bitch.

February 7, 1999

Called Dad all morning, no answer. Sitting here feeling melancholy. Think I'll write a poem. This is a first memory.

DADDY'S GIRL

I see my dad; he is handsome,
with a mound of soft brown curls and olive skin.
He is wearing a black tuxedo,
and his deep brown eyes are sparkling at me.
We are at a wedding, his sister's, Aunt Ellen,
A big Jewish wedding with lots of food and happy people.
Daddy and I are dancing.

We have been dancing for hours.
Mostly I twirl, because I like to watch the floor spin, and
I love the way it blows out my dress.
When I plop down on my bottom from dizziness,
Daddy laughs and lifts me up and twirls me some more.
We are so happy,
But where is Mommy?
Oh, I see her.
She is alone again, like always, in a corner, my quiet mommy.
She is a watcher,
Not a doer like Daddy and me.
She has flowers in her hair.

February 7, 1999 5:00 p.m.

Mom took me shopping when she came home from church (ritual, see?). I got nothing; just wasn't in the mood. Mom bought herself a long flowing hippie skirt. I think she has the same skirt in two other colors. Now Mom is walking around feeling sorry for me. I must have looked completely deflated after I ran to check the phone messages when we got home. No call from Dad.

February 7, 1999 – 9:00 p.m.

Still haven't heard from Dad, but Jimmy Safco drove by about 7:00 p.m., and Mom was so relieved to have me out of the house that she forgot I was grounded. Well, Jimmy ended up getting lucky, and I ended up with a small bag of weed all my own. Not a bad deal. I get to screw someone I'm actually attracted to and get a little reward to boot.

I got it over on all the other high school sluts. They're just trying to build self-esteem. I'm building a little business arrangement. Now that I have my pot, I can get some sleep tonight.

February 8, 1999

Shit, I'm freaking out. Alan Chafin just asked me to the Valentine's dance. Fuck! Why did anyone have to ask me? I'm such a freak. Don't they know I can barely even make it into this building every morning? The thought of being at school is enough to make me vomit and shake and run crying. I hate my teachers, and what's worse, I hate the kids. I feel them look at me, sneer, whisper. Why in the fuck would Alan Chafin want to take me to a school dance? I have never been asked on a date. I have only been asked to bed. I lost my virginity two years ago and still have never been on a date.

I like Alan. I really do. He's a nerd. He's quiet and he's shy and he is smart. I think school is hard for him too. He doesn't have a lot of friends, just your other basic nerds. He gets along well with the teachers, though. They love him, and he respects them, which doesn't help his social status among the youth at all.

I told him I had to check my calendar, and he looked at me as if I were a freak, which I am. I told him I didn't know if I would be seeing Dad that night, and he acted like he understood, but he knows it's just an excuse. Fuck, the only problem is, I didn't make the excuse because of him. I made it because of me. I'm the dysfunctional one. I'm the outcast, the loner. Run, Alan, run, fast and far away. I give blow jobs to boys who couldn't care less about me, just to smoke pot. I'm a secret pothead, and the potheads don't even like me. I fit nowhere. I am no one. I thought I walked the halls invisible until you had to notice and ask me to a dance. Guess what, Alan. A vicious dog lives inside my head, and the only time I can freely let him out is when I play racquetball. Crazy, huh? Do you still want to take me on a date? I guess Alan is not as smart as I thought.

February 8 – late

I can't sleep. I eat and then I get sick and then I eat some more. Great, now I have a fucking eating disorder to add to my problems, except I don't make myself sick. It just happens, and it's not coming from my mouth. It's shooting out of my ass. Attractive.

YES, I AM BEAUTIFUL!

My stomach is full of knots. It feels empty and hollow, so I fill it with food. It's something to do, trying to cut the boredom, you know? But five minutes after I eat, I can feel it all turning inside me, and I cramp and then I shit, and it's gross and it's disgusting and it's who I am, a gross and disgusting creature.

My bowels are much worse when the dog is out, and guess what, he's out. I don't know if it's because of Dad standing me up or because of Jimmy using me up or because of Alan asking me out. It's all too much! Why can't I just die? I would love to just sleep—a death sleep!

A DEATH PRAYER

Now I lay me down to sleep.
I wish to God my soul to keep.
I wish for death and not to wake.
I wish for God my soul to take

February 9, 1999

Staying home from school today, only this time it's legit. Mom heard me up and down all night long, and I told her I have diarrhea. She gave me some Pepto-Bismol, made me some toast and oatmeal, and then went on to work. The oats were good with lots of butter and sugar. I made myself some hot chocolate to go with it. I probably shouldn't have hot chocolate, in my condition, but I like it. Hot chocolate makes me feel happy.

My belly is full; I put thick, warm socks on my feet and mittens on my hands. Warm hands and warm feet also make me feel happy. I have wrapped myself up in my soft green comforter as if it were my cocoon. I feel warm and content and ready to burrow down and sleep. When I wake, I will be a beautiful butterfly, and it will be spring.

February 9, 4:00 p.m.

I managed to sleep the entire school day away, and although my dreams were beautiful (not the normal nightmarish hell I endure during sleep), I am still the same girl I was before entering my sleep. I am still plain old Libby, and there is still snow and ice on the ground. The only transformation that has taken place is the one inside my head. It is calm in there; let a sleeping dog lie.

I would love to get up and shower. My hair and skin feel dirty, and I have a sour smell to my body, but showering would involve getting wet and then being cold, something I cannot face. I will sit here for two more hours, not even leaving my comforter to pee until I have to. My mother will walk in at 6:00 p.m., feed me, and make me get up.

February 10, 1999

I am a champion above champions, except it is unknown. Only I know how tremendous a feat I had today. Yes, I crawled from my cocoon. Yes, I undressed and allowed my sunken, cold body to get wet. Yes, I emerged from the shower, even though it took forty-five minutes and pounding on the door from my mother. I stepped out. Yes, I even did my hair with a blow dryer, and I dressed in jeans, not the warm sweats that I want to live and die in. But I dressed in actual jeans, cold and crisp, and a sweater that fits tight. Did I stop there? No, I did not. This unknown champion then ventured out into the cold, into the morning, having smoked my last cigarette last night. I bravely walked the two blocks to high school.

This unknown champion then did the most remarkable of all remarkable things. I told Alan Chafin I would go to the Valentine's dance with him. Well, actually I told him I would meet him there. "I'll be at the doors at 7:00 p.m.," I said, actually smiling at the young brave soldier who smiled back at the unknown champion.

February 11, 1999

I have smoked half a pack of cigarettes since school let out. I must slow down. The guy at the gas station around the block sells them to me when he's working, and he works Monday through Friday. How convenient; those are actually the same days I am given lunch money. Tim, the gas station guy, knows I'm underage. He also knows I'm a good lay. I like sex with old guys. Tim is actually only twenty-four, but that's still pretty old. Old enough to sell me cigarettes. Old enough to pump my mom's gas and change the oil. Old enough to take me to his small dirty studio apartment, give me a beer, and have sex with me, which we have actually done only once.

Back to the reason I smoked ten cigarettes in three hours. I am now frantic about this fucking dance. The champion of champions is scared. First of all, what do I wear? I cannot tell my mother I need a dress to go to a dance. She would be too happy, the pressure too great. With the news of the dance, my mother's mind would begin to play with her. She would become elated, and then she would think that maybe I am not the freak that I know I am. She would question herself, and she would question me. She would scoop me up in her arms and take me shopping, pulling cute red dresses off every rack (red for Valentine's Day, you know). There's bound to be a sleeveless one in the bunch that she would insist I try on, and then she would see my scars, and all her elated emotions would come crashing down in one big heap.

No, I have decided she cannot know about the dance. It is best for her to just live with the disappointment in me that she has always known, rather than allowing her to hope, then ripping away the rug and letting her land, once again, on her ass.

Since I have no girlfriends to speak of that I could borrow from and no money and no job, I am left to rummage through my own closet. I guess it could be worse. I could have been given a non-materialistic father who buys me nothing nice. As it has worked out, I have two prospective dresses to choose from; three, if you count the skirt and top ensemble worn to my cousin's bar mitzvah, but I believe it to be too casual. So I am left to choose from a black dress with long lace sleeves and a sweetheart neckline worn on my seventeenth birthday when Dad took me to a five-star restaurant and then to see *Evita*. Good night. Good dress. I also have a red velvet dress with shoulder straps that is worn under a black, short-cut velvet blazer. The blazer successfully takes the sexy look away from the red dress—important to my parents, and it covers my arms—important to me. I wore the dress to my father's New Year's Eve party. Both dresses could work. I have one pair of black heels, and my mother has an endless supply of black pantyhose. The plan goes as follows:

Get ready at home before 6:00 p.m.. Sweats over hose, coat over dress, heels in my bag. Walk to dance at 6:30 p.m.; 6:45 p.m., arrive at school. Go to the alcove doorway at the west side of school building, strip off sweats, change shoes; place discarded items in a bag; stash bag in bushes; walk around to the front of the building to meet Alan at 7:00 p.m. At the end of the night, retrieve items and head for home. Home by midnight.

I am going to tell my mom that I am spending time with a friend from school, Alana. Mom will be so happy that I have found a friend that she will let me leave. Oh, must give her fake phone number.

2:00a.m. - can't sleep

The Valentine's Day dance is actually today, Friday, February 12.

I am in such a tizzy, I cannot sleep. My mind keeps hurling thoughts my way. What if I get into a fight? I know that seems irrational, but it's not. The girls in school are not nice to me, and their sneers and fake smiles will cause me to lunge across the room and pound their heads into the ground.

I need to stay grounded. I have been counting my breathing, trying out the relaxation exercises that my mother prescribes for me. "Count your breaths, Libby. Count your breaths." This is a direction I have been given repeatedly, since babyhood. As I held my breath and turned blue, my mother would frantically try to appear calm and say, "Count your breaths, Libby. Count your breaths."

So I count my fucking breaths. Just spend time counting my breathing. I wonder how much fucking time I have wasted in my life counting my own breaths.

February 12, 1999 4:00 a.m.

I have been awake the entire night. I am going mad, too mad to even write.

February 12, 5:30 a.m.

I tried to relax myself with a hot bath and music, but it does not work. The music just pounds in my head and the bath makes me cold—I can never get it hot enough. I am going to wrap myself up in my cocoon and try to sleep.

It is now 6:30 a.m., and my mom just came in to wake me. My hair had dried into a tangled mess, and I swear my skin has faded. I almost look like a ghost. I am just a remnant of myself. I should call Alan to tell him I'm sick, but I don't know his number and I do not have the energy to look it up. Maybe I will feel better by tonight.

Still February 12, morning

My mother is worried about me. I think she may call off work and stay home with me. I told her that was not necessary. She asked if my diarrhea was gone. It was, but it's back. She doesn't think it's good to have diarrhea for three days. She says I'm wasting away to nothing. I do look sunken. My eyes have fallen into the back of my head. My lips are white. If my bowels stopped moving, I would believe I was dead.

February 12, 1999 afternoon

I can't believe I'm not at school, I'm sure Alan is looking for me. Maybe it's good that I'm not there. Maybe he will think I am sick, or maybe he will think I took the day off to get ready for him. Oh God, I think girls do that, cut school on dance days and go get their hair and nails done (so much fucking pressure). I hate high school. If I can't even handle the pressures of a f-ing Valentine's dance, f-ing prom is out of the picture.

Since I didn't have a fever and my mom's boss has been giving her shit, Mom reluctantly went to work. I am alone. I am free to get out of this bed, smoke a cigarette, eat junk, and watch MTV. Instead I lie here comatose, unable to move.

February 12, 1999 3:00 p.m.

I want to die. I truly want to close my eyes and not have to open them again. I want to lie down, cover myself in warmth, and sleep forever. I have looked through my mom's medicine cabinet, hoping to find something that would let me sleep for a lifetime. I find nothing. She believes in homeopathic remedies only, so unless I want to overdose on garlic pills or Echinacea, I'm shit out of luck. That's the problem with having a spiritualist for a mother. Everything in this house is organic. Have a cold? Drink tea. A sore throat? Warm salt water. Upset stomach? Peppermint. I can't O.D. on tea, salt water, or peppermint. It would be much easier to kill myself at my father's house. He's Jewish, which allows him a chock-full medicine cabinet.

Since I can't die and I no longer feel like living, I will sleep.

February 12, 5:00 p.m.

I have cut myself. I tried not to. I tried sleeping and eating and listening to music, but the urge and the pain inside of me is so great that the wolf woke up, and I cut myself. I made parallel lines across my forearms, which were actually looking quite good and had healed up nicely from the last incident.

I watched blood run down my arm and felt no pain. At one point I flipped over my wrist, exposing my bulging blue vein—so easy it would be to slice it, finally end my misery, bleed it all out. But then I remembered my mother and how she would find me with slit wrists. I thought about the blood stains it would leave on my soft blue carpet and how my mom would have to rip it up and how she would want to sell her house, because of all the memories we made here and how I died here and haunted her at night.

I couldn't slit my wrist. Instead I cried.

CUTTING

I sliced my white flesh and watched my red blood.
How quickly down my arm does it run,
and the pain on the inside is now on the out.
Will somebody take notice? This is my shout.

But now my flesh with horror I hide.
I felt the pain and cried.
To drain all the pain from within I did try,
Because if it stayed in, I think I would die.

February 12, 1999 7:00 p.m.

The phone rang from 3:30 p.m. until 6:30 p.m. I know it was Alan, but I couldn't pick it up. My thoughts are racing. There is no possible way for my mouth to keep up with my mind. I cannot talk to him. What do I say? One hundred things cross my mind, but none of them make much sense. I ignore the phone. Maybe he will get the picture.

February 12, 1999 7:30 p.m.

Mom just came home. She brought me chicken noodle soup and hot rolls from Bob Evans. She said, "I'm sorry you're sick, honey."

I said, "So am I."

She meant physically ill, but I know my mind is sick. It must be. Other girls can go to a school dance. They do not hide in their beds; they do not cut open their arms or have their shit turn to water. They look forward to dates and they make friends. They love crowds and parties and malls.

I lay panic stricken within my dark, glowing room. It is my five lava lamps that illuminate enough glow for writing, and if I lay my notebook at my head and prop my pillow up, I can maintain my warm fetal position and comforter-cocoon while I script.

I should be in front of the school right now. I close my eyes, and I can see Alan standing in front of the long red brick building. I bet he keeps ducking in and out of the doorway for warmth, every few minutes stepping out into the ice and wind, scanning the parking lot and walkway, anticipating my arrival. Happy, giddy, excited teens pass him. Giggling, flirty girls and obnoxious cocky boys. A sea of red dresses and black suits.

Inside the school are balloons and flashing cameras. Music and dancing light, laughter, and drama pour out the windows and door of the school building and layer Alan's background. Yet he stands there, freezing his fucking ass off waiting for me. I can see his black suit, the same suit worn by the jocks, yet they still look like the jocks, and he still looks like a nerd. I can see him holding the silly, stupid wrist corsage, probably purple, a fucking overrated color, but most likely red for Valentine's Day.

I bet his parents are happy for him, proud of their boy. I wonder how long he will stand in the cold before retreating home. How long is his endurance, how strong his idealism? How long will it take before he knows that the crazy bitch stood him up? Then he will toss my frozen corsage into the trash bin and head for home.

The wolf has been awake since the cutting. He prowls around my head, and I pace my room. I did try the dress on. Okay, I tried the fucking dress on, the black one, and I looked like shit and the lace rubbed my new cuts, and I ripped the fucking thing off and left it lifeless on my bedroom floor. Why did I tell that fucking boy I would be there? Why would I accept such a proposal? I HATE MYSELF! I HATE MYSELF!

February 13, 1999

Saturday!

I made it through the night. It is the weekend, and I feel much better. The dance is over. I did not die going, and I did not die by not going. Alan has the weekend to be angry and then think things through. I had breakfast this morning with my mom, and I surprised her by telling her I was better and asking her if we could go to a movie. I need to get out of this house, but I also need it to be dark and quiet. A movie would be best. a movie with Mom, who loves movies and needs a date.

Saturday evening

Had a good time with Mom, but I saw Jimmy at the theater; he was with a bunch of friends. Actually I saw a couple of people I knew, but I only talked to Jimmy. He stood beside me in the concession line. Asked me if I was busy tonight, asked if he could drive by. I don't feel like making out in a cold car. I told him I was busy, but Mom was going to church tomorrow, 11:00 a.m. service and some fellowship afterwards. He said he would come by. I now feel incredibly happy.

February 14, 1999

Happy f-ing Valentine's Day. I got a dozen roses delivered from Dad, a heart-shaped box of chocolates and a teddy bear from Mom, and laid from Jimmy.

Despite all that, I am fucking pissed off, but I don't know at whom.

Maybe Alan, maybe Jimmy or all the fucking kids who are happy and well adjusted, who go over life's little bumps with ease. Maybe I'm just mad at myself because I can't.

Jimmy came over this morning, and we ended up having sex in my bed. The sex part was great, and I was feeling good with myself. I was feeling powerful and sexy after days of just incompleteness and pain. It felt great to watch Jimmy melt in front of me. He is putty in my hands. He is so into me; those popular girls at school can't do for him what I can. I know this, and Jimmy knows it too. That's why he keeps coming back for more.

After great sex, Jimmy and I sat on my bed smoking cigarettes and talking. He told me about the Valentine's dance, what everybody was wearing, who looked good, who came with whom. He was rating them, giving them titles. Most slutty dress worn by Misty Miller. Best-looking couple, Brandon Foster and Emily Wood. Jimmy was just having a great time. He was standing on my bed, wearing only boxer shorts, and he was using my curl brush as a microphone.

"Pimp Award goes to Alan Chafin."

"What?" I asked, in total fucking disbelief.

"Oh yeah," Jimmy states, " My man Alan's a pimp."

I was in total shock. Jimmy tells me how Alan entered the dance all alone, looking around, like maybe he had lost something. Jimmy's group of friends start snickering and joking as Alan stands in the middle of the gymnasium, the center of the freak show, looking lost. Soon Amy Gold and her table call him over.

Amy is the leader of the nerdy girls. Not really nerds, just different people—square pegs. They've actually got a pretty big clique going on. Jimmy goes on to tell me that Amy and all her friends were there stag. I think they go to all the dances like that. I don't believe any of them ever has a date; they just hang together full of school spirit and giggles. They probably have the most fun.

Alan ends up sitting with them. I guess a total of six girls—Amy Gold, Mandy Wilson, Andrea Barton, Natalie Flint, Jane Sweet, and Jennifer Crum. I guess Alan and his six girls started the dancing, which doesn't surprise me. I bet Amy Gold's group starts the dancing at every dance. It's easy for them. They are just there to have fun. They know the others kids laugh at them, but they get to be a group and laugh at the other kids. There's safety in numbers.

Jimmy said they danced the freaking night away, and during slow songs, each girl took her turn with Alan. For pictures they all went up there together and posed together. And since it was seven stag people, the photographer took seven pictures. Seven different poses. All six girls framing Alan and hanging on him. Jimmy said it was wild, and he bets every guy there was jealous of Alan Chafin. Sure all the girls were geeky girls that the other guys would probably never ask out, but there were six of them. I guess one geeky girl by herself is a no, but six of them together is a yes.

I got rid of Jimmy shortly after the story. He wanted to have sex again, but I couldn't. He had woken the wolf with his tale of "The Pimp," and I needed him to leave before I blew. Jimmy left a little freaked by my mood swing, but oh well, he'll get it someday. I'm crazy!

I cannot believe that I sat here cutting myself and crying, feeling for Alan Chafin. While I contemplated suicide, he was fucking dancing with six girls. I bet he had the time of his life.

I did him a favor. He had a much better time with healthy, happy, Amy Gold and her freak crew than he would have had with me. Things worked out for the best for Alan, and I made it happen. I accepted his invite, he got dressed and went for me, and I graciously backed out and allowed him a limelight he will never feel again. It was a night that would go down in history for Alan Chafin and Westmore High. A night when one young man took on six young, naive, hyper, oddball girls and became known as the Westmore Pimp. A night to be remembered.

THE DANCE

Paper signs of red and white,
Balloons and streamers wave like kites.
Young girls in dresses stretched so tight
Cocky boys pretend to fight
and everything seems so right.

Not quite.
One young man stands out of sight,
No date to be found—a woeful plight.
Fights back the tears with all his might,
Pulls himself up to full height,
Decides he'll try to take a bite.
Silly girls in the corner, looking just right,
and as it turns out, he had the best night.
By Libby—Dedicated to Alan. You're Welcome!

February 14, 1999 10:00 p.m.

The day is gone. I spent it in my dark room. I did nothing today. My mom is freaking out 'cause I'm such a nut. She came home from her church service yesterday expecting me to be the pleasant teen I had been earlier that morning, but the pleasant girl had disappeared and left me in her place. I know that what I'm having is a pity party, but I can't stop. I tell myself to see things differently—words from my mother. Just as she says "Count your breaths," she says, "Libby, you have to look at things differently. Find the good and choose to be happy."

Can you really choose to be happy? Mom believes you can. She believes that you not only choose your emotions, but you choose your journey. She says we create our own destiny and that there is no such thing as luck—good or bad.

So it's not fucking luck that all those giddy girls were sitting around a table fantasizing about boys, when all of a sudden an available one (that would not snub them) walked through the door. I bet people in third-world poverty-stricken countries believe in luck. You're fucking lucky if you get to eat or your child does not die or a natural disaster does not tear down your shack on any particular day. But hey, choose to be happy!

So all the miserable wenches and poor bastards who have shot their brains out or choked to death on pills or hanged themselves in a basement and were found by a horrified family member—well, they chose their destiny. They chose to live their lives, sad and depressed, to feel frightened all the time, always to feel alone, especially when surrounded by others.

Oh, Mom, you don't f-ing get it? You have a healthy brain, so how dare you comment on people as a whole? I thought you didn't believe in judgment. I thought you stood on the soapbox of acceptance, yet you say these miserable souls had choices. You think I choose to sit alone in my room hating myself? You think I choose to sweat and shake every time I enter a crowded building? You think I choose for my heart to race at the thought of high school football games and pep rallies? I choose not to be able to do what so many teens do, and then I choose to be sad about it? Well, fuck you. You can't choose your feelings like you can choose between chocolate and vanilla. You're given your feelings, and if you're given chocolate despite your violent allergic reaction to it, you'd better choose to fucking eat it anyway. Right, Mom?

CHOOSE TO BE HAPPY

You're born to a mother with ten other kids,
not enough food, not enough beds.
You could choose to be happy—instead you chose SIDS.
Your children have left you; your husband has died,
So you sit all alone in your mansion and hide.
Your phone does not ring—no one stops by.
You could choose to be happy—instead you just cried.
Your country's at war; your sister's been raped,
and your genitals they mutilate.
You could choose to be happy—you tried to escape.
Found you, they did, and beat you to death.
It's your destiny, child—just count your breaths.

By Libby
Dedicated to my mother and every other spiritualist out there who believes you can choose your own fate.

February 15, 1999

Didn't go to school today. Just couldn't get up the courage. Instead I went to my Dad's. I woke when my mother woke me. I dressed for school in faded Levi's and a sweatshirt. I stuck the shorts in my backpack. I took the bus to my Dad's and had to sit next to a very smelly man who was actually dressed in a suit and probably going to work, but that didn't stop him from smelling like a big armpit. I wonder if he is miserable too, if he would rather be in a death sleep, but instead he has to pull himself up at the last minute, put a wrinkled suit on top of his uncleansed body and go to work. I bet he's miserable at work. He can hear the sneers of others. He can hear them say he smells and that he is odd, but he makes more money than they do and he is much smarter, so he says to himself (the only person he really talks to) that they're just jealous. The sad thing is, they're not. They really do believe they're better than he is.

I let myself in Dad's apartment, which I love to do. I imagine it's mine and I'm grown and living this fantasy life. Dad's place is clean. Today there were two coffee cups left on the counter, two. Oh well, he has proven he can't live with anyone long, so I don't know why that would worry me.

Dad is the master of picking up after himself and keeping things neat and orderly. He is very different from my mother, who lays stuff everywhere. Mom is sloppy; not a slob, just sloppy. Dad can wash a sink full of dishes in a double-breasted suit, white crisp shirt, and monogrammed cuffs and not get wet. When Mom leaves the sink, she is always wet up to her elbows and across her front. I don't know how those two ever got together, except for knowing that Dad loves all women. I do know why they are apart.

After eating food at Dad's house that we never have at home, crazy stuff like garlic bagel chips with humus and seltzer water, I went over to the gym. Carol, one of the resident managers, just looked at me and smiled. She knows I'm supposed to be in school. I wonder if she will say anything to my father. I know she has slept with him. I can tell by the way she acts when he is around, flirty and sexy and unsure of herself all at the same time. My dad eats it up.

I played racquetball all morning, me all alone in that closed room, beating the hell out of the crazed blue ball. I felt good and strong. My adrenaline was pumping. My racing thoughts have a home in the racquetball room. I love the deafening sound and sweat and speed. I don't like to play with others. Dad sometimes asks me to play racquetball. I've gotten better than him, faster and stronger. He say's I'm aggressive. He just doesn't like having his ass whipped by a girl. I used to love when Daddy asked me to play tennis or racquetball, but now I think he just crowds my space, gets in my way, and interrupts my thoughts. I'd rather hit my tennis ball up against a brick wall than play with someone else, and I'd much rather shut myself into a white box and beat up a blue ball than play with others. I do better alone in my box.

Two hours passed before I even realized the time. I headed back to my dad's apartment, out into the cold all sweaty and hot, not a good idea, but better than showering in a public bathroom. I showered in the privacy of my father's house and had to be very careful to put everything back the way I found it. I popped myself a bag of popcorn and grabbed a Tab to take with me on my bus ride. I was home by five, and I was starving, so I decided to cook dinner for Mom and me. I made spaghetti and garlic bread and even two small salads. Mom was overjoyed when she came home. She thinks I'm back to normal, as if I've ever been normal.

She made a big deal about how great the pasta was, even though it was just pasta from a box and a jar of Ragu. "All this meal needs now is a glass of wine," she said as she surprisingly poured two glasses of wine. I can't believe how good today was. I sit here writing, all sleepy-eyed from a big meal and wine, after a day of playing hard. How I wish today could be my everyday.

February 16, 1999

I'm at Dad's again. The same smelly man was on the bus today, and we made eye contact. I think I grinned. He shoved his head back into his newspaper. Only one coffee cup on the counter this morning. I'm feeling very good, ready to go play.

February 16, 7:00 p.m.

God, I can get used to this. The day can't get any better, me in the white room for two more hours. That must be my time, two hours. It flies by, but I always seem to come back to reality, exhausted and unable to play any longer. Dinner tonight was Tuna Helper with milk to drink. I guess I'll have to make spaghetti again soon.

February 17, 1999

Tonight at dinner (French toast, scrambled eggs, and hot tea) my mom talked to me a lot, and I actually enjoyed it. It had nothing to do with finding myself and creating my path—the shit she usually spoons me. She talked about herself, something she shares very little of. She talked about hating her job. I never knew how much she hated her job. She goes every day without complaint and stays late every evening. Who would have thought she was miserable?

My mother is an office manager for a bunch of doctors. I always thought she liked it; she's done it since I was born. The doctors always call our house to ask her questions, and she jokes with each one of them like they're all best friends. How can you pretend to like something and someone for so long? "Money and insurance," she said. "I've got really good benefits."

"What do you hate about it?" I asked.

"Everything else." She quickly corrected herself and said that wasn't true. She likes the patients. They are probably what has made the whole ordeal bearable.

I asked about her coworkers, the ones who invite us to big Christmas parties and call our house, the ones that she pretends to like.

Mom responded by explaining that the doctors are arrogant and rude. She said they can't help it. It's their mindset, so she does not blame them. She told me the nurses do not respect her. She is not in medicine, just the boring insufficient office worker. She is their servant and treated as such. She doesn't blame them either. She said there is a pecking order.

Surprisingly enough, she hates the Christmas parties too. She doesn't like the huge houses and pretentious beliefs, values, and dispositions. I guess that's why after we leave every party we take blankets down to the homeless. I never got the connection. The blanket thing was just a tradition, and I just thought she was multitasking, by doing them both on the same night. I should have known. Everything my mother does holds a deeper meaning.

I guess I should feel closer to Mom after finding out the truth, now knowing that she is stuck somewhere she doesn't want to be., but as I sit here writing, it just makes me angry. It all goes back to her being a hypocrite. My mother is the only person I ever heard say things like, "Be true to yourself" or "Don't follow the crowd, follow your heart." "You have the power to create your own identity." "It's important to hear the voices of others, but more important to listen to your own voice."

My mother has preached to me from birth to be an original. All my life I have been angry at her for having the strength that nobody else has. She was the only one who didn't give in to the standards and ideals of society. I was always jealous of her courage and insight. Now I'm just angry, because she's not so different after all. Another letdown.

February 18, 1999

Another day home from school—I wonder how long it can last. I've decided I'm not going back until I have to. I have gone too far to turn around now. If I went in today, they would give tons of homework and have tons of questions, and I would be had, so I'll just wait it out. I brought my bathing suit today and have decided to swim after racquetball, as long as nobody is around. My cuts are now scabs, but I still don't want to advertise.

February 19, 1999

The man on the bus held my stare; he knows we are the same. I wonder why it took him so long. I was so damn tired last night, two hours of racquetball and then lap after lap in the pool. My body aches but my mind is calm, so it is well worth the workout. The wolf has been contained. He wakes only in the white room, and chases his ball. He zooms back and forth in my mind as I zoom back and forth in the white room. I tire the wolf out and then I go home and eat and sleep and wake the next morning, only to tire the wolf out again. It's working for us.

February 19, 5:00 p.m.

I'm home from my dad's only to get ready to go to my dad's. Surprise! He has made time for me this weekend. He will be here in an hour, and we will go out to eat. I'm hoping this time it will just be the two of us.

February 21, 1999

Oh, where do I begin? This weekend was horrid and beautiful and sad and happy and all feeling and all experiences wild. First, I was busted. Then I exploded. Then I ran and hid, and then I talked and lived and found my true self, only to come home and crumble. Now I must compose myself and pour all my dirty and beautiful thoughts, acts, feelings, and frustrations out on this paper.

It started at dinner. Dad and I sat across from each other, both of us enjoying our $15.00 plate of food.

"Libby, you've been coming to my house this week, haven't you?"

"No," I said, spooning in another mouthful of linguine.

Dad accused me of lying. He told me he hadn't said anything to my mother yet, because he wanted to talk to me.

I don't know why I lied. I guess I just didn't feel like talking about it. I mean get a freaking clue. Why would I want to talk about this in a crowded expensive restaurant? But this is so typical of my father. Of course he dresses his ladies up and takes them out in public to talk to them about things they don't want to hear. This way nobody can cry or yell or shout at him. He can be in control and look handsome and smug while ordering himself creme brulee and pouring his sad wench another glass of wine.

The whole thing pissed me off, and when Dad leaned over to speak to me again, I just flipped. "We need to talk, honey," was all it took. The next thing to happen was a moment of temporary insanity (or maybe it's permanent). I picked up my big round garlic butter roll like it was a baseball and flung it at my father's head. It hit him in the forehead, leaving a big round buttery red mark (which just goes to show you that the rolls are too hard for the price) and bounced from his forehead onto his plate, splashing marinara sauce all over his baby-blue Armani shirt and tie.

"Jesus Christ!" my father said as he slid his chair back, his mouth curled up in a perfect O.

"Leave poor Jesus out of this," I said and then giggled hysterically."

My father just stared at me in amazement, not knowing what to do with his crazy daughter. Should he go wash his tie, run from the restaurant, scream, or shit his pants? He had no idea, so he just calmly sat back down and motioned for the check.

I stopped laughing and began to eat, knowing that my barely touched plate was about to be snatched out from under me.

After we left the restaurant, instead of turning left toward his house, he began to drive toward mine. With this one turn, the wolf woke up and leaped to the front of my brain.

"So what now, Dad?" I began, not able to stop myself. "Take me back to mother's? Leave me? That's what you do, right? Leave the women who upset you a little, challenge you, make you fucking realize you're not all that you think you are? So you're gonna bail out on me again. You fucking coward!"

My father just drove, and the more I talked, the faster he drove, and the faster he drove, the angrier I became. I screamed some more. "Everything has to be just right, doesn't it, Daddy? And since you can't get it right, you would rather just leave it. Leave every fucking relationship you make, even the relationship with your own daughter. I'm not perfect. Dinner wasn't fucking perfect. The rolls were too hard, weren't they, Dad? So now just take me back to my mother and dump me, because it all wasn't going the way you thought it should go. You are such a selfish, pompous prick!"

My dad pulled the car over and turned to me. Big fat tears were rolling down his cheeks. "Libby," he said in a cracked voice.

What had I done? I had hurt my father, my very favorite person in the whole world. I had hurt him. I grabbed the door handle and bolted from the car. My dad tried to chase me, but it was dark, and I've gotten surprisingly fast, and he had no idea where I was running to. When I started weaving in and out of back yards, he gave up and went back to his car.

I guess I really didn't know where I was going either, at least not until I got there. Tim was just closing up shop. "Hey, you okay?" Tim asked as I wiped the snot and tears from my face.

"No. Can I go home with you?" Tim just put his arm around me and walked me to his truck "Only for a little while, Libby."

I ended up spending two nights. We stayed up all Friday night talking and drinking. I poured out my heart, and surprisingly enough, he listened. He didn't try to attack me or scream at me or make me call my parents. He just sat silently in his chair drinking his beer and letting me talk. I talked to Tim all night long. I told him about my racing thoughts and how school sucks and I haven't gone in a week. I talked about my father and mother and how screwed up we all are. I told him about not being able to go to the dance and how Alan went and ended up getting the pimp award. I talked and cried and talked. Tim gave me beers and cigarettes and a roll of toilet paper to wipe my snotty face.

I don't know when I fell asleep, but sometime during my story and after my beers, I closed my eyes and drifted off. I woke Saturday afternoon to the smell of fries. Tim had gone out and bought us each McDonald's. We ate and talked some more. This time I let Tim talk. He told me about regretting dropping out of high school. He talked about fighting with his stepfather and being pissed at his mother for never taking his side. He told me his girlfriend just broke up with him for some college guy, because she wants to do better than a mechanic. I felt relaxed listening to him. I knew exactly how he felt, and it was such a relief not to be alone.

We didn't even start having sex until late Saturday night. Oh God, did we have sex! The whole thing was so f-ing educational. You can't believe the difference seven years makes in a person. I was put into positions I never knew were possible, and the time he spent with me—the tenderness and relaxation. I'm used to urgent little Jimmy. Tim was sensual and slow. It was his mouth that was on me, not the other way around. I had my very first orgasm, and not just one. We had sex for hours, and each time lasted so much longer than I thought possible. Tim held back. If I thought he was gonna finish, he would stop and just lie quietly kissing me here and there, and then he would start again. He saw my arms. This was the first time I have ever been completely naked with a man. He saw my arms and he kissed them and he rubbed them with lotion and then he flipped me over and rubbed my back and massaged my body. Most of the time I kept my eyes closed. I couldn't look. It would have killed it. It's true, you do moan when you feel good. Little involuntary gasps left me. I sighed and exhaled. I giggled when my ticklish spots were found. I had been lifted and transformed. I had emerged from my tightly woven cocoon. I was a butterfly. As my spirit fluttered around Tim and my body lay in his bed soaking him up, my parents were frantically looking for me.

I came home late this morning, thinking my mom would be at her fellowship. She wasn't. She was sitting on the couch crying over me, waiting for the phone to ring. I guess while I was gone, I didn't really think about how scared my parents would be. I just thought I needed some time to get away, clear my head. My mother jumped up from the couch when I walked in. First she hugged me, and then she abruptly pulled away, looked me in the face and said, "You spoiled little brat! Go call your father now; let him know you are home!" She then walked away from me. At the time I didn't think she ever wanted to talk to me again, but since then, I have heard it from both my parents.

First they both let me know that they had to call the police and file a missing person's report. They went through old phone numbers and called every kid I have ever associated with. They drove the streets, looked at the malls and movie theaters. They cried and fought and then cried some more. They both want me to go back to counseling, I'm not surprised. My mother has been dragging me to counselors since I was six. She usually stops taking me and starts looking for another counselor after about six months or twelve visits. It takes about that long before the counselors start to blame my parents for all my problems. It's blamed on either my rich, materialistic father (I'm overindulged) or my hippie mother (I'm not disciplined) or just quickly summed up as only-child-syndrome.

I will go to their counselors and I will go to their schools. I have no choice. I am expected to fit into society, despite the pain it causes. This is exactly why I would just rather die. Maybe I could just go live with Tim and never leave his apartment. He can go to work; I like that he is a mechanic. It is an art, a gift. It is a brilliant mind that can fix things. Maybe he will just let me stay there. I can be a prisoner of love, and when he comes home tired and greasy from work, we can have lots of sex. I do believe that would work much better than counseling.

February 22, 1999

I'm at school. The teachers at school are acting all concerned. It's pure bullshit. They didn't care when I wasn't here; they didn't even call my house to check on me. My mom actually did a pretty cool thing. She wrote me some doctor's excuse on a prescription tablet from work—even forged the doc's name. She sternly stated as she handed me my excuse, "As far as we're concerned Libby, this is an excused absence. There is no way in hell I want you to be suspended for missing so much school." Then she added, "Get all your work, because you have plenty of time at home to do it." My mother rambled on and on as she drove me to school. The new plan is to drive Libby to school and watch her walk into the building. I truly hate being here. I wish I could go see Tim.

February 22, after school

I made it through the day, but I don't know how. I walked the halls in a daze. I sat in class trying to listen, but was completely unable to focus. As each teacher handed me my list of missing assignments, I felt as if I were drowning. Honestly, my chest became heavy, as if it were filling up with water. My breath was stuck. I tried to blow it out and count, but it was like trying to blow up a balloon. As I sit here now, I can barely even write. I just want to curl myself up in a tight little ball and cry.

February 23, 1999

I went by the gas station after school today. Tim was uncomfortable, just at the sight of me. He tried to look past me, ignore me, act like we hadn't just spent a weekend together, but I wouldn't allow that to happen. You're not going to get off that easy, I thought. Pretend I don't exist, so I don't? Well, fuck you! I took a Snickers bar from the candy shelf and started to eat it. I don't know what possessed me to do such a thing. I then plopped myself down in a hard and dirty, cold plastic gray chair, eating my stolen Snickers bar, and waited for him to respond. Finally, when he had to do something, and nobody was around, he kneeled in front of me and broke my heart.

"Libby, you're a great kid, but you're just a kid," he said.

I didn't want to cry, but as soon as he began, big tears started rolling down my face.

"Hey, Libby don't do that."

Good, at least I was making him uncomfortable.

"Look, it's just that the guys said your parents were here this weekend asking everybody if they knew who you were and where you might be. Of course none of the guys had a clue, but Libby, I can't risk this. You're seventeen. I'm twenty-four. Your parents can put me in jail for rape."

"You didn't rape me," I tried to argue.

"I know that and you know that, but it's your age," Tim argued back. He said he knew this dude that was twenty-two and his girlfriend was sixteen. It would have been no big deal if she was twenty-two and he was six years older, but since she was only sixteen, he did time for corruption of a minor or some bullshit like that, and now he's on probation. Tim said, "I can't risk that shit." Then he had the nerve to suggest, "Maybe we can try again in a year."

"Fuck you!" I blurted out as I threw my Snickers wrapper into the trash, bundled myself up to my nose, and walked home.

The phone was ringing as soon as I walked in the door. It was my mother. "Libby, you're an hour late. Where have you been?"

"I'm home now," I said and then slammed down the receiver.

I swear I hate my life. I hate the way my mind works. I hate the way the minds of everybody else works. I hate Tim and his sex that made me feel so good and tricked me into thinking I could actually have pleasure and love in my life. I hate Jimmy for using my body for his own pleasure, and I hate Alan for asking me out when I find myself undesirable. I hate all the girls at school because I am different than them, and I hate my mother and father for not knowing how to help me. But mostly, above all, I hate myself.

I wish I could turn my hate into a passionate art form. I wish I could sit here and write poems of love and betrayal and broken hearts and broken dreams and a broken mind, but it is too much work. It takes too much thought and too much energy, and mostly I just would rather die.

February 24, 1999

Back at school again, and it's almost unbearable. I hear laughter, and I think it's automatically about me. The other kids look at me, and I can't stand their faces. So much of me wants to punch at people's faces. I saw Alan in the hall. I tried like hell to avoid him, but I can't seem to avoid unpleasantness. Strangely enough, Alan smiled at me and started to walk toward me. I think he wanted to talk. The whole thing just freaks me out. Why would he want to talk to me? Why would he smile at me? I ducked into a classroom to avoid him. God, I don't want to see him again. Maybe I'll get lucky and drop dead by next period.

SAME DAY!

I hate it here. I want to claw my fucking eyes out. I think I am truly losing it. I can't eat or talk or think. I can't even hear the lecture; I just see mouths opening and shutting. Dear God, am I going crazy? I am! I know that I am! I have to run from this building.

February 25, 1999

Where do I begin? Do I first write that I am officially expelled from my school, or do I write that I was arrested and charged with assault? February just hasn't been my month. Winter is not my season.

It started with a walk during my lunch period. I really wanted to leave, but when I opened the door of the school, the wind and snow blew me back in. Besides, I couldn't leave. Everybody has been watching me, so I started walking. I must not have heard the bell ring, or it did not register that lunch was over. I needed to be in my English lit class. I guess I did realize that everything was quiet and I was the only person walking the halls, but that only calmed me and made me walk faster, steadier.

I could see Vice Principal, Mr. Phillips, watching me as I made my laps through the hall, down one side, up the stairs, down the hall, down the stairs, down the opposite and adjacent hall, up the stairs again. I passed Mr. Phillips every three or four minutes in the west wing. I heard, "Stop, Libby!" It echoed from the hole in his face.

Shut your pie hole, I thought, but didn't say.

Mr. Phillips was only a presence, and I was not of his world. I was in a parallel universe, an adjoining world. I had leaped the boundaries of sanity, and I strolled the world of crazy, or maybe unconscious mind. Yes, I could see Mr. Phillips, but I could not respond. It was as if he had come to me in a dream. We were in separate places. He was talking to the supernatural.

I passed him quickly and began another lap through the connecting hallways. My brisk steps were silent as my Hushpuppies swiftly swam the current of the tan-and-blue linoleum. Tan square, a blue square, tan square, a blue square. I focus my gaze on the floor. The squares, the lines, the symmetrical shapes of color—it calmed me. As I jolted down the science hall, Mr. Phillips blocked my path and broke my stride, stopping me on a tan square. I was unable to reach the dark-blue one I had to step on next.

My mind swirled. How was it that this man had entered my hemisphere? He was an intruder. He had trespassed into my realm and upset the balance. I tried to bring my mind back to school and out of the blue-and tan-checked world that it had been walking in. I tried like hell to focus. I told myself, *Libby, come back.* I thought that I was reaching my senses, gaining ground, when suddenly two strong, hairy, manly arms gripped me.

"Libby Goldstein, stop this instant!" The short-clipped nails on his short, tan, fat fingers dig into the muscles of my arms. I noticed the white line that surrounded his wedding band, another white line on the edge of his watch. I thought, *It's February; how in the fuck did you get a tan? I'm a ghost in my white turtleneck. A person made of powder.*

"Get the fuck off me!" I shouted as I tried to pull my white-powdered arms from the vice grip of his fingers. He was crushing me. As I yanked, he tightened his grip. I was caught, tan, muscled fingers pressing into my white thin flesh and bone. His fingers held me like the jaws of an animal tearing at a frightened white rabbit. "Get off me!" I screamed over and over, thrashing my body. I was lost within. I saw nothing but red. I heard faraway voices and angry shouts echoing into my red world. The next thing I knew, a tremendous force was pressing against my back and brought me down hard, onto my stomach. My chest was pressed into the tan-and-blue squares. I couldn't breathe. I was being attacked by school personnel.

"What the fuck is a matter with you people?" I was yanked to my feet and pulled down the hall by Mr. Phillips and the bull dyke administrator who had just plowed me to the floor. "Bitch!" I spat, coming back to reality.

I expected my mother to be called and she was, but not before the school police officer. I was actually cuffed at school. I was no longer fighting them. I was quiet and would have walked out the door and into the car without a fight, but instead they felt the need to wrench my powder-white arms behind my back and lock my wrists into cold metal handcuffs. I was led outside into the wild winds and blistering cold without a jacket and was then driven downtown.

I did not see the inside of a jail cell. Instead I stayed in a room of orange carpet and blue chairs and the smell of coffee. My mother picked me up there. We were both informed that Mr. Phillips wanted me charged with assault. "I didn't assault him. He assaulted me!"

"Miss," the officer began.

I quickly retreated inside myself. I could hear the firm monologue that was being shouted at me, but none of it made sense. It flowed in one ear and out the other and didn't stay long enough even to be recognized. After hours of paperwork and lectures, the officer released me to my mother, who took me home. We drove in silence.

I now sit in my room burning incense and smoking cigarettes. My mother has not said much to me. I don't believe she knows what to say. She is in her own room with her own door shut. I know she is lost in her own little thoughts; it is a look that I recognize. I don't believe she has called Dad yet, because he is not here acting smarter than both of us. It is okay if she cannot talk to me, because I cannot talk. I have slipped inside myself and am watching the world through glass. I am Alice in Wonderland. I have no words that they can understand, no thoughts that they can relate to. I am foreign, an alien, with chalk-white skin and bulging blue scars down my arms. You can look at me, but you can't touch.

Still February 25, 1999

Well, I was wrong. My mother does want to talk. She has come into my room three times to yell at me. I say nothing in return. She cannot get a rise out of me. I will not sass; I will not defend myself. I will not explain to her that I am no longer sane. This is a concept she will refuse to grasp, so why even bother? I will just sit here alone being crazy.

February 26, 1999

After much thought, it has occurred to me where and who I am. I have become the groundhog. I must have followed the poor creature back into his hole and have been there this whole long winter.

Not to frighten myself so, I must admit that some of the groundhog's hole is beautiful and mysterious and has been painstakingly tunneled by the groundhog himself. The tunnels are beautiful, like Jimmy and marijuana and sex with Tim and racquetball. When I'm up and not too tired, I can walk the hole and experience these things, but mostly in the groundhog hole, I just want to sleep or try to sleep. I burrow myself down against the cold-packed dirt and curl my body into itself.

The problems occurred when I mistook the sullenness of my groundhog hole for a chrysalis and started to believe I would metamorphous into a butterfly. But now I see my cocoon for what it truly is: a deep and dark hole that I have tunneled myself. Some of it is fascinating, but mostly just dark. I will no longer disappoint myself with fantasies. It's much easier to accept that I am a groundhog than to try to become a butterfly. What terrifies me about being a groundhog is just that. At least when I was a caterpillar, I was heading for better and more beautiful things. The caterpillar is much more blessed than most creatures, because it is certain that it will become beautiful and graceful and loved before its death. The groundhog just stays a groundhog. For almost his entire existence, he will live in a hole and be seen as the groundhog; that is, until he is seen as road kill, which answers the question of my method of suicide. I'll just throw myself in front of a car.

March 21—SPRING!!!!!

It's been over three whole weeks since I have written.

Why haven't I written?

Well, the answer lies among the four white walls that make up my new room. Comically enough, I have been hospitalized, institutionalized. I have flown over the cuckoo's nest. It is my mother's doing.

Three weeks ago I walked into my room after taking a very long, hot bath and found my mother sitting crossed legged on my bed, soaking up the words of my journal. She was reading and then rereading all my thoughts and fantasies of death, discovering that a wolf lives in the head of her daughter, who is actually a groundhog, but wishes she were a caterpillar ready to emerge a butterfly.

Well, it was all a little much for her to endure, and she looked up at me crying and simply stated, "You need help." It was after that, that my journal made it into the hands of a psychiatrist, who decided, after reading all my words and then asking me things that I could not explain or respond to, that I was a threat to myself and needed full hospitalization. My shoestrings were taken away from me, along with my journal. I have not been given back my shoestrings, but I was given my journal today. This is only because they want to read my secret words after I write them. They want to discover me by my writings, because I do not talk to them. They want to hear the yells and shouts of my diary.

At this moment in time, I'm not interested in verbalizing. I just listen. I listen to girls scream, "Bitch!" I listen to crying and cursing. I listen to doctors order nurses and nurses order teens. I listen to many "Fuck yous" and excuses and stories. I listen to diagnoses and theories and thoughts. I listen to my mother and father every night at seven-thirty, when they arrive for family time and I listen to the voices of other parents during family time. All of them sound the same, scared and pathetic and pretending not to be. I listen to truly crazy kids talk off-the-wall bullshit, and I listen to truly sane kids rationalize every not-so-sane thing they do.

I hear it all. I hear terms such as anxiety disorder, bipolar disorder, borderline personality disorder, obsessive-compulsive disorder, schizophrenia, depression, antisocial disorder, eating disorder, and so, so many other disorders. I do not know which one I will be labeled, which mental disease will be slapped across my forehead, which ailment will make up my identity. I don't believe they know yet.

They are trying to discover me through medication. I know this is killing my mother. Give me meds for bipolar—if they don't work, I'm not bipolar. It's all a bunch of crap. It is a conspiracy to stop the out-of-the-box thinkers; just medicate them back into the box. I know that I will be out of here soon. I have heard them talk of insurance coverage.

I also know that this is just the beginning. A jar of worms has been spilled (the jar a metaphor meaning my brain). The worms are being analyzed. Who knows? Maybe I hold all the answers to all of life's questions. Wouldn't that be poetic justice? And maybe just, maybe, I will emerge a butterfly.

ANGELA

I was thinking that I might fly today
Just to disprove all the things that you say.
It doesn't take a talent to be mean.
Your words can crush things that are unseen,
So please be careful with me; I'm sensitive,
And I'd like to stay that way.

"Sensitive" by Jewel

MONTHLY JOURNAL UPDATE

Men of the Month

Carl: Distinctive features are BIG *Rough* hands with greasy nails. He's a mechanic, worked on my brakes and rotors. Carl has hair on his penis. NO KIDDING! Not a lot of hair, but enough—like ivy growing up a tree. First hairy penis I've ever seen.

Matthew: I totally love his soft and sensual voice. He talks of love and life, BIG TURN ON! He has beautiful long brown hair that smells of apples, ANOTHER BIG TURN ON! (Matthew must use apple shampoo.) His penis is little, **not** a turn on; however, he has long staying power. BIG-BIG TURN ON! Just goes to prove that size isn't everything. FOUR STARS****

Phillip: Boring! Boring! Boring! I must have been completely brain dead to even go there. This man is as boring in bed as he is out of bed. I was hoping to be pleasantly surprised; no surprises with Phillip.

Marcus: BIG MAN, at least six foot five, huge equipment (African American). Little attention span. *Too bad, so sad. I still give him two stars***

In conclusion, I am still looking for my soul mate.

GRATEFUL LIST FOR APRIL

YOU! Most importantly I am grateful for YOU! I am grateful to be able to pick you up every month and fill your pages with my experiences. You make them real. You make them mean something. You make me reflect. *It's so cool to reflect.* YOU are my soul.

Every month I come to this coffeehouse. I sit by the window. I drink café mocha, and I write my soul stories. I am **grateful** for this coffeehouse. I am **grateful** for café mocha. I am especially **grateful** for you. The coolest part about you is that one day when I'm gone, my children—or even grosser, my grandchildren—will discover you. Then they will discover me. I will be young again. I will be alive again. My life on this earth as Angela Ann McClan will have been recorded:

the men that I have loved, the little things I am grateful for, the losses and pain I have felt and suffered, and my reflections on it all, as well as my goals for another day. Angela Ann McClan was here. She lived, she loved, she lost, and she won, every minute of every day of every month of every year.

More things to be grateful for

I am **grateful** for the RAIN! *April showers bring May flowers.* Next month I'll probably be grateful for flowers. This month it is the rain that calls me. *I love the rain!* It's a damn good thing, because it has rained steadily for three weeks straight.

The rain has ruined my only pair of white Keds, and still *I am grateful.* My umbrella broke the day I wore a white T-shirt. *I am still grateful.* I got drenched walking to my English class. *I am still grateful.* I had to sit through an hour lecture with titty hard-ons. *I am still grateful.* That was the day "Boring Phillip" asked me out. *I'm trying to be grateful.*

I am so **grateful** for my GUITAR and SONG WRITING; however, I am having an incredible block of the inspirational mind and have not been able to write a poem, lyric, letter, or decent English paper. *I am still grateful.* June will be my song-writing month. I always feel poetic in June. A good thing, 'cause I'll probably have to retake English this summer.

I am **grateful** for my NEW JOB. Yes I know, another new month, another new job, but this time I am TOTALLY and COMPLETELY FULFILLED with my employment. I now work part-time evenings at a health food store. I have always secretly wanted to work at a health food store, so when the sign appeared in the window, it was like TOTAL DESTINY. They hired me on the spot, DESTINY. *I love my minimum-wage job.* How many people can say that?

P.S. Sensual, apple-smelling Matthew is the manager: DESTINY?

I am **grateful** for school, even though I am in debt up to my ASS and I have switched majors NINE times. I am undecided at this particular time. *I am still grateful.*

I am **grateful** because there was once a time when women couldn't go to school. "*We've come a long way, baby.*" If a chick was allowed to go to school, she had to become a nurse or a teacher. Those are actually very humanitarian positions, but hey, so is being a firefighter or cop or doctor.

THANK YOU WOMEN of the past, for fighting for all us women.

THANK YOU for EQUAL RIGHTS and EQUAL RESPECT. Even though we are still working on those issues, a hell of a lot of progress has been made.

I am **grateful** to all women. I am **grateful** for school. I only wish I had more male professors. Personally, I find it comforting to know that I could play the "*pussy card*" if I'm in fear of failing.

I am **grateful** for the TREES that give me oxygen. I am **grateful** for the WIND that blows through my long blond hair. I am especially **grateful** to have LONG BLOND HAIR. *I think it would totally suck to have short brown hair.*

I am **grateful** for my APARTMENT. I am **NOT grateful** for its cockroaches and leaky pipes, but it's okay, because these experiences are helping me grow. I am **grateful** to live on my own, out of my parents' suburban home with its trendy porch and finished basement. I am **grateful** to learn to pay my own bills. Even though Daddy sends me a check every month, I still have to deposit it in my own account, write out all my own checks, and pay the bills on time. With Daddy's allowance and my new job, I am still just barely making it. I am **grateful** to be TWENTY-TWO years old, and to have a FLAT STOMACH and PERKY TITS. I know that these are blessings that DO NOT KEEP.

LOSSES SUFFERED THIS MONTH

This month has been the most difficult so far this year. I usually fill this part of my diary up with words like car keys and patience, but this month my losses are huge.

Pokey died. My beautiful beloved cat of sixteen years died April

2 at 1:00am. He went peacefully in his sleep and I sat by his side stroking his long black-and-white coat. It was the saddest moment of my life. Pokey was given to me by my daddy for my sixth birthday. Since then, Pokey and I slept together every night, with him curled up on my pillow. I named him Pokey, because he was always poking his head into things—paper sacks, trash cans, laundry baskets, cupboards, etc. A year later, he kept poking the female cat next door. That was until he got his balls cut. My nosey cat Pokey, I can't believe he's gone. Every time I walk in the door, I expect to see his nose poke around the corner. Every morning I am tempted to put food and water in his silver bowls. At night I miss his warmth on my pillow and his weight on my head. God, take good care of my Pokey.

Other Losses Suffered This Month

I lost FOCUS after losing Pokey. Losing focus caused me to **lose** my CAR KEYS, BACK PACK, ASSIGNMENTS, three PAIRS OF SUNGLASSES, and MY MIND. I have been walking around in a funk for weeks. I can't drive. I make stupid mistakes like forget where I'm heading. I have **lost** DIRECTION. I cried for days, hours upon hours. I have **lost** all my TEARS. I have **lost** my APPETITE, causing me to **lose** FIVE POUNDS.

I know I need to move on. I need to acknowledge my feelings by writing them down, and then I need to move forward. It's been three and a half weeks of *total* sadness.

Still More Losses!

I again have **lost** SIGHT of my future. I realize I do this every other month, but it is so hard to have to prove that I am an artist.

I am a writer. I know this. It's simple and natural; however, this is not known by my writing professors, the arrogant dickheads. They stifle me with all their stupid rules. "*That's a run-on sentence.*

That's a run-on sentence. That's a run-on sentence." What kind of COCKAMAMIE BULLSHIT is that?

I am a singer. This too is natural, so it kills me to have to write that I have been rejected from the music program. REJECTION SUCKS! Who sets the standard? Who acknowledges talent as talent? Who? An opinion is just an opinion. Have these "holier than thou" people ever listened to Cher or Bob Dylan or Stevie Nicks? These three wonderful singers most likely would have been rejected also. Knowing this makes it easier to keep singing. I have also been rejected from the dance and theater programs. I was not too upset about dance. All those people want to be ballerinas, and I DO NOT. I just want to learn how to dance, while I play my guitar and sing. I figure I can teach myself that. I have been watching a lot of music videos, trying to catch all the female folk singers and do like they do.

As for the theater program, I was not surprised. Basically I BOMBED the audition by forgetting three lines of my monologue. After I dropped the BIG STINKY BOMB, I joked to the professor about the casting couch. I said something like, "I know I wouldn't forget any lines there." The old bastard just scoffed at me and then asked me to leave. Oh well, he probably couldn't get it up anyway. He is at least **FIFTY** years old.

Photography fell short of a nightmare. My professor was a big ugly BITCH! I did exactly what I was supposed to do, and I was still treated badly. Our first assignments were on lighting, and my photos were TOTALLY AWESOME. I photographed my lovely cat Pokey lying on the carpet in a beam of morning light. Pokey's long black coat shimmered, and he looked peaceful. I took shots from all angles as the sun rose in my window and my beautiful cat basked in its glow. LIKE, HOW ARTISTIC IS THAT?

My photos on shadows were just as GREAT. This time I put Pokey under the pine trees of my parents' back yard. I lie on my stomach and shot straight into the shadows that held my beautiful cat.

Action was much more difficult, especially since Pokey was so old and would not run anymore, so I took Pokey to the park to play with the kids. The pictures on the merry-go-round proved to be the best action shots, plus I had a lot of kids in those shots with Pokey.

Do you know what that FAT UGLY BITCH said? My subject matter was always the same. Call me stupid, but *Children and Kitty Playing in Park* IS NOT the same as *Sleeping in the Sunlight* or *Creeping in the Shadows*. (Those are actually the real titles. Catchy, huh?)

I was so **pissed off** and **hurt**. Dr. Rice (THE BIG FAT UGLY BITCH) had to pass me, because it was obvious that the photos I shot were the **BEST** in the class. My technique cannot be beat; however, she gave me a C. I admit normally I would have been ecstatic with a C, but this time my work was an A+. That woman just has a prejudice against cats. Anyhow, my feelings were so badly hurt that I dropped photography as a major.

The bright side of the story (remember there is always a bright side) is that I took all my BEAUTIFUL photographs down to Kinko's and made cat calendars for all my loved ones. Everybody is going to get a "Millennium 2000 Cat Calendar" this Christmas from me and my beloved Pokey, may he rest in peace.

REFLECTIONS IN APRIL

Another school year has passed, and I feel lost and misunderstood. After three years of higher education, I am no closer to a future. I have managed to retreat further from my original goals, as well as every goal made along the way. My father is pissed off. My mind is more clouded than it's ever been, my future more unclear. In fact, the only class I find fulfilling is yoga. *I love yoga!* All I have ever wanted to do was write my poetry and play my guitar. I did not realize I would have to endure TONS of criticism from VERY SMALL-MINDED PEOPLE.

My father is expecting—no, demanding—that I graduate from this university with a degree that gives me security. That is not who I am. I don't want security. I want to create. My father says,

"Take some teaching classes; teachers get summers off. You can create in the summer." How can I tell my artist soul that it will be fed only in the summer? It will *starve* to death, *crumble,* and *die* by mid-November.

I try to tell my father that **I am a songwriter**, but it falls on deaf ears. My father says terms like 401(k) and health insurance. I tell him those are just **evil** necessities and that I have to be true to my artist soul. Our conversations go in circles.

I think I need to take another trip into the counselor's office for career counseling. Every time I do, which has been many, they make me take this stupid questionnaire. This "test" is supposed to help me find my true calling by the answers I give. Last time it said I should be either a florist or a circus clown. Although lovely, some flowers make me sneeze, and I can't ride a bike to save my life, so I seriously doubt this test works. Maybe this time.

GOALS AND INTENTIONS

As for now, I **intend** to keep WRITING. I will write my SONGS and SOUL STORIES because they fulfill me. I will continue meeting with my poetry group on Sunday nights. This is my favorite night of the week. I will continue with yoga and will take an advanced yoga class next semester. *I love yoga!* I will continue to play my guitar and work at the health food store.

I **intend** to find my TRUE LOVE. My men-of-the-month/soulmate search will continue as is, looking in the bedroom first. My reasoning is that the search for the soul mate is the *most important* and yet *most difficult* task we set out to do on this earth. I am not naive when I write that it may take years to find my soul partner, so I do not believe in wasting time with dating. I honestly believe that I will know my soul mate the instant I fuck him. "*We will become one in our act of love making. Our hearts will beat the same rhythm. We will take in the same breaths. Not only will our limbs be entwined, but so will our hearts and souls. We will fit together like puzzle pieces, and we* *will both know instantly that we were created for each other."* Until that time, I'll keep test driving all other makes and models.

I **intend** to keep COUNTING EVERY BLESSING, ALWAYS TO BE GRATEFUL. To remain INNOCENT and IDEALISTIC (I think those two qualities are totally sexy.) To LEARN FROM LIFE and to ALWAYS LOOK ON THE BRIGHT SIDE.

I **intend** to keep COUNTING MY LOSSES. I will accept my pain as I accept my pleasure. Each loss shapes me. I will not hide my feelings of loss or gain. I will be true to myself.

April has been a difficult month, but it is now ending. The rain has stopped, and the flowers have begun to bud. The trees all have their leaves, and the air has been much warmer. I plan to clear my head during the month of May, to pull out my entire summer wardrobe, and most importantly, to live each day to its fullest.

I will now leave this coffee shop and walk three blocks down a wet sidewalk to Pet Town Pets. Who knows? Maybe I'll go home with a kitten. As for now, this is Angela Ann McClan ending this soul story. Until next month, I will live, love, and lose with acceptance and grace.

BROOKE

Because I feel that in the heaven above
The angels, whispering to one another,
Can find, among their burning terms of love,
None as devotional as that of "Mother"

"To My Mother" by Edgar Alan Poe

May 16, 1999

Happy Mother's Day to Me!

Dear Camden James Fisher,

You are my beautiful baby boy. It is so hard to believe that you're here and that I'm a mommy. It's especially hard, since you're not even supposed to be here yet. My eager baby boy arrived six weeks early. You broke Mommy's water on prom night as Daddy and I were dirty dancing. I thought I was going to be embarrassed as your waterbed gushed down my leg and left a large pool on the dance floor, but everyone was kind and excited and mature about it all. After all, we are graduating seniors. Mrs. Evans and Mrs. Powell, my two favorite teachers, helped your daddy get me into the car, and away we went. Even though you're early, and even though we have all been really worried about you, I still think it's kind of cool that you decided to be born on prom night. It's like really freaky, maybe fate, because you were conceived on Homecoming night. Both nights were incredibly special and beautiful; however, I did happen to ruin two very expensive dresses, one stained by you in your eagerness, and one stained by your father in his.

Everybody at the hospital said that you came fast. I don't see how they can consciously make that recollection. Do these people not remember the screams, pain, sweat, horribly bad mood, and the things I said over the entire five hours? Besides, when did five hours become fast? That's not fast. I must admit it's so much better than women who say they were in labor for some ridiculous amount of time, thirty hours or something, but five hours is definitely not fast. Fast is like those stories of babies being born in truck beds en route to hospitals or behind someone's desk at work. Five hours is probably perfect, just like you.

I have heard that women forget the pain of childbirth after the baby comes, and that is why they are able to have more than one child. Well, Camden James, you may be an only child, because Mommy hasn't forgotten, and I don't believe that I ever will.

How can someone forget the tightening that pulls across her stomach and the unbearable pains that shoot across her back and down her legs? The pain itself was so intense, it caused me to kick and blow involuntarily. Whether a woman has taken Lamaze or not, she's going to blow. It's simply a survival skill. The relief between contractions is just a small break that God has fit in, so that the mother can catch her breath before tightening again to prepare for the next attack.

The whole labor process is a contradiction in itself. When giving birth, I had the most incredible pain interrupted by relief. I was hot and cold; my body was wet; my lips were cracked and dry. My mouth was a sand pit, my vagina an ocean. My legs trembled, uncontrollably, but my fists were clenched and my arms were tight. I intensely felt opposite emotions at the same time, such as love and hate. I needed someone beside me and then I felt bothered by the person's presence. I would think *Just talk to me*, and then I would think *Just shut up* or *Hold my hand, but stay out of my space.*

I was such a Dr. Jekyll/Mr. Hyde that it wasn't long before they came in with the epidural. Thank God for the epidural. Why anyone would put herself through natural childbirth is beyond me, especially when there is medicine to help. When you have a headache, it's okay to take an aspirin, so when you have a baby, it should be okay to take an epidural. This is my advice to the world of pregnant women.

The only thing not pleasant about the epidural is how they give it to you, but after that, it's great. Having a needle poked in your spine while simultaneously hard contractions are controlling your body and mind is not such a good time. It would be so much nicer if they could somehow figure out how to get that numbing medicine into a person in a gentler way, like by mouth, through a medicated, ice slushy umbrella drink. If only I wanted to go into medicine, I could invent this technique and be rich.

Soon after getting the epidural, the pains felt more like little inconveniences and less like brutal attacks. I was even able to do my hair, which got totally messed up during the pushing process.

Pushing you out, my son, was the hardest amount of work I have ever had to do. It made cheerleading camp and workouts seem like a breeze (which pains me to say, as captain of the cheerleading squad). The first thing about pushing was the position in which I had to put my legs. Gross. (Please know, my child, that I do not blame you. I'm sure if you could speak, you would have your own version of the story and have a lot to say on how uncomfortable, painful, or cramped my body was for you).

Back to the stirrups. First of all, they're entirely too cold. It would be much more appealing if they would line those steel get-ups with pink fur, like a giant house slipper that can be taken off and washed (another brilliant invention). Then there is the mirror that hangs down in your face so you can watch. Like who in their right mind wants to see their vagina get big enough for a human head to emerge? GROSS.

I didn't watch, and I didn't let your dad watch, either. He wanted to, though. He was completely intrigued by all the blood and your head and my vagina, and he kept sticking his face in the way of everything, so much that he had to be yelled at. I'm sorry I yelled at your daddy and everybody else while you were trying to be born. I hope that I did not scare you. What I needed was your dad to get his head out from between my legs and help me. That damn (but beautiful) epidural that they had given me made it impossible for me to push on my own. Pushing is actually holding a crunch while your legs are up in stirrups. I needed your daddy to help push my shoulders forward, bend me in half, count to ten, and then let me rest, and once he finally got his head out of the doctor's way, he was a good help at that. I think he was a natural at pushing me forward and panting. It comes from all the football conditioning he does, and since he's captain, he leads the whole team in strenuous exercise.

Both of your grandmas were a big help too. Grandma Fisher (Daddy's mommy) held my right hand and cried, while Grandma James (my mommy) held my left hand. Pushing took an entire hour of the five hours it took you to come out.

Then there was the split second of your arrival, when everything and everyone became motionless and silent and you did not cry. When that wee second of time was up, it was a mad rush. The doctor barked at the nurse who barked at the other nurse. Oxygen was thrown on your face, and within seconds, you were whisked away. I lay in a daze as both grandmas went in and out of the room with questions, and Brandon, your daddy, said nothing. That pumped-up school boy was silent for the first time in his life, and I became frightened. I tried to talk to your daddy, but he wouldn't talk back, and then the doctor was between my legs again.

I saw you for the first time after I was already settled in my room. They didn't bring you to me, like all the other mommies who cheerfully had their babies in their room, with an overflow of happy visitors. Instead, I was taken to you, pushed down the hall in a wheelchair by a worried nurse. She pushed me past all the well babies that were bundled up in pink or blue and pushed me into the frightening silent room of the Neonatal Intensive Care Unit. I was parked in front of a hooded bassinet that more resembled an animal cage than a child's crib.

Camden James, I'm going to be honest with you. I am your mommy, and I will never lie to you. I will tell you the truth, because you deserve the truth, and because you will hear our story from others. You terrified me. You were small and thin. You weighed only four pounds, five ounces, and your body seemed incredibly long for its weight, nineteen inches. During the pushing process, your head had been sharpened to a fine point, and you had no hair. Your skin glowed florescent yellow and green under the bright light that kept you warm, and there were tubes and wires hooked up to you all over. In your hooded bassinet, as you tried to stay alive, you reminded me of a very sick animal. As I write this, tears stream down my face, and I am full of regret, but you did not look like my baby at all and kind of looked like a lizard or alien.

You have to know that through my pregnancy, I envisioned a healthy, chunky, happy baby like the ones in the Pampers ads. Those are the only types of babies I had ever seen. As I sat beside your bed peering in at you, I became freaked out with fear. The lights and numbers on your machine blinked and beeped anxiously and kept reminding me that you were a fragile little being.

You were on a ventilator, because they said your lungs were not fully developed. They went on further to say this happens mostly with premature white boys, and they even referred to it as wimpy-white-boy-lungs. This pissed your father off. The nurse then explained to us that for some reason, white premature males have the hardest time. Black females were the strongest of premature babies, and then white females, and then black males, and lastly white males.

We could stay with you for only a few minutes, because your heart rate kept going up, so they told us to leave. Your daddy pushed me back to the room, and he seemed all happy again, just to see you and be sure that you had help, but I was frozen.

I'm so sorry, Camden James, but you were a very fragile little being, one that I couldn't possibly take care of, at least not without breaking. I was so scared that I refused to see you anymore. It wasn't your fault. I didn't mean to reject you in your first four weeks of life. I just felt overwhelmed and unsure of myself. I knew that I could never handle your care. You were here and you were sick and tiny, and I couldn't believe that I was responsible for your life and you were so helpless.

I lay in my hospital bed for two days, refusing to see you. My reaction so unsettled the nurses that they sent people up to speak to me about adoption. I am telling you the truth when I write, I never, ever considered giving you up for adoption, but I did let them talk. I sat in my bed silently praying for your health as they rambled on. I could hear their words floating around my hospital room like flies, but I could not put the words together or understand. I was lost in my own thoughts. Then your daddy and Grandma Fisher came rushing into the room and ordered everybody out. Grandma Fisher wants to adopt you, but she is your grandma, not your mommy, and I love you. I was just scared.

When I went home, I didn't go back to the hospital. My mom did though. Your Grandma James went three times a day, before going to work, on her lunch hour, and again after dinner. I stayed home in my room, not talking to anyone. I refused phone calls from friends who were so eager to hear about you. My mother would come into the room every night and give me daily reports. She said things like, "Brooke, good news; I got to touch Camden James today." "Brooke, good news; Camden James is off the ventilator." "Brooke, good news;

Camden James is slowly learning how to suck." With each report I felt as if my solitary prayers were being answered and that I could not break the rhythm. I was serving you best by closing myself in, shutting everybody else out and praying.

I have walked around in silent prayer for the past four weeks. I pray when I wake every morning, and I pray in the shower and while I brush my teeth and before going to bed and through each and every task I have started and finished over the past month. I know that my prayers were helping to heal you, but how could I explain this to anybody else? I mean, I'm not a religious person at all, and saying that I was in meditation and prayer would sound clumsy and stupid coming out of my mouth.

Your daddy and Grandma Fisher have been very angry at me. They think I am heartless and selfish. Mrs. Fisher said so, right to my face, and Grandma James had to kick her out of our house by saying, "Darlene, if you have come over to upset Brooke, well, you succeeded, and you can now leave." Your daddy, however, gave me a sweet smile and a kiss on the forehead before Grandma Fisher pulled him through our front door, so I know that he is more concerned and less angry at me than his mother.

Grandpa Fisher called that evening to apologize to my mother. My mom told me that he said, "This is a very scary time for everyone, and we all love and care about Brooke very much and are willing to do anything to help her through this." He's much nicer than his wife. Grandma Fisher hates me. While you lived inside my tummy, she did nothing but cry and moan about how I have ruined her son's life and future. Now that you are here, she's concerned that I will ruin yours.

Grandpa Fisher has spent the last nine months running interference on his wife's emotional state. Once he said, "Brooke didn't impregnate herself. Brandon does carry some fault, Darlene." I smile from ear to ear every time Grandpa Fisher puts Grandma Fisher in her place. It just needs to happen more often, to be effective.

Camden James, I'm sorry to insult your grandma. I am only trying to be honest with you the best that I can. Since I'm going to lay my faults and imperfections out for you to see, then I'm going to lay everybody else's, along with them. Grandma James, or actually "GiGi," which she has informed me she wants to be called, took the news of your coming like a soldier, which is exactly how she takes all news since Grandpa James's death.

Camden James, you will never get to know my daddy, because he died two years ago in an accident. Sergeant James, as he was known by everyone, was a strong, brave, handsome man who also happened to be the town hero. Your Grandpa James was a policeman. One rainy night in September 1997, he pulled over a drunk driver, who drove away as my dad approached his vehicle. The man's blue Chevy Ranger hit my dad head on, killing him. The man, Willie Sparks, was later caught, and I guess he had warrants in three other states. I don't believe Willie Sparks meant to kill my daddy; he just meant to get away. He's in prison, however, and labeled a cop killer for life, and my daddy died a hero.

The whole town of Butler shut down to attend your grandpa's funeral, and every year on the anniversary of his death, the police department puts together a beautiful memorial that's held in the town square, and the whole town of Butler shuts down again. I'll take you this year.

Sergeant James would have loved you very much. You are named in his honor, and even though James was his last name and not his first, it was what everyone called him. I changed Sergeant (his title) to Camden. My dad's real first name was Clifton. I believe that your grandpa, Sergeant James, has to do with a big part of your healing. I have felt my daddy's presence a lot. Sometimes I smell him; he was a Stetson man. Sometimes I just feel him near me. During the past four weeks, his presence has never been stronger. He has been beside me in my prayers. He has been helping me pray, giving me the right words to say. How else would I know what I'm doing?

It is also important for you to know that through these past four weeks, there has never been one time when I didn't think I would be bringing you home. I always knew and believed that you would be in my arms, once my prayers were answered and you were healthy.

To prepare for the arrival of my baby boy, I redecorated your room, actually our room. During the time I carried you inside my body, I was completely and totally sure that you were a girl. I called you Jamie Lynne—Jamie after your grandfather and my last name, and Lynne from my middle name. I must have absolutely no psychic ability whatsoever. I even gave you a pink baby shower, which I called a princess party. The number of mistakes I've already made as a mother is embarrassing.

The princess party was held in our back yard, and the cheerleading squad went out of its way with the decorations. Large pink, white, and red bows were tied around everything. Bundles of pink, white, and red balloons were strategically placed along our white picket fence. Three long picnic tables were draped in red-and-white checkered tablecloths, and a large bowl of cherries was placed in the center of each table, with white and pink pillar candles burning alongside the cherries. We ate from real china; no paper plates touched a table at my princess party. We drank a deliciously pink fruit punch out of large burgundy glasses. The stereo was set up outside on the patio, and we played Whitney Houston (definite princess music; I have the whole collection.) The princess party was held at sundown, my favorite time of day, when the sky is both pink and purple. You received enough gifts at the princess party to fill a real palace. The only problem was most everything was made for a princess and not for a prince.

As a result, during my prayer and meditation and while talking to Grandpa James, I've been trying to create a space to bring my little boy home to, and not one that is so frou-frou that you're bound to grow up gay. I started my creative process by giving GiGi a list of things I would need: material, batting and thread, paint, brushes, and maybe a few baby patterns. My ideas flowed from a miniskirt I had made myself last summer. The skirt is crisp white material with bright blue and teal-green polka dots. I gave the skirt to my mother and told her to buy up the rest of the material. From the yards and yards she brought home, I covered the pink quilt and bumper pads that were already in your crib. I then made you and me matching bed skirts and six matching pillows. I sewed matching curtains and a valance for our bedroom window, and with what was left of the material, I made you a polka-dot teddy bear and dog (who knew I could make stuffed animals)? The blue and green spots make your white crib much more masculine, and I ripped down the gay pink canopy I had made when I thought you were a girl.

Next, I painted. The wall behind your now polka-dot crib is soft baby blue and the remaining three walls are mint green. On your baby-blue wall, above your crib, arching like a rainbow, in my best big block-letter cheerleading print, I wrote out Camden James in a very bright blue. GiGi was so tickled by the newly painted walls and polka dots that she went out and bought me a new bed spread in the same bright blue color as in the arch of Camden James.

Lastly, I made your clothes. First I had to pull all the pink and purple that hung in my closet and lay in drawers and replace them by making boy clothes. During our pregnancy, I had become obsessed with sewing little sundresses. Since you were to be a baby girl born in the summer, I created for you the most beautiful little dresses and matching floppy hats. I spent all my money from my part-time retail job and babysitting to buy material. I made you dresses in every soft pastel color and floral print imaginable. Night after night I sewed dress after dress. I showed your pretty collection to Mrs. Wilkes, the home-ec teacher, and she was quite impressed. When I ran out of money to buy material, I made your daddy take me to the fabric store and use his money. I loved making the dresses. I loved them so much that I made myself a couple matching ones, mine not nearly as cute as yours. By the time I was six months pregnant, you already had a princess wardrobe, and I hadn't even had your princess party yet.

Your beautiful little dresses and floppy hats are now neatly packed away in an enormous plastic tub and shoved in my closet. GiGi picked up a pattern for baby bib overalls (the kind that has two buttons at the shoulders and two snaps at the crotch) and material in bright red and navy blue. I made the baby bib overalls out of the bright-colored fabric, but wasn't having nearly as much fun as creating the sundresses. Then out of the blue, the inspiration hit and I feverishly began sewing brightly colored diaper shirts and matching baby boxer shorts. Oh, they are so adorable. You can imagine, the tiniest baby boxers, just like your daddy wears, and then, just like the idea of the floppy hat, I decided you needed something for your tender bald head, and what better to wear than a matching do-rag, cut like a bandana, only much smaller.

Oh, Camden James, you are going to look so adorable in these beautiful outfits your very own mother created for you. I am so pleased with myself. GiGi is pleased too. When I showed her the entire ensemble, she laughed out loud and exclaimed, "Oh, Brooke, you've never made anything cuter." The next day she brought home a huge stack of material, adorable plaids and paisleys. Camden James, you are going to be a GQ baby.

Through all of this craziness, I am most surprised by my mother. I know money is tight. Who knows how much your hospital stay will be, whether GiGi's insurance will help, or if I will have to apply for state assistance, and will the state even help? All these unanswered questions I know taunt my mother endlessly, yet she allowed me to create all these things for you and even encouraged me. She took my orders for paint and material (which are not cheap) and brought me supplies each night after visiting you. She never said we didn't have the money or told me what she was spending. She never even showed me the receipts. Maybe she believed my creative explosion was cheaper than therapy.

You are now four weeks old, Camden James. You are strong and healthy and weigh more than five pounds. You can breathe on your own and you can suck a bottle and a pacifier. The nurses have fallen in love with you over the past month, and they call you "Little Sergeant." They know that you are the grandson of Sergeant James. It is still two weeks before your due date, and you are already here. Ironically you are to come home on Mother's Day. I have nothing for my own mother except a card that I made from thick, pink construction paper and a flower stencil. Inside it I wrote a heartfelt thank you. I also sewed do-rags for GiGi and myself that match the outfit you are going to wear home. (Won't that be hysterical)? Our true gift today, however, is you, Camden James; your health and your life.

In a few hours, when the world wakes up, my mother will take me to the hospital to retrieve you, and we will come straight home. The neighbors have sent over food. They are so nice to us now that my daddy is dead. We will feast all day on cold cuts and salads, and your daddy will come by for a visit. The sun is slowly rising. The flowers have decided to bloom this week in anticipation of your arrival. Things are looking good, Camden James. You have grown to a healthy new-baby size, and I have slimmed down. In only a month's time, I am almost back into my old jeans.

In less than three weeks, your father and I will graduate from high school. Instead of walking across the stage with a big belly or missing graduation altogether, to give birth, which is what I thought was going to happen, I will be able to attend with a slim figure and beautiful baby boy watching from the audience. You will get to meet all of Daddy and Mommy's family and friends. Cousin Tiffany is the valedictorian. Aunt Pam is proud. Your great-grandparents will be there and your great aunts and uncles. Afterwards there will be parties and celebrations all week long, and I will take you with me and everyone will love and admire you. After that, we have the summer to get close, and you have the summer to bond with your daddy.

He will leave us in September, but don't be angry; be proud of him, Camden James. Your daddy got a football scholarship to play for a small university a couple hours away. He wanted one of the big schools to recognize his talents and pay his way. It didn't work out that way. Oh well, maybe he won't go pro, but at least he will get to play in his freshman year. Daddy wants us to go with him. He has already proposed marriage and has promised me a diamond ring. I guess your daddy thinks he can do it all, be a college student and football star as well as marry his high school girlfriend and start a family. I have not accepted your daddy's proposal. I just smile and kiss him when he talks of marriage. I figure time will tell. I do not want to ever get in the way of his dreams. I don't want us ever to be resented. We will stay with GiGi when daddy leaves. We will take enjoyable road trips every Saturday in autumn to watch your daddy play ball. I will still be his own private cheerleader.

As for you and me, Mommy has a plan—a big, beautiful plan. It came to me because of you. I need to talk this over with GiGi, because it requires using the money that I received when my daddy died, the money that is to be my college fund. I want to fund something else, however. I want to fund my dream, a dream that has carried me through these four long weeks.

I want to open a baby boutique. I want to rent a trendy little site in the downtown square and fill it with my line of Camden James clothing. I believe I have enough sundresses and floppy hats to start the process, and I can sew my diaper shirts and mini boxer shorts quite easily. GiGi crochets and knits, and I was hoping she would believe in my dream enough to fill it with blankets and sweaters. I've thought about starting out by selling on the Internet or at craft shows, but my true dream is to own *BROOKE LYNN'S BOUTIQUE*. I believe I can make it happen and still go to college. I can take my classes at night. I have known since the age of eleven that I was going to be a fashion designer one day. It's going to happen sooner than I thought. It's going to happen now.

Very truly yours, forever and ever,

Mommy

JASMINE

The Princess looked at her more closely.
"Tell me," she said resumed
"Are you of royal blood?"
"Better than that, ma'am," said Dorothy
"I came from Kansas."

Ozma of Oz, L. Frank Baum

Dear Diary,

My sixth-grade teacher, Ms. Hutchins (I'll be in seventh grade this fall), told our class that we should keep journals for the summer and write in them every day. Ms. Hutchins said journaling is a nice way to hold your memories. She said it's fun to go back later and remember what you did and what was happening in your life at that time.

I seriously doubt that when Ms. Hutchins made this suggestion she knew that all hell was going to break loose in my house this summer, but it has, and it has me feeling frightened and excited and nervous and angry, all at the same time. Since I have all these emotions twirling in me at the same time and absolutely nobody I want to share them with, I thought I would take the suggestion of Ms. Hutchins and start a journal. So here it goes.

Dear Diary, I am scared right now, plenty scared. Momma is scared too, and Tye, my little brother, if he has any sense at all, he's feeling it too. Momma has scrubbed both Tye and me clean and has bought us new clothes, including new underwear. I doubt anybody will be looking at my underwear, but I'm glad she bought them for me just the same. Tye's and my new clothes match, which is just plain ridiculous, if you ask me. I am getting way too old to be dressed in an outfit that matches my six-year-old brother's. I don't think Momma realizes twelve-year-old girls want to match their outfits only with their best friends, and not a first-grade boy. But they're nice clothes, and I love to get new clothes. I like new clothes even better than a new toy, and if all I ever got for Christmas were clothes, I wouldn't mind a bit. Daddy laughs at how much I love clothes. He shakes his head and smiles his big white smile and says I'm just like my Aunt Teresa. Aunt Teresa is forever shopping.

Momma bought me blue jean capri pants with a little white T-shirt and a new pair of white sandals. Capri pants are really "in" this year. Momma wears them all the time, and her long, silky-white calves look beautiful sticking out of the bottom of her pants. Momma is what Aunt Teresa calls a leggy woman. Tye's clothes are blue cargo shorts and a white polo shirt. He has on new white leather running shoes, and he's been running all over the house making squeak marks on the floor, and Momma is so nervous she has just ignored him.

Momma is getting herself ready now, and she has done and redone her hair about a hundred times. My hair is done too, but Momma doesn't know a thing about fixing my hair. She tries really hard, but it never looks as good as when my aunts do it. So after trying, she asks my aunts (Daddy's sisters) if they would do it. My aunts just laugh at Momma and call her "Blondie," and then they braid my hair up just like my cousin's. Momma thanks them and laughs at herself, like she's dizzy or something.

Momma is not some dizzy woman, even though she never did finish high school. They think it's a big secret that Momma is a drop-out. But I've known since I was eight. I heard her talking to Daddy about wanting to go back to school and get her diploma when Tye started kindergarten. Tye will be in first grade this fall, and Momma hasn't gone back to school yet.

My momma's life has been hard ever since she fell in love with my daddy. It's like when you love someone so much you become them, but not really them, just a part of them, like an arm or leg or even more removed, like a hand. Something that sticks out from that person and is separate, but is still attached. Then you are a separate thing, but you are still part of the big thing, and you need that big thing to live. My momma loves my daddy so much that she is lost in him. She is lost in his life. The only family Momma has is Daddy, Tye, and me. The only friends she has are Daddy's friends (Momma is painfully shy). The only big family Momma has is Daddy's family. Oh, how my momma sticks out like a sore thumb among us all. There's not even a shred of evidence that Momma existed before she fell in love with my daddy. Daddy is Momma's living circle. The air that she breathes, the water that she tastes, all of it is my daddy.

Momma is going to try and step out of that circle today, out of the circle of warmth and love and stand alone. The reason I'm scared is because she is taking Tye and me with her. Tye and I are being forced to leave our own circle of light and Daddy's love and step into a cold, dark and angry place, our grandmother's house.

I don't want to meet my grandmother. I have never seen the woman in my whole lifetime, and I don't want to see her now. I am afraid that she will look me up and down and shake her prejudiced head, like I'm pitiful. I'm afraid she will call my Daddy a nigger, 'cause I know that's what she calls him. I'm afraid that she will call Tye and me niggers, and if that happens, I don't think I can keep myself from punching her in her old white face.

My daddy has these same worries, and he does not want my momma to take Tye and me to our grandmother's house. Momma has said that she would not let that woman hurt Tye or Jasmine, and that is something he should know. Momma said that she needs to do this for herself and for her children, and Daddy said, "Bullshit!" and then walked out of the house and Momma sat down and cried even harder. She cried like there was no stopping her. She cried the way Tye does when he falls down and scrapes his knee, which he does all the time and should be used to by now. But he cries every time, like his skin is soft and smooth and has never been hurt before. That's how Momma cried, just like it was her first pain, and it was a surprise. Momma then stopped crying, as if she never even started. She just stopped and washed her face and made Tye and me dress in these matching outfits and then went to take her shower, and my daddy still hasn't come back.

I don't think he will tonight. I think it is too hard on him to see my momma worry so much about pleasing a mother who has been so mean to her. My daddy told Momma that her mother has rejected his children ever since they were conceived, and she should not have the privilege now of even being in their beautiful presence. My daddy said it was our grandmother's loss, not ours.

Momma cried from her bright-blue crystal eyes. Her eyes are so blue I can see my reflection in them, just like when I look into the water of a still lake, and when she cries, they are even more blue. Momma is a beautiful crier, just like some director screamed, "CUT!" and a make-up artist came running over and put teardrops in my momma's eyes and blushed her cheeks a rosy red. While Momma was crying her pretty blue tears, she said to my Daddy, "What about my loss? I've lost my whole history." It would have been nice if Daddy would of just hugged Momma, instead of leaving. What Momma really needs is a hug and Daddy's strong arms around her to make her feel safe.

I know I sure do feel safe in Daddy's arms. Daddy's arms are big and strong and as dark and mighty as the night. Daddy's big bulging muscles pop out if he does so much as bend his elbow. Momma's arms are long and skinny like her legs, and with her summer tan, her arms are the same color gold as her hair. I wish I looked like Momma, but I don't. I look like my daddy, and Tye gets to look more like Momma. Sometimes I just sit with Momma and I lay my arm next to hers and just stare at the contrast. Momma says I have beautiful skin. It is the color of coffee with double creams. Tye's is even lighter. Momma's color is lighter than peach but darker than white with a tint of beige freckles sprinkled across her skin, like God's glitter or confetti or something wonderful thrown lightly on her skin. I would love to have freckles. I have no freckles, just a few ugly moles.

The most beautiful thing about Momma is her hair. Her hair is what I envy the most. It's straight, completely straight, not one single kink in it. It is the longest and silkiest and straightest hair on earth. It nearly touches her bottom. The color of it is a million and one shades of gold, all falling down her pretty head, shoulders, and back. Some of her hair is the color of wheat and some of it is the same shade as the maize crayon in the 64-box of Crayolas. Then there are the streaks that look to be as white as lightning on the night sky. Momma's hair is beautiful and powerful, just like the lion's mane. My hair is just brown, brown, brown, and more brown. My eyes are the same color. I can only guess my momma must look like her momma, but this I do not know for sure, or at least not yet.

My grandmother kicked my momma out of the family when she was seventeen years old, when Momma got pregnant with me. My grandmother and great-grandmother (they raised my momma in my great-grandmother's estate) told my momma that if she did not get rid of that nigger and his child she carried inside her, she would no longer be part of their family, so my momma left my great-grandmother's estate, and she was not permitted to take anything with her, just the clothes she had on. Momma moved in with my Aunt Carmen, my daddy's sister. Momma had to quit school and get a job. My daddy was already finished with high school (my daddy is three years older than my momma), and he was working in a fancy restaurant. First Daddy was a bus boy and then he was a waiter and then he was a cook and a bartender, and now he is the manager. We lived with Aunt Carmen until I was four years old, and then we moved into an apartment. When Tye was two years old and I was eight, we bought the house we live in now.

Our house is a nice house. It is a pretty blue color with big white shutters. It reminds me of a sky with clouds. The back yard has a fence around it, so Momma is going to get Tye a dog for his birthday this year, and I CAN'T WAIT! Tye and I have our own bedrooms, and my carpet is light pink and his is dark blue. Our whole neighborhood is built up the side of a Virginia mountain (the Shenandoah Mountains). The streets just climb right up the side, We live near the top.

Right now, I don't want to leave my pretty blue house in the mountains to go visit my grandmother's estate. *Estate* is not even a nice word. It sounds cold and crisp and formal, just like I think she will be. Momma talked to me a little last night about our visit. She told me not to be afraid and to remember that my grandmother is more afraid.

My grandmother is alone now. My great-grandmother died three weeks ago, and my momma read it in the paper. It made the social section. She had a whole page written about her and how much she did for her little Virginia county. She never did anything for Tye and me. Momma called her grandmother "prominent." Daddy called her a "social-climbing-ass-biter" and then said, "Scab"!

Momma went to her grandmother's funeral. Daddy stayed home and cooked Tye and me steaks on the grill and let us drink Coca-Cola with lots of ice. He told us that we were a princess and a prince. My Aunt Teresa and Aunt Carmen came over to our cookout and even brought us presents. After supper, Daddy let Tye and me run through the sprinkler while he and his sisters whispered secrets to each other. My aunts kept hugging Tye and me that day and telling us how much we were loved. They kept rubbing Daddy's back and patting his hands. Later they went and rented movies and came back and stayed with us watching TV until Momma came home. When Momma walked in, they suddenly jumped up without even seeing the end of the movies they had just rented and left our house in a hurry, kissing my daddy and making a big fuss over him as they left. Momma stood in the doorway like a beautiful stone statue, quiet and far away from us.

Ever since that night, Momma has stayed quiet. Momma is quiet anyway, not like me, who Daddy says can talk from sun-up to sundown and still have something to say. Momma is naturally quiet. I think Momma is usually quiet, just because she doesn't have anything she wants to say, but lately Momma is busting with things to say. You can look in her eyes and tell that she is having a long, wordy, secret conversation all in her own mind and that she is deliberately choosing not to share her words.

Momma has seen my grandmother two other times since the funeral. Each time she has visited my grandmother, she has done so by herself and has stayed only a few hours. Each time she has come home lost inside herself. Lately you can talk to Momma and she will nod her head one way or the other without even knowing what you asked. Last week she drove straight through a red light. At Aunt Teresa's birthday picnic, she started crying right in the middle of the barbecue, and for no good reason that I saw. For just a week now, Momma and Daddy have been talking about my grandmother wanting to meet Tye and me. My daddy says my grandmother is evil and bigoted and that she will hurt Tye and me. My daddy says in his deep, strong tone, "Why do you need that woman? Isn't my love enough?" He tells my momma that she has made her own family with her husband and children who love her and need her. He says, "Please don't put Jasmine and Tye through this. They don't need that woman's acceptance."

Momma cries her beautiful tears and argues back quietly.

Momma's words are whispers. She begs my daddy, "Please try to understand. It's not about acceptance. It's about a missing piece, a part of myself that my children do not know."

My daddy believes my Momma is separate from her past. My momma believes she is made of her past.

So here I sit filling a notebook that I picked up only an hour ago. I pray that being introduced into the part of my Momma's life that I had been earlier banned from and then protected against won't hurt me as much as I'm afraid it will. I pray that my grandmother will be nice to Tye and me, and I pray that she will be nice to my daddy. I pray that Momma and Daddy will stop hurting each other's feelings, and I pray that my momma is happy.

Oh, Dear Diary, my daddy is home. I heard his red truck pull into our driveway, and now I can hear their hushed voices rising under the crack of my door. I can close my eyes and picture my daddy.

He is big and strong and dark as the night, and he is hugging my momma. Momma is pale and delicate and golden like the sun. I am so glad that my daddy came home before we left to see our grandmother. For my daddy, this is a grand gesture. This means he is going to support my momma, even though he doesn't understand her. This means my daddy will forget about being afraid, just so my momma can feel good. This means my daddy loves my momma, every bit as much as she loves him.

Oh Diary, Daddy and Mommy are done kissing and hugging and making up, and now Momma is ready to leave. I guess she wasn't quite prepared until she knew my daddy would be here for her when she came home. I'm So Scared!

I suppose if this visit goes well and Momma can talk Daddy into it, he will be joining us next time. Well, Tye is in the car and Momma just rapped on my door twice. Ms. Hutchinson was right. This is going to be a summer to remember.

Sincerely,
Jasmine Renee Johnson

SISSY

Dark and dusty, painted on the sky
Misty taste of moonshine
Teardrop in my eyes
"Country Roads" by John Denver

July 9, 1999

My life has forever changed;

Beau has left me, simple, pure, and true. He's been gone three weeks today. He left on Sunday, June 20, 1999, Father's Day, at 10:00 p.m. After confirming that the kids were truly asleep, he pulled an already packed suitcase from underneath the bed, gathered up his crayon drawings from Henry, an ashtray made of clay from Roman, and a Dixie cup full of wildflowers that the boys had given him from Sabrina. He left my gift on the table, a baseball cap inscribed #1 DAD. He placed his hand on my shoulder, and in a sympathetic, yet matter-of-fact tone, told me that he no longer loved me. He then walked out of our small and rusted mobile home, letting the frail, thin door slam shut behind him, and stepped into the deluxe Winnebago of Judy Mathers. There was no fight, no apologies, and no explanations, and with his pathetic exit, the lives of each of us were changed forever.

Before Beau left, there had been red flags. First, I knew that Judy Mathers was a slut. I knew from the day she pulled her fancy-shmancy Winnebago into our KOA campground. She entered the camp store in cutoff jean shorts that entered the crack of her ass and a string bikini top that managed to cover only her nipples. I knew when she grabbed a large bottle of Evian spring water and rolled it back and forth across her sweaty chest as she talked to Beau about renting a campsite. I remember disgustedly asking her, "Are you gonna buy that?" That was after I had watched her roll it over her fake tits approximately twenty-six times. She sighed, rolled her eyes, and then handed me a dollar. I remember Beau giving me a look of embarrassment and anger like, "How could you have said such a thing to this beautiful, slutty woman?" That was ten months ago, and I was nine months pregnant with Sabrina at the time.

Looking back, I see that carrying Sabrina was the worst pregnancy I have ever endured. The heat is what caused my misery. At least while I was pregnant with the boys, we were living in a decent state. The boys were born in West Virginia, Beau's and my hometown. How I miss home!

In West Virginia, even when it's hot, a gentle and welcome breeze will soar through the mountains and trees and gently wisp your hair or blow at your dress like an old friend, not like here in Florida. In Florida the heat cracks and dries up the earth instantly after the rain has stopped falling, and little red fire ants crawl out of the cracked earth to plan their attacks. I tell you, being pregnant in Florida is the equivalent of Hell. I honestly believe that any woman who has had more than one child while living in this state is nothing but a masochist and a victim.

I gained sixty pounds while pregnant with Sabrina. I was sick with toxemia, bloated and fat from heat and exhaustion. I was so swollen and weak that I stopped looking like myself and instead had been replaced with some fat, tired person. I lost thirty pounds in the first six months of Sabrina's life, and I've lost the remaining thirty pounds within the last three weeks of Beau's abandonment.

It was during the time I spent in fat hell that Judy Mathers, the ol' slut, pulled her Winnebago into my life and began enticing my husband.

Sabrina Marie Jaspers was born two days after Judy arrived, and I was no longer pregnant, just fat. A large, sleep-deprived, lactating, grouch. It was the beginning of September, and Roman and Henry had just started back to school. I tried to take six weeks off after the baby, but that's not easy to do when you live and work, in the same place. Most days, after getting the boys off to school, Carla would cover the store for me and let me nap with the baby. But she now had the duty of running most of the family activities, instead of splitting them up, like we usually do. By noon I would be sitting behind the counter on a hard wooden stool, ringing up hotdogs and marshmallows for some fellow camper, a baby attached to my nipple, a large pad in my bra wet with breast milk, and a large pad in my pants wet with post-partum blood.

It was during this time that Beau would be zooming around the campgrounds in a golf cart checking and rechecking complaints, cleaning up the grounds, and stopping by Judy Mathers' place, the ol' slut, on invites for a cold glass of iced tea and a stolen moment in her air conditioning and out of the heat.

Judy Mathers! I refer to her as "the ol' slut," but what I should call her is "Mrs. Robinson." That's what she is, an old seductive Mrs. Robinson. I knew she was older than I, but I wasn't sure by how much. That was until I saw her driver's license. I almost flipped when I looked at the date on the hard plastic card when "Mrs. Robinson" paid for another month's rent. Forty-five! That ol' slut is forty-five flipping years old! That's seventeen years older than me and fifteen years older than Beau. She's old enough to be our mother, at least where we come from. What pissed me off most is that she looks so damn good. I mean Raquel Welch good.

I hate to admit it, but that's who she reminds me of, a flipping redneck version of Raquel Welch. Judy's hair is short and stylish. It's cut high off the neck with soft and sexy brown curls that lay sideways across her forehead and cover one brown bedroom eye. She has a damn little waist and huge fake tits. She has long, thin legs that are always oiled and naked and reach her flipping throat. Even her teeth piss me off, because they are so sickening straight and white, and she's a smoker! The ol' slut just looks like sex.

It's not fair. I could never look that sexy, even if I tried, which I don't. I just don't have it in me. I'm twenty-eight, and I still look like a kid. She's *Hustler* and I'm *Teen Beat*. She's "Oh my God, would you please have sex with me?" and I'm "Would you like to babysit my kids? And while you're at it, can you lend me five bucks?"

The whole thing just totally sucks!

July 10, 1999

An emotional day

I don't know what to do. I'm flipping back and forth through emotions like Beau with the remote control and a television set. I'm sad and then I'm angry. I'm scared and then I'm glad the son of a bitch is gone. I'm overwhelmed and then I'm completely lonely. These emotions are not new. They have held me hostage for ten months now. First there was the roller coaster ride of knowing the ol' slut wanted my husband, and then the ride of knowing my husband wanted the ol' slut.

Remembering all this is painful.

I knew the first time they had sex. I saw it in his face as soon as he walked through the front door. He wore their sex like a cloak. It hung on his body. It hid in his sorry voice and lived in his guilty eyes. I was sitting in our La-Z-Boy chair, breast-feeding four-week-old Sabrina. Henry and Roman lay on the floor in front of the television. Beau walked in, spoke a simple sentence, looked at me, and I instantly knew he had slept with her.

"Want me to fix you something to eat?" was all he asked, and as I looked up from watching my infant daughter find and then take my nipple, I saw their sex written on his face. It would have been less obvious to me if Beau had been wearing a neon sign around his neck that said, "Sissy, I'm sorry, but I've decided to have sex with another woman."

"No, I'm not hungry," I managed to answer. He fixed me a cheeseburger anyway, grilled it to perfection on our little Hibachi. I nibbled on the sandwich some and then had diarrhea. Beau, however, ate like a pig. Sex always makes him hungry.

At the time Beau began his affair with Judy, he and I hadn't had sex in months. During the last part of my pregnancy, I was just too big, too hot, too sick, and too tired. By the time Judy Mathers made her move, I was recovering from childbirth.

I knew there was flirting between Beau and Judy. I knew there was sexual attraction, and I had prayed that he wouldn't act upon it, if not for me, then at least for the kids. I believed that Beau was bigger than that. I honestly believed that the kids and I were important to Beau. In fact, I believed that we were his life.

Life with Beau

I knew we were in a rut. We had three kids in eight years and a job and home that we couldn't get away from. But this is the life that Beau had wanted, the one that he had carved out for us. I never wanted to get married fresh out of high school, but what else was there to do? College wasn't in the cards, not with a dead mommy and a daddy who couldn't understand why I even wanted to finish high school. Daddy, bless his heart, would bribe me with money to stay home from school and hang out with him.

So when I ended up pregnant at nineteen by Beau Jaspers, a sexy, blond, country boy who every girl in the county wanted, I thought, "Hell, why not just produce beautiful blond children that look just like their daddy? Why not be someone's wife? Why not love sexy Beau Jaspers for the rest of my life? Why not?"

I'll tell you why not. Because Beau Jaspers will leave you with your three beautiful, blond babies that look just like him. He will leave you with no money, no explanation, and no hint as to the future. He will leave you in a rusted-out mobile home that's parked in the hottest state in this country, far away from your family and best friends. He will leave you for a hard-looking Raquel Welch. He will leave you with no babysitter, a piece of shit car, and a life in a KOA campground. Who would have thought?

Marriage

Beau was the one who thought the KOA campground living was the ticket. He was convinced, and he managed to persuade me that we would have this incredibly cool life.

I remember when I told Beau that I was pregnant with Roman. I must have conceived on New Year's Eve. That was a good night. Most couples just kiss at midnight; well, Beau Jaspers got the idea that he wanted to be doing something else when the clock struck twelve, so I obliged. I took the EP test early in the morning on Valentine's Day. I didn't even realize the holiday until Beau showed up at my door with a gigantic box of chocolates and a teddy bear (he couldn't afford roses). I just stood there in the doorway crying, holding onto a bright blue EP stick. In my mind, I had just ruined our lives, but Beau was ecstatic. He picked me up and swung me around and kissed me on the mouth, and then he got down on one knee and proposed immediately, right in the doorway. I was so touched by his happiness that I instantly fell in love. I now wonder if he ever loved me.

Beau and I were married in May before my belly was too big, but soon enough for everyone to know there was a reason for the season. Our wedding really was beautiful, especially for being thrown together so quickly. For that I give all the credit to Mama Jaspers and her litter of daughters (Beau is the youngest of nine children and the only boy. Explains a lot, doesn't it?).

The wedding ceremony was small but quaint. We were married in a little white Methodist church with a little white steeple on a big, green, grassy hill; very picturesque. The reception was a barn party at the Jaspers and it was a blowout. The dancing and music were outrageous and fun. The food was delicious, and the decorations were just beautiful. The Jaspers went out of their way to make the day special for Beau, their one and only boy. They even got us a live DJ, and everybody square danced. My daddy helped by paying for most of it.

It was on our honeymoon that Beau got the KOA idea. We went camping for two weeks after we were married. We started out in the mountains and moved our site every third day. We would hike all the trails in that area and fish all the streams, and then we would move on. It was real pretty.

On the last stretch of the vacation, we ended up in Beckley. Beau wanted to do some white water rafting and climbing. We decided to stay in a KOA campground in the area, because I was in the mood for some pool swimming. Well, Beau went up to the camp store one morning for some ground coffee, and he came back happy as a lark. "Did you know the people who work here can live here?" he exclaimed. "They have mobile homes for them already set up. It's called a perk." What he meant to say was "a trap."

"Oh, Sissy, wouldn't that be cool?" Beau went on, beaming with a new, exciting idea. "Just imagine a life on vacation, fulltime vacation, and being paid to go on vacation, even given a vacation home; sounds too good to be true." But it was true, and when we left Beckley a few days later, it was only to go home to say good-bye and get what we needed to come back and live. Beau Jaspers had spent the rest of our honeymoon landing himself a job.

In the beginning, I have to admit I was as excited as Beau about our new life. We were going to seize our moments while we were young and start out our life together on an adventurous journey. We were going to leave home together, live together, work together, and spend all the time we could enjoying the outdoors, swimming, and cooking out. Our child's life would be blessed, being raised by two loving, free-spirited, parents in a campground. It was cool, it was earthy, it was awesome; and it was so much better than the alternative.

Beau comes from a family of West Virginia miners. Coal mining and the Jaspers date back generation after generation. It is in their blood. As dangerous as mining is, it has always been the Jaspers' livelihood and something they seem grateful about—everyone, that is, except Beau Jaspers. Beau had already told everyone in his family that he would not be a coal miner, and in fact, he would not set one foot in a mine, not one day. That's one promise Beau has held true to.

Beau had found an out. He didn't have to mine coal. Beau, was going to make his living by doing something he loved, running a campsite. We lived in Beckley for five years, and our lives were truly awesome; however, Beau wasn't completely satisfied. He not only wanted the outdoor life, he also wanted twenty-four hours of sunshine, so he worked his ass off in Beckley and continually asked for a transfer to his ideal place, Florida. Two years ago, his wish was granted and we moved our little family, Roman being six at the time and Henry, four, to this hot little hell hole, and I had never been more depressed (except for now).

July 11, 1999

They hired someone to take Beau's place yesterday. He seems nice enough. Fortyish, friendly. He would have been a great match for Judy Mathers.

Everyday mornings

I woke early after no sleep last night, fixed two bowls of Fruit Loops, and left them on the kitchen table with spoons in them. I then poured two glasses of milk and put them in the refrigerator. The boys and I have worked out a system. They wake and go looking for me. They find the cereal instead, so they glance out the window and over at the camp store directly across from our home. I wave from the camp store window. Sabrina, seated nicely in her backpack, waves over my shoulder. This is usually around 7:30 a.m. The boys then leave the window, flip on the TV, retrieve their milk from the fridge, dump half of it on top of their cereal, and enjoy cartoons and breakfast.

A half hour later at 8:00 a.m., after Carla has come in to relieve me, I go back home and check on the boys. By that time Sabrina has usually fallen asleep on my back and we are both sweating profusely. I lay the baby down and dress the boys, always in the same thing, a bathing suit, T-shirt, ball cap, water shoes, and lots and lots of sun block. After the baby has napped for about an hour, the kids and I go back over to the store. I feed Sabrina from the store shelves and leave the money in the register at the end of the day. Then I take the kids out to the pool for pool duty. This is where the stress begins to build.

The boys are good at the pool. They keep floaters on their arms, usually play nicely, and stay in the shallow end of the water. Sabrina, however, drives me crazy. She no longer wants to be on my back, and really, she shouldn't be. I can't possibly save a drowning child with a baby strapped to my back, not without drowning my own child first, so I am forced to lug Sabrina around while I check chlorine levels; unclog the drain; pick up glass bottles, food wrappers, and pop cans; retrieve balls and goggles and shout, "No running!" a hundred times each morning.

In the meantime, Sabrina goes from one hip to the other, to the baby pool, to the stroller with its shade up, back to the baby pool, and then into the big pool with me, where she is passed around by her brothers and then to other campers I do not know, trust, or want holding my baby; however, every day it happens. My daughter is in the arms of some stranger from Nebraska while I squirt water on a scraped knee and remind the vacationing children not to run. "Can I have my baby back?" I find myself asking too many times a day.

By noon, my pool time is over. I have just spent two and a half to three hours outside in the hot sun, with my young survival children. I am now relieved by Brian, a high school kid who doesn't live in the park, but who comes in to work four hours a day, the hottest hours of the day, the hours Carla and I refuse to work at the pool. Carla goes out from four to six. After that it's swim at your own risk, because Carla and I are busy with "family fun" evening activities, mostly crafts in the rec room until dark, and then it's campfire stuff, sing-alongs and weenie roasts.

After pool duty, I am off to the laundry room, kids in tow. I enjoy laundry duty for a couple of reasons. First, I love the smell of a laundry room, scented clean linen. I also enjoy the swirl of the washing machine and the hum of the dryer, but mostly I like the laundry room because that's where I shop. Sounds terrible, I know, but it's true. Almost every single time I check the dryers and clean the lint vents, I find the abandoned, stray clothing of another person, mostly kids' clothes, small shirts and socks that a parent missed. My children have as many Disney T-shirts as the actual Disney store. They could wear a new bathing suit every day, and they do. I neatly fold the found item and place it on the table. If the item is still there in three days, I claim it. Carla doesn't even do that much. She just brings me the newly washed clothing and says, "Look at this Gap Kids bathing suit some moron left in the dryer. I think it will fit Henry." Carla is good at taking care of herself and her friends, but screw everybody else.

It was while I was refilling the detergent dispenser that I noticed Randy, Beau's replacement. I actually didn't even notice him, the kids did. I was busy refilling laundry detergent and emptying trash cans when I heard Roman ask, "Is that my daddy?" I looked out the window and over at the miniature golf course where a man sat in the driver's side of a golf cart, facing away from us. He was about the same build as Beau, which is strong. He wore a ball cap, so I couldn't see his hair, which I doubt is anything like Beau's. Beau's hair is beautiful; it's long for a guy, and it's golden blond. Randy had on a new white camp T-shirt. "No, that's not Daddy," I answered Roman as I lay my hand on his shoulder. Roman shrugged off my touch, and I instantly began to cry, not for me, but for Roman.

I feel so helpless. I don't know what to say to my kids, to explain the disappearance of their father. What does abandonment do to a child? I know a little of this from my own life, but my mommy died; she didn't just walk away from me.

Roman is eight years old. He is my man-child, strong-willed and stubborn. He hides his true emotions deep in anger. He kicked over the trash can, walked out of the laundry room and into the rec room, where he began to throw pool balls into the corner pocket.

Henry is six years old. He is much softer than his older brother, Roman. He lives within his emotions. He hides nothing; he feels everything. Henry began to cry. I left Roman in his anger and comforted Henry. Wrong? Probably.

Sabrina is ten months, beautiful and innocent. She sat most of the day on my back in her pack and pleasantly cooed out "Dada" every time Randy came into sight.

July 12, 1999

Today sucked! It's nearly midnight, and I am just getting the kids to bed. I can't keep up this pace. I never really knew how much a help Beau was until he was gone. We had such a good tag-team going. When the kids and job were too much for me, I could simply radio Beau, and he would take over. The kids would happily ride around in a golf cart and talk to all the campers as their daddy tended to their needs. Roman and Henry loved delivering firewood and making the rounds. Every one of the regulars referred to them as "Beau and his boys." There wasn't a damn thing in this site that Beau didn't have his hands in. He was the master, the all-knowing, all-doing, the kingpin. He was Super Camper, and Roman and Henry were proud to be his sidekicks. WHAT AN ASSHOLE!

July 13, 1999

Sabrina keeps throwing up, which is unlike her, especially since she is still being breast-fed. I think it's the heat and lack of sleep she has gotten. Maybe it's stress. Can a ten-month-old baby have stress? Can she feel my stress as she rides side saddle on my back? Is it making her sick? Whatever it is, she keeps puking in my hair and down my back. If I wasn't so worried, I would be pissed.

July 14, 1999

Sabrina is now running a fever. Poor thing, she has been so good. She sits in her pack on my back and lays her hot head between my shoulder blades. She is not wrestling to get down or grabbing things off shelves when I walk past. I feel guilty, because I just keep going, plugging along with a sick child strapped to me. Roman and Henry know their sister is not well. They know I am an emotional wreck. They use these misfortunes to their advantage, getting away with everything. When I need the boys to be their very best, they are at their worst. When I am on the verge of tears, they begin fighting. When I want to scream, they beat me to it by screaming and tearing through this small house. When I am overwhelmed with work, they create gigantic messes. Yesterday they cracked eggs on the floor. Henry said, "Roman is sick of cereal for breakfast; he wanted sunny-side-ups." I stood at the stove top sobbing while I scrambled three eggs.

It is as if my children are feeding off my negative energy. The baby is sick, the boys are out of control, and I feel as if I'm living someone else's life. We are all falling apart, slowly crumpling, and Beau has not called.

July 15, 1999

Oh, what a day I have lived! Today I reached my lowest point. The only good that can come from falling into a hole is pulling myself out.

I was up with Sabrina half the night while she cried in pain and pulled on her ears. I opened the store in the morning, but when Carla showed up, I told her the baby was sick and I was taking her to the doctor. Carla would have to cover it all or call in some help. I got everybody ready and put the kids in the car, and then that piece of shit Buick would not start. I hate that damn car. I decided to take the golf cart.

The doctor's office is only two miles down the road anyway, right? I don't know what I was thinking. I should have just asked Carla if I could borrow her car. But I didn't. I could tell Carla was already pissed because she had to do everything; besides that, she looked hung over. Mostly I'm just tired of having problems that everybody knows about. I guess it's not surprising that I barely got a mile down the forty-five miles-per-hour road (driving on the berm, of course) before being pulled over. My two little boys were seated beside me and my baby was strapped to my back. I can only plead temporary insanity, because that's what it was. The police officer was appalled by my behavior. He screamed that I was reckless. He sternly berated me in front of my kids. Roman sneered back at the officer, refusing his pity. Henry cried, and so did I.

It wasn't too long after being pulled over that I totally lost what mind I had left. Here I am, parked at the side of a busy road, the driver of a golf cart. Motorists in other vehicles driving by slowed down and pointed. The teenagers thought it was hysterical, and I could hear their laughter floating in the air. The old people were not amused. They shook their crooked little fingers at me in shame.

As the cop threatened to take me to jail, charge me with child endangerment and slow speed, I began to blubber. All that I have not said came soaring out of my mouth. I couldn't stop myself. With my scared children nestled next to me, I told this police officer that I have a sick baby and a broken-down car. That I live in the KOA campsite down the road and my husband of nine years just left me for an old slut with a deluxe Winnebago. I don't know if the cop was shocked or truly saddened by my life story, but for whatever reason, instead of arresting me, he drove me to the doctor's office. He even let Roman sit in the front seat of the cruiser. The golf cart stayed parked along the interstate, and I had to call Carla to come pick us up and then take us to get Sabrina's prescriptions filled. I thought for sure I was going to be fired immediately, but everyone feels sorry for me, so I still have my job. Randy went out and brought back the golf cart.

Sabrina has double ear infections (swimmer's ear) and a summer virus. The boys will probably get sick next. I am truly a terrible mother. How could I be so stupid? How could I put my children in harm's way like I did? I'm a fool. What's worse is how I unloaded to that police officer, the boys listening to my panic. A mother is supposed to make her children feel safe. I completely failed. Carla thinks I'm being too hard on myself. She thinks it's a hoot that I stole a golf cart. "Lighten up, Sis" she said. "You're just trying to survive."

How can I ease up on myself? Even if I accepted every horrible mother thing I did today, I would still have a ten-month-old baby with swimmer's ear. Pathetic.

July 16, 1999

I slept in this morning. We all did. The boys climbed right in beside me with Sabrina, who was already in my bed, and we all slept until 10:00 a.m. It was awesome, waking up late, well-rested; a warm, tangled mess of arms and legs, my bed not so empty.

Carla opened the store for me this morning, and Amy, a part-timer, came in to work Carla's shift when Carla took over my pool duty. They have given me a day off. I guess when your husband leaves you, your kids are sick, your car breaks down, in desperation you steal a golf cart and get pulled over by the police and have a mental breakdown on the side of a busy road, you qualify for a sympathy day. I took it, and the whole day brought well-wishers.

My first visitor was Randy. He came bright and early, before the kids and I were even up. I noticed him while I started to prepare breakfast. I looked out my dirty window into the hot day, and there, underneath the hood of my car, extended a man. His head was hidden, and what I could see was faded Levi's, a white muscle T, and two big strong arms. My first thought was Beau, and instantly without conscious effort, my heart sped up and then leaped into my throat. My stomach filled with fluttering butterflies, my temperature rose, my palms became sweaty, my mouth dry. I ran to the door and jumped down the first step, startling the man working underneath my car. Oh, how embarrassing that was! As instant as the emotions had taken flight, they landed HARD and left me feeling dizzy.

When I stood there in awkward shock, Randy let me know that the problem was with my starter, and he was going to fix it. Feeling like an idiot, I tried to tell Randy that I didn't have the money right now to fix the car, but when I get the money, I would appreciate it if he would do the work. Instead of closing the hood of my car, Randy continued to work (as if he hadn't heard me), all the while talking to me about his past.

He told me that he was the oldest of four boys, and that he was twelve years old when his dad took off. He said he and his brothers were a rowdy bunch that caused his mom a lot of trouble. He also told me about his neighbor, Mr. Nelson, and how he would help out and watch over him and his brothers.

Mr. Nelson worked on his mom's car whenever needed. He kept it running for her so she could continue to work. He also taught Randy and his brothers how to work on cars. Randy said that for the numerous times Mr. Nelson worked on their car, he didn't think his mom paid him anything more than a turkey sandwich and a Coke. Randy went on to tell me that dear, kind Mr. Nelson died two years ago, and that Randy felt it was in his destiny to keep my car running.

I went back inside crying and humbled and made Randy a big turkey sandwich and took it out to him with a plate of chips and an icy Coke. I then gave Sabrina a bath. I wonder if there really was a Mr. Nelson.

My next visitor came around two p.m., hot and sweaty, from the walk from her trailer to mine. Mrs. Bumgardner surprised me when I opened my door, and she stood there in a bright floral house dress fanning herself. "Can I help you?" I asked. She didn't answer, just pushed past me into the house and plopped her large frame down on my sofa in front of the air conditioning. I quickly poured her some ice water and gave her a minute to catch her breath.

Hazel Bumgardner is a regular in the trailer park. She and her husband Harry have been setting up house in this park for more than ten years. It was a retirement thing. They have pulled their beautiful recreational vehicle in every October and stayed straight through until April. Returning home to see the forsythia bloom, Mrs. Bumgardner would tell us every checkout.

Harry Bumgardner died of a heart attack a year ago in June. Mrs. Bumgardner surprisingly pulled in alone last October, but this time she didn't leave come April. She stayed, for whatever reason. Maybe it took everything she had to pack up and drive that monstrous vehicle here by herself. Maybe it's just too much to do to return home. I've often thought about asking her if she needs help getting back, but then I decided it would be rude and that she must have somebody who could come retrieve her if she wanted.

"I got a proposition for you, Sissy," is how she began. She went on to tell me that she had heard about my troubles and how surprised she was that my handsome husband, Beau, turned out to be such a bastard, and how was it that such a doting father, would leave his children?

I was trying to figure out how I could politely kick Hazel out of my home, while she just kept talking. I surely did not need her affirmation that Beau was a bastard. By the time I had worked up enough courage to ask her to leave, she was off the topic of Beau and me and my life and was talking about herself.

I believe something happens when you live your life's dramas in the view of spectators. The ones who choose to get involved with you do so, so they can tell their own stories or work out their own pains and somehow come full circle, so just like Randy this morning, I heard Hazel Bumgardner's history and what it was that pulled her to me.

Hazel talked of loneliness. She admitted to having no purpose. She told me Harry had been her purpose. They had married when she was sixteen years old and just because they loved one another so much. They had been married fifty-six years when he died. Hazel told me that she and Harry had no living children, that she had trouble during her pregnancies and must have had a dozen miscarriages in her lifetime. Besides the miscarriages, she had three babies, two live births and one stillborn.

Hazel's first baby was a girl that weighed only one pound. She named her Hope, and Hope died three days after birth. Hazel had a second daughter, this time a little bigger, almost four pounds. She named her Grace, and Grace lived for a week. Hazel stopped trying to have babies after Angelo was born, her son, a stillborn.

I cried all the way through Hazel's story, and she apologized for making me sad, yet she continued to talk about loneliness, death, dying children, and a deceased spouse, and when I could barely take it anymore, she offered up her proposition.

Hazel Bumgardner wants to babysit my kids. More than babysit. She wants to come to my home every morning, so the kids don't have to rise so early. She wants to keep house for me and mother my children while I run this campground.

Of course I refused Hazel's lavish offer. After all, I don't truly know her, nor can I afford to pay anyone to watch over my children. When I told Hazel that I could not afford a nanny for my kids, she scoffed at my words. "I'm not suggesting that you hire me to be a nanny," she said. "On the contrary, I don't work for anybody." After my dreaded insult of employment had left her, she softened and asked that I give her a purpose. A purpose is what Hazel called it.

Hazel confessed that she had left her home in a deep, sorrowful mourning and drove here because she didn't know what else to do or where else to go. Hazel has been waiting to die. She has been wishing to join Harry and her babies on the other end, but it doesn't look like she's going to die anytime soon, and while she waits, she needs a purpose. Hazel starts tomorrow.

My last visitor was Carla. She came after family evening activities and brought with her a six pack of beer and a Bonnie Raitt CD. She told me the CD was her breakup music. I popped it in and played it, low and mellow. I informed Carla that I couldn't drink any beer, because I'm still breast-feeding. "I know," Carla responded in a matter-of-fact tone. "This is for me."

Carla and I sat on the floor with a big candle burning between us and Bonnie Raitt softly filling my home with music and allowing my children to sleep peacefully through the night. Carla killed her six pack of beer while I drank pink lemonade, my favorite, and ate popcorn. We talked for hours. She made me laugh and she made me cry. It was nice to have someone there with me. I felt young again, like I was hosting a sleepover with my best girlfriend or like a single girl in her first apartment. It was a liberating feeling. It was freeing, and it was the first night in a long time that I did not miss Beau.

Carla is good for me. I know there is not a thing she wouldn't do to help me. She is a good friend to the people she lets in (we are truly a small and select bunch). Carla can be intimidating, however. For one thing, she has no problem and may actually enjoy telling someone to "fuck off." Carla lives life based on her own set of rules and doesn't give a damn about impressing anyone around her. It really is quite impressive.

Carla is trying to talk me into sleeping with her brother. Carla's brother, Manny, short for Emanuel, is just about the sexiest thing walking. Not only is he a young, dark, strong, stud man, but he is also very charitable, lending out his services to poor pathetic women in need. He calls it "mercy fucking," and he is quite proud of himself. Manny has managed to help probably hundreds of desperate women get over losing their spouses and start to feel good about themselves again. As tempting as it sounds, I think I'll have to pass on Emanuel's pity sex.

About 1:30 a.m., Carla stumbled out of my trailer down the road toward her own. I thought I saw her at Randy's front door, but I could be mistaken.

July 17, 1999

Hazel Bumgardner, good to her word, showed up at my door at

sunrise this morning. I was just about to pull my sleeping baby from her bed and strap her on my back when I heard Mrs. Bumgardner's soft tap on my door. She came with a Thermos of coffee and some breakfast rolls. Since I didn't have to wake the baby, I was able to have half a cup of coffee with Hazel and a few bites of a pastry. I had been feeling embarrassed by Ms. Bumgardner's offer. Poor, husbandless Sissy needs help, but after seeing the look on Hazel's face and the new bounce in her step, I felt good—really, really good. She was right. We all need a purpose.

When I finished at the store and went home, the boys had eaten a breakfast of scrambled eggs, sausage, and toast. Their bowls of Fruit Loops had been poured into a Ziploc bag and placed on the counter like some colorful snack. Sabrina was not only dressed, but she had also been bathed and then lathered in lotion and powder. Her diaper, in fact, carried so much baby powder that every time Sabrina stepped away from cruising around the couch or table and tried to take a step, she undoubtedly landed on her bottom, causing a white powder cloud to rise up behind her and give my house a powder-fresh scent. It's like having a live-in air freshener.

Roman and Henry loved the idea of going out to pool duty without Sabrina, but Sabrina, however, held up her little arms to me, waiting and wanting to be lugged along. I've carried my petite baby girl around on my body for the entire ten months of her life. She has been parented as if she were a baby chimp and is more than willing to swing from my neck. Sabrina does not understand naps in a crib or time away from a parent.

She was crying when the boys and I headed out the door. It's a good thing Hazel Bumgardner didn't hesitate to scoop up my little monkey and lay her across her enormous bosom. Thank you, God, for Hazel.

My day ended as well as it began, with my three children and me sitting around a campfire helping host family-fun activities. Tonight was a campfire sing-along, and to my surprise, Randy showed up with an acoustic guitar. After Carla and I finished making fools out of ourselves teaching children songs from our Girl Scout days, Randy entertained the adults with tunes written by John Denver. Of course, being from West Virginia, I grew up on John Denver, and hearing Randy softly sing those same songs that played loudly on my father's turntable was like taking a trip home. I can honestly say that this has been my happiest day since moving to this awful state.

July 18, 1999

I'm writing at the store, because it's a quiet, early morning, and I already have a story to tell.

Last night after the campfire and sing-along, I had all three of my kids lying in bed with me. Sabrina was under my shirt, latched on for dear life, while Roman, Henry, and I went over our day. Henry and Roman had spent the better part of the evening catching anoles to add to their collection. Anoles are little lizards that live all over the place in Florida, and the boys love catching them.

The boys collect all sorts of critters, and we have numerous little aquariums and fish bowls. I make the boys keep their collections outside. One terrarium holds toads; another holds lizards. They have a couple bug catchers full of big spiders. They have even been known to catch a snake, which happens to scare me the most, because you never know when you're going to come across a poisonous snake. I am forever saying, "No snakes!"

The rule is that they can keep their catch for one week, as long as they catch some crickets to throw into the terrarium for food. After one week, whatever is still living, whether it's the critter or the critter's food, must be released. The boys can then begin again. It's a never-ending cycle of catch and release.

Well, last night the boys were out-of-their-minds excited because they had caught twelve of those fast little lizards, so I let them bring in their terrarium, so we could all sit and watch the lizards interact. Very educational, is what I was thinking. Actually, it was entertaining. The boys and I had a great time watching those little lizards jump all around that glass cage. We were fascinated. It must have been hypnotic or we were just all very tired, because don't you know, we all fell asleep, and at some time during the night, the terrarium fell over and a dozen of those little creatures escaped, IN MY BED!

Well, I thought I felt something on my face a few times during the night, but I just figured it was Sabrina. She likes to rub faces, and I was exhausted. In fact, I slept straight on till morning. When I woke up, it was to find that these creepy crawlers had spent the nighttime hours nesting IN MY HAIR.

I felt the first one stretched out across my forehead like a sunbather, and I screamed. I was jumping all over my room screaming like a crazy woman. The kids woke up with a start and they began screaming. "Get 'em out! Get 'em out!" I shouted as I jumped around pulling out clumps of my own hair in a search for lizards.

Hazel, who now has a key, was on her way to the house when she heard my screams and came running through my door in a panic. "Sissy! Sissy! What is it?" she said in heart-attack mode.

"My hair! I can't get them out! Lizards!"

The boys were screaming, "Momma's got lizards in her hair." Ms. Bumgardner was frozen with amazement, and she looked at Henry, who could no longer contain himself, and they both began to giggle.

Henry's laughter is not only the cutest sound I've ever heard, it is also the most contagious. Roman started laughing, and then Hazel began to howl with a belly laugh that I'm sure has been aching to come out for a long time now. Poor Sabrina didn't know what to do. She stopped crying and looked from her brothers to Hazel and then to me. Her big tears rested on her cheeks. I was still jumping around like a mad woman.

"Hold still!" Hazel commanded after she had calmed herself a bit.

"Get 'em out! Get 'em out!" I began again.

Hazel sat me on the bed and Henry retrieved the terrarium from the floor. Very gently and carefully, Hazel and the boys searched through my hair, catching lizards. It was a terrible experience, and I think I've been traumatized by it. It wouldn't have been so bad, if they could have just pulled the creatures off me, but the damn lizards are fast as hell and don't like to be caught, so every time they felt someone's fingers, they would scurry through my hair to the other side. That made me scream again, jumping up and shaking my head. Hazel and the boys would break out in laughter, and we would all have to compose ourselves again. To make matters worse, my hair is long, to the middle of my back, and it's auburn. Well, those damn little anoles turned a brownish red to match my hair and hid themselves in my tangled strands! It took nearly a half hour to free me from those creatures, and when we thought they were all gone, I gave another shriek and went into the shower. Hazel and the boys started laughing all over again.

Well, now I'm over at the store, still feeling jittery. I don't quite know when I'll be the same again. I'm sure Hazel, Roman, and Henry are still laughing as I write.

July 18, 1999 - Still

This day has gone on forever. It is my longest yet.

The inevitable has finally occurred. Mama Jaspers knows her son has abandoned his family. I have been so good at fielding Mama Jaspers' phone calls, missing them on purpose twice, and having to lie about Beau's whereabouts once, but this time she tricked me by calling earlier than her usual Sunday at 7:00 p.m.

The call came while I was in the shower, and Roman, my man-child, answered it. He spoke only briefly to Mama Jaspers before informing her that his daddy left us and went with another woman, and he's not coming back. Roman then hung up the phone and went back to watching *The Simpsons*. Mama Jaspers called back immediately, but Roman ignored her call and focused on Bart Simpson tormenting his father. On ring number fifteen, I retrieved the phone, soaking wet from the shower and wrapped in a towel.

Mama Jaspers' voice was full of shock and concern. She told me that Roman had just told her his father had left us and was not coming back. She wanted to know what the hell was going on. I looked over at Roman, who was sitting quietly, poking his finger into a small hole on the arm of the couch.

"Stop that!" I viciously whispered to him.

"Why? It 's already ugly!" spat back my angry son.

I turned my back on Roman, allowing him the satisfaction of winning. Besides, he was right. Mama Jaspers raised his daddy, who had left us, and what the hell did it matter if the ugly couch had a hole?

"Yes, Mama, it's true," I told her, "Beau left."

She wanted to know when, why, and how, and when I informed her he had been gone for more than four weeks, she went into hysteria. She yelled at me for not calling and then began spouting accusations of Beau's being a missing person. She asked if I had filed a report. She suggested that he had been kidnapped or in an accident. Basically she called me irresponsible and went into denial.

It took all the strength I had to tell Mama Jaspers the truth. I love Beau's parents very much, and I know how much they love him, and I know how much of a disappointment he can be.

Then it happened. In that still moment when I had finished telling Mama Jaspers about Beau and Judy, I could hear her deflate as she exhaled. She sounded as if everything had just emptied out of her. Her breathing became hollow. In that same moment, I heard Roman sniffle behind my back. I heard my own heart beat against my chest. It felt like an eternal moment of loud silence in which we three were connected solely by a strand of despair.

Before hanging up, Mama Jaspers asked if we needed any money. I lied and said, "No"

She then asked me if my daddy knew. It was then that I could no longer contain myself, and I know Mama Jaspers heard my tears when I answered, "Not yet."

Mama Jaspers apologized to me, like it's her fault Beau ran out. Why do we mothers always do that? We wear our children's problems on our chest like a big scarlet letter *F* for failure.

I know why I hadn't called Mama Jaspers. It's because I have been hoping that this situation isn't real and that Beau would come home any day, but I can't explain why I haven't called my daddy. I know in my heart that he would be there for me and that he would give it his best Skip Cooper shot to help the kids and me out. Maybe I didn't call because Daddy has always seemed so emotionally absent to me. I know he must feel things, but he shows no good responses. He is the type of man you can always count on for a good time, but a shoulder to cry on consists of his buying you a beer and letting you win at a game of pool. He wouldn't know what to say. He wouldn't know what to do.

I remember when Mama died. I know it must have been hard raising me and my brother Charlie, but he never said so. Daddy never complained or whined or cried about being left alone to raise two young children. I was nine and Charlie was just six when our mother died. Daddy continued to work the same long hours roofing or siding someone's house, building a deck or shed, finishing a basement, or repairing a barn. It was with whatever work Skip had come up with for that week that we lived off of.

Skip Cooper had a reputation of being the best handyman in our county and all the surrounding counties in West Virginia. Daddy is never without work or a crew of scraggly but nice fellows to help him out. It was usually a wife or girlfriend of one of those scraggly guys who would watch Charlie and me during the week. Friday night was payday, and everyone ended up at our house drinking Daddy's beer and eating Charlie's and my pizza while Daddy counted out tens and twenties and placed them in white envelopes for each fellow and the babysitter. Daddy didn't work on the weekends, contrary to what you would believe about most handymen.

No, Daddy's weekends were made for Michelob, poker, bowling, motocross or whatever else he stumbled into. Charlie and I were a part of it all. It didn't matter if it was a Harley gathering with topless women or a bluegrass concert with lots of weed. We were right beside our daddy being treated to cotton candy on paper cones and salty hotdogs. By Tuesday all of Daddy's money would be gone, and it would be back to plain peanut butter on white bread for Charlie and me to eat all week. We didn't care, 'cause we knew, come Friday night, our kitchen would be filled with greasy pizza and buckets of chicken and it would be party time for the next four days.

I think now most of Daddy's and Charlie's days are spent living large and less on P.B. and white bread. Daddy has built the fine reputation for his work, but it is Charlie who has grown to have all the business sense and good looks to boot.

Charlie is our mother's son. He has her thick raven-black hair and her deep brown-black eyes. He has her creativity, her wit, her charm, and her common sense. Combine that with Daddy's friendships and reputation, and the Cooper boys are doing just fine. I know Mama would be proud of them.

Mama was only thirty years old when she died, and Daddy, Charlie, and I lost our muse. My mama was an artist, but she never did anything more with her talent than to paint beautiful murals all over the small, dingy walls of our home. Mama had a way of creating what she wanted out of nothing. We had no fireplace in our tiny two-bedroom house, so Mama painted one with a beautiful roaring fire in it. We had no kitchen window, either, so Mama painted one of those too, with an ocean view.

Charlie's and my bedroom was painted like a carousel, a mystical, magical carousel, with life-sized mythical creatures painted on all four walls. Our carousel didn't contain horses, which would have been too common for my mama. This one consisted of a dragon, unicorn, griffin, lion, and gargoyle. There were also two other mythical-looking creatures that Mama conjured up from her own mind. I used to pretend I was riding a different one each night. Charlie's favorite was the griffin.

The painted brass bars from each creature reached the top of the wall. Our ceiling was the top of the carousel and resembled a brightly jeweled canopy. From the light in the center of our room, Mama used wire and silk ribbons to make a wind sock-mobile. It is my best childhood memory.

Mama was not only an artist, but she was also a beauty, striking, to be exact. I have never seen another woman as beautiful as my mama, Marie Ann Cooper. Marie had thick black, wavy hair that she blew dry and sprayed into place every morning. She had perfect lips that she painted bright red and porcelain skin she caked with powder and sheltered from the sun. Marie had large dark eyes that she lined in black with eyeliner. My mother was a Maybelline girl. She bought it by the purse full from our local drug store. Maybelline, Rave hair spray, the color red, and the smell of Wild Musk all remind me of my mother.

I look nothing like my mother, although I am her only daughter. I look just like my father, which also means I look nothing like Skip Cooper.

There you go! The secret is out. I am a bastard; however, it's not much of a secret. It has always been the whispered talk of the town, and I'm not even much of a bastard, because Skip Cooper stepped in when needed. I am proud of my dad, Charles A. Cooper Sr. He brought home a baby girl that looked nothing like him or his wife and loved the baby and continued to love the baby, even after his wife and the baby's biological father died—together.

That's right. I'm also an orphan, but not even much of an orphan, because again, Skip Cooper continued to father me.

My mother was only nineteen years old when Dr. Phillip Johnson came to our small town and opened up a new practice. Dr. Phillip Johnson was a fresh and young face to replace Doc Lewis who had spent his life doctoring our town and died at age eighty-two right after performing his last house call.

Dr. Phillip Johnson was handsome and smart. He had a lovely wife who had a lovely voice and sang in the church chorus. He had two little girls, old enough to toddle around his office and make him seem more charming. He hired my beautiful, young mother to be his receptionist.

When my mother became pregnant with me, she could have shook the whole town with scandal, which actually seems to have been more her style, but for whatever reason, she didn't. Instead she went to Skip Cooper, who had been totally and hopelessly in love with her since puberty, and confessed her problem.

Skip joyously married my mother, who continued to work for Dr. Phillip Johnson, who had now been accepted by the town's people and was called Doc. Their affair never completely ended. I believe they had a few hiatuses, mostly when Mrs. Johnson put her foot down.

Skip, however, showed no emotion regarding the affair, although it must have hurt him badly. My brother Charlie is Skip Cooper's son, born during a hiatus, but always, after a small break, Mama and Doc Johnson's love affair would start up, and Mama would once again be working late.

It was during one of those late-night working sessions that Mama and Doc Johnson drank a little too much wine, drove a little too fast, and maybe got a little too frisky behind the wheel of his sports car, not paying enough attention to the dark and curvy mountain roads that tempt drivers each night with danger.

Doc Johnson took a hairpin curve at about seventy miles an hour. He and mama were both ejected from his car and died on impact a few feet from one another. His little red convertible Mustang lay in a crumpled mess at the bottom of a cliff.

The whole town gossiped about the death of the respectable doctor and his very beautiful receptionist. Soon the gossip turned to me. Wasn't it strange how much I resembled Misty and Mandy Johnson, Doc's two girls? I had their same straight auburn hair, while my mother, father, and brother's hair was all dark and wild. I had the same creamy Johnson complexion and auburn freckles. My Mama had porcelain skin and not so much as one tiny mole, let alone a colony of freckles to dot her body. I also had the same flat body as Misty and Mandy Johnson. Mama had curves that would stop traffic. Lastly, I had the same pale green eyes as Doc Johnson himself. Soon Mrs. Johnson couldn't bear the gossip or the obvious resemblance I bore to her children, so she packed up her two girls and moved away.

None of it seemed to bother my father. He continued to work, play, laugh, spend his hard-earned money easily, and raise Charlie and me like two lovable little puppies.

So there, I have it all written down in front of me, my past and my present, a series of events that has always left me in unpredictable situations, being rescued by the unpredictable. First Skip Cooper, and now Hazel and Randy and Carla. Thank you, God, for my earth angels.

I think in writing this I have sorted it all out. I didn't call Skip

Cooper because he has already done so much for me. He loved me, raised me, and fathered me the best he knew how, and in all reality, I was dumped on him.

July 19, 1999

Hazel woke me this morning. I had overslept. I still had my journal in front of me and pen in hand when Hazel whispered into my room. I was already in gym shorts and a T-shirt, so I brushed my teeth real fast and threw my hair back into a pony tail before flying out the door. Hazel came over a couple minutes later and brought me a sweet roll and coffee. I do believe that Hazel Bumgardner makes the best cup of coffee in the world. It's smooth and light and has a comforting flavor. I don't know if I have ever tasted anything that has comforted me like Hazel's coffee. Her sweet rolls are good too.

Later that morning, during pool time, the boys, some camper children, and I were having great fun playing a water game we call sharks and minnows. I, of course, was a shark chasing little minnows all over the water, when Hazel came out with Sabrina. Sabrina was happy to see me and started squealing immediately in apprehension of getting into the water. I have never known a baby to like water as much as my baby. Hazel got a kick out of watching Sabrina kick and splash in the water. She even put her face in the water and came up smiling. Sabrina may not be able to walk yet, but she sure as hell can swim.

While I was swimming with the kids, Hazel went back to her place and filled a picnic basket full of good things to eat. So full, in fact, that she had Randy drive her and her basket back to the pool by means of the golf cart. Hazel had made enough egg salad sandwiches to feed the entire pool, which really wasn't that crowded. Henry and Roman, who both love egg salad, ate two sandwiches apiece and then spent the rest of the day expelling egg-smelling farts.

Hazel, Henry, and Roman cracked up every time one of them let a stinker. Poor little Sabrina crinkled up her nose and closed her mouth really tight, probably so she wouldn't taste one, since she is right at butt level. It was all pretty gross and irritating, and I kept yelling at them, but then I decided if I couldn't get them to stop farting or laughing about their farts, I would just have to try to see the humor, and I did. Soon I was giggling too.

Hazel and I joked about the other campers' children who had eaten her egg salad and those vacationers cooped up in a tent or camper with a smelly egg-farting child. I told Hazel all those farting children at the campfire tonight might start a forest fire. She said, "Or worse, and blow us all up" With that, Hazel and I laughed for about five minutes. During that time, I could tell Hazel was grasping the same emotion that I was, knowing what a blessing it is to laugh.

July 20, 1999

Today the FedEx man came to the camp store to deliver a package from Mama Jaspers for the kids. Inside the big cardboard box were wrapped gifts for the kids and me. I made a big deal out of the presents from their grandma and let each child open them up one at a time, so I could lavish the same amount of attention on them. Roman acted like he could not care less. He really didn't even want to open his present, but Henry kept insisting.

Henry was given a bug catcher and a book to help identify his catch. Sabrina got a soft baby, perfect for her little arms, and a new set of blocks. Roman got a pocket knife, a beautiful, blue Swiss Army knife with his name engraved in the side and a sterling silver and marbled blue case to keep it in. It was a special present, meant for a little man, and Roman eyed it silently as he rolled the knife back and forth in the palm of his hand. At the bottom of the box was a new journal for me. Inside the journal was a card, and inside the card was a check for three hundred dollars. Money the Jaspers can't afford to give away. The card was one ordered from paralyzed veterans. This one was a watercolor vase of flowers done by a foot artist. It's incredible what some people can do using their feet. Inside, Mama Jaspers had written me a small note:

Sissy,

I can't even begin to express how heartbroken Pops and I feel right now. Please know that you are and always will be my daughter and that I will cross any and all mountains to see your babies. If you are in need of anything at all, we are a simple telephone call away.

I love you, Mama Jaspers

P.S. Call collect

I put the note into the journal and put them both up in a safe place. I will use that journal only when I feel whole again. I will not fill it with negative thoughts and energy.

July 21, 1999

Roman got into a fight today, and he ended up beating the other child. The parents, who are regular campers (they come twice a year), are pretty upset. I'm pretty sure they're going to be calling my boss to complain about Roman and me and how I handled the situation, which wasn't exactly great.

The truth is, I feel Roman's anger and frustration. He's hurt beyond comprehension. Beau was Roman's best friend, his mentor, his father, and he sneaked away without so much as a good-bye, like a coward in the night. It's stupid shit like that which makes a child angry, and who better to take it out on than some snot-nosed, spoiled, bully that pushes you around for a couple weeks twice a year?

Tad Holden is an over-indulged, self-centered little punk who takes it upon himself to pick on my boys ruthlessly. He's a year older than Roman and two sizes bigger. Evidently Roman took all the bullying he could take, because he ended up plowing the child to the ground full-force and then swinging his fists into Tad's body like a mad man. I saw some of what was happening from the camp store, and I started calmly out the door, but when Mrs. Holden shrieked like a murder witness, I bolted to Roman's side and plucked him off her child.

Tad's nose was bleeding and his face was puffy and red. He was hurling insults and threats at Roman while his mother cried and tried to smooth down his sweaty hair. I simply held Roman in a hug, blocking out the hysterical suburbanite. After a few minutes of clutching my son in an embrace that only we understood, I tried to walk away so we could go talk and I could figure out what had happened.

"Make him apologize!" Mrs. Holden screamed at me. I ignored her and kept walking. I wanted to get Roman out of the situation, so I could calm him down and get some answers. As I walked across the lawn, Mrs. Holden kept shouting at me. She yelled that Roman was a brute, whatever the hell that means. She screamed that my children were heathens and I was raising them in a zoo. I was doing a good job of allowing her insults to bounce off me, and then she yelled out at the top of her lungs, "Sissy Jaspers, you're trailer trash! Not even good enough to keep a redneck man! No wonder Beau left you for prettier trailer trash!"

It was with those words that my "redneck" roots emerged, and I covered the ground between us in three quick movements. I stopped dead in her face and spoke as harsh as I ever have. "How dare you judge me and my children, you obnoxious, pompous, pampered woman! You don't know me or my babies, so don't pretend you do. You live in a bubble with hair salons, shoe stores, and Disney vacations. You are not permitted to have a say in my life or any life that resembles mine, because you're too shallow and sheltered to actually know anything. As for your kid, he's deserved that ass-kicking for some time now. I hope it teaches him more than it taught you."

I turned with Roman at my heels and began to walk away from that snob and her silent child. Suddenly a thought occurred to me, and I turned back around and shouted, "And another thing, if you're so hifalutin rich, why the hell do you stay in a KOA with trailer trash? Go check your pretty ass into a Disney hotel, bitch!" I heard Roman giggle and knew I had gone too far. I looked and saw all the gaping mouths of the campers.

I tried blocking everything out while heading into the house with Roman, but as I passed by Carla, I heard her whisper, "You go, girl!"

Once in the house, I turned my anger on Roman. "Great, Roman!"

I shouted. "Now tell me, what in the hell are we supposed to do when I lose my job?"

Roman threw himself on his bed and cried into his pillow, and I walked away.

Here I go again, being an awful, horrible parent, and the truth is, a child's fight won't get me fired. It's what I did and said to Mrs. Holden that has me worried. Oh, God, how come I always say and do the wrong things? What in the hell is wrong with me?

Hazel brought over chocolate chip and walnut cookies and I plated three for Roman and took him a glass of milk. I humbly apologized to my forgiving child for yelling at him, and of course he accepted, as children always do. I asked if we could talk about what happened between Tad and him. Roman told me, "No," that there was nothing to say, so we said nothing. Instead, I sat on Roman's bed silently, eating chocolate chip and walnut cookies together. Roman was right again. It was better than any conversation we could have had.

July 22, 1999

Mr. Holden came in this morning to the camp store to check out. I owed him money for the rest of this week and next. He was quiet yet direct, and I was just about to apologize to him, when he stated, "We will be reporting this, Sissy." He left immediately after getting his money, with his nose in the air. I suppose they will drive two miles down the road to Trails End Family Campground and set up home there.

Later in the day, Henry came to me dragging a laundry basket. What I thought was rolled up black socks in the floor of the basket turned out to be puppies, nine little black Lab puppies, not more than a few weeks old.

"Henry," I gasped, "where did those come from?" I'm used to Henry's creepy-crawly collection, even if I am a little wigged out from the last episode. What I'm not used to is watching my young son tote around a basket full of newly birthed mammals. Henry informed me that the Wilsons had left the pups when they checked out. It was hard to believe, but it was true.

The Wilsons consisted of a father, two boys, and a black Labrador retriever. They showed up here about six weeks ago in a pop-up trailer. Mr. Wilson had told me that he and the kids' mom were divorced and that he had his boys for half the summer. He is a school teacher in Michigan, off for the summer. He had decided to spend his time with the boys vacationing in Florida. I was impressed with Mr. Wilson. He seemed like the nicest man ever, and after Beau left, he looked even more genuine.

Every morning he would come into the store to say, "Hi" and purchase a little something for the day. He always bought a little extra for the kids. Later I would see him and his boys getting ready to fish, their black Lab in tow. In the evenings they were always at the campfire.

I had no idea his dog was pregnant, let alone that she had pups, and even if I had known, I would never think he would be the type to abandon his puppies. For Pete's sake, the man checked out early this morning. His boys were with him when he came into the store, and his dog was poking her head out of his truck. I talked to him for ten minutes or more, inviting them back and saying how much I enjoyed their stay. Not one of them mentioned they had left puppies. I would at least think a kid could have said something. One of his boys could have told on him while he had the chance. His dog could have at least cried or barked or jumped out of the car window like Lassie would have done. I mean, they all had to be heartbroken. I can't even imagine teaching my children to abandon dogs. What a shitty father! What a shitty teacher! No wonder he's divorced.

I put the puppies behind the store counter and called Randy on the walkie-talkie. Randy seemed as puzzled I was. He admitted to not having made it over there yet to check things over and collect the trash. You have to work pretty hard to beat Roman and Henry over to a vacant campsite. They usually watch the trailers pull away and then sprint to the empty site, looking for left or lost treasures. Henry sure as hell came upon one today.

Randy guessed that the pups were about two weeks old. He said we may be able to take them to a vet or pet store to be cared for, but Henry would not have it.

"No!" my sensitive son screamed. "You can't take them from me! I found them!"

I tried to explain to Henry that the pups needed a mommy or a vet to keep them alive, that it was too big a job for us, but Henry refused to give up the puppies. While I calmly tried to reason with him, he became more stubborn and then he began to cry. Henry's face was tear-streaked and made muddy from his dirty hands and wet eyes. His nose was snotty, his lips wet and red. He looked beautiful and angelic, like a little dirty angel, the keeper of small creatures. Randy saw it too, and he pulled me away to talk.

Randy let me know that he didn't have the heart to take the puppies away from Henry. He said instead he would go to the vet or library or whatever and see what we needed to do to help keep the pups alive. "Well, God damn, Randy," I yelled at him. "You're about as sensitive as Henry!" I told him if that's what he was willing to do, then he'd better go do it. I felt bad for yelling at Randy, but gee whiz, we all have our breaking point, and I guess three kids, nine dogs, and no husband is mine.

Randy left and went to the vets, and Henry sat on the floor most of the afternoon petting whining black pups. Carla came in, and Henry told her the Wilsons left those puppies for him, which I acknowledged by nodding my head, and after she got done cussing up a storm about that asshole Wilson, she carried two of those puppies around in her shirt for about a half hour.

When Henry and I took the pups back to the trailer to check in on Hazel and Sabrina, Hazel about fell over with glee. She picked up Henry in a bear hug and swung his little body from side to side. She and Henry then sat together on the floor, showing the puppies to Sabrina, who tried to climb into the laundry basket and sit on them. Well, Hazel laughed at that too, and Henry laughed, the puppies whined, Sabrina squealed, and I thought, "Oh Shit, I am in for it now!"

July 22, 1999

Randy came back from the vet with formula, baby bottles, a warming blanket, and instructions three pages long. Puppies eat more than human babies, or at least more often. A human baby can be tricked with a pacifier, and sometimes you can get four hours between meals out of them, but not puppies, and there's nine of them. By the time I'm finished feeding the last dog, the first one is hungry again. Henry helps me, but it is so much work that I don't know how I'm going to survive this.

Later, same day

I called a meeting at the house with Hazel, the boys, Carla, and Randy. I let everybody know that my plate is about as full as it can get. "I'm calling in for support," I told them. I suggested that we work out some sort of schedule with the pups, or they are surely gonna die. I also said, "I'm not about to deal with the death of a litter of pups on my hands." The pups can stay at my place, because I don't think Henry would have it any other way, but damn it, people are going to have to sign up to take a turn at feeding.

Hazel agreed to add puppy feeding to her mornings. She can feed Sabrina from the high chair while Henry and Roman help her feed the pups. Carla and Randy agreed to take turns in the afternoon. Everybody said they would come after the nightly campfire to help me get the pups fed so I can get my kids to bed. I guess I'll be the one up all night. In a month, if they survive, they will be old enough to eat on their own and be given away. I have to work on preparing Henry for that one. Hazel reminded me that the Lord doesn't give us more than we can handle. I just wish he didn't think I could handle so damn much.

July 23, 1999

Drama! Drama! Drama!

Mr. Carey, my boss, showed up today. I saw his long, silver, Lincoln Town Car pull into the campground, and my stomach flipped. I knew he had been called about Roman's fight and the nasty things that I said to Mrs. Holden, and I knew I was in trouble. Just as I knew, right at that moment, Hazel, Roman, and Henry sat in my trailer feeding nine hungry puppies while Sabrina threw eggs on the wall from her high chair.

"Oh, dear God," I prayed. "Deliver me from this hell."

Both Randy and Carla saw Mr. Carey too, and they both headed over to the store to see if they could be of any assistance. Mr. Carey wasted no time in asking them both to hold down the fort, while he and I went over to my place for a talk. "Oh, shit." their eyes blinked at me as I headed out the door.

Mr. Carey and I walked into my trailer just as Hazel was helping Henry place a puppy back into the basket and grab another one to start feeding. Mr. Carey peered into the basket in astonishment and then quickly asked if the dogs belonged to me. I was readying myself to tell the man "Yes," when Hazel started in on a big lie.

She told Mr. Carey that the puppies belonged to her and that the mother dog was at the vets sick, and she wasn't sure if the dog was going to make it. She said that the boys have been a big help with the feeding of the animals, and she didn't know what she would do if she didn't have us. As Hazel lied, the boys stood still with gaping mouths. Hazel continued to ramble on as she gathered up each pup and placed it back in the basket. She handed the basket to Roman and scooped Sabrina from the high chair and scooted all three children and nine puppies out of my house before the boys could tell on her for lying.

As soon as they left, I quickly looked around my home scanning the place for remnants of harboring dogs. To my surprise, the place looked good. The puppy formula was on the table, but that could be explained through Hazel. The rest was surprisingly clean. Even though I'm not a very good housekeeper, Hazel is an excellent one, and the whole place smelled of her delicious coffee. In fact, the only uncomfortable thing in my home was the tension that filled the space between Mr. Carey and me. So I did the only thing I knew to do to ease that tension and offered up a cup of coffee.

Mr. Carey began "our chat" by acknowledging my stress and predicament. He also apologized for Beau, which always puzzles me. He hinted that my life was impossible (imagine—impossible),"with running a campground and trying to run a family, too," he said.

As if I hadn't been humbled enough, I felt the desire to defend my pathetic existence. I told Mr. Carey that actually I was doing fine and that I had taken the opportunity of hiring a nanny for the kids. I explained to him Hazel's situation, and he seemed a little better knowing that my children are not running the grounds unsupervised or as the heathens described by the Holdens.

Mr. Carey questioned me about Roman's fight. I explained that Tad Holden was a bully and that Roman had taken enough, and that's when the questioning turned to me. "Is Mrs. Holden a bully, too?" he asked.

I will tell you, humble pie tastes like shit. I ate it anyway, as I apologized for every harsh word I spoke to Mrs. Holden. There was a moment of silence, and I felt we were done, but then Mr. Carey worked up the nerve to mention the golf-cart incident. He asked me if I thought I needed counseling to overcome my problems. It was then that my humble attitude turned defensive, and I told Mr. Carey to rest assured, I can handle my own problems. I reminded him that my husband has only been gone five short weeks, and considering all the adjustments I have made, I feel I'm doing a damn good job, with an "impossible" life.

Mr. Carey chuckled—I think at my southern accent and the way I quoted *impossible*—and then he agreed that I am a strong woman. As he headed out the door, he thanked me for the delicious coffee. I was accepting the compliment that should have gone to Hazel when I looked up and saw my supporters. They stood in front of my home like a redneck posse. There was Carla, Randy, Hazel, my three children, and behind them, about twenty of the regular vacationers, and I sucked back in my exhale and began to pray.

Carla was the first to step forward in my defense, and she was loaded for a fight. She stood barefoot with one knee bent, her hands on her hips, and her head swinging back and forth in a ghetto motion. Carla, never intimidated by anyone, talked to distinguished Mr. Carey as she would talk to anyone she felt wronged her. She told Mr. Carey that if I was going to be fired over some unfair bullshit with one hoity-toity little bitch, she would quit. She also said that every vacationer standing behind her would not be coming back to these grounds if I was let go. I was scared for Carla and kept praying that she would stop her redneck monologue, but as I watched it unravel, I noticed that Mr. Carey seemed more intrigued than insulted. I kind of got the impression that he enjoyed Carla's spunk.

After Carla finished, Hazel began. She wasn't nearly as dramatic as Carla, but she too was more forceful than I thought she ever could be. Hazel mostly just complimented me. She told Mr. Carey that I did an incredible job running the grounds. She said I went out of my way for every family and made the site a real community atmosphere. She said the reason the regulars return to his grounds when there are so many more options in the area was because I made it feel like a home away from home. She also told him she would never return if I was going to be fired. All the residents behind her shook their heads in agreement.

It was all very sweet, yet extremely conflicting. My friends were prepared to fight a battle for me, and as flattering as that was, I kept wishing that they would just all go back to their campsites and homes. As I prayed for the drama to stop, Mr. Carey turned to Randy and asked his opinion, which was further validation that Mr. Carey was indeed enjoying the show.

Randy was far more respectful than Carla, but he admitted to agreeing with her. He also stated that my personal life truly should not be a factor, and besides the fact that I live here, I keep my personal issues private. He ended by saying that he too would have to leave if I was let go. Basically he let Mr. Carey know that he would not work for a man or company that put out a woman with three babies.

As everyone quieted down and waited for a reaction from the tall, good-looking Mr. Carey, Roman worked up the courage to shout, "Don't you dare fire my mommy!"

That does it, I thought. *I'm done for.* But Mr. Carey only smiled. Then he thanked the vacationers and Hazel. He chuckled at Carla and shook his head in her direction. He shook Randy's hand, and then he started down to his car, only to stop in front of Roman and grip his shoulders in a firm embrace. "Take good care of your mama, son. You're the man now," he said.

Once seated in his long, silver Town Car, Mr. Carey called me over to his window. He told me that he felt much better knowing that I have a strong support team. He advised me to lean on them when I have to. He said he had a grandson about to turn twelve, and he would be needing one of those pups to give as a present. I told Mr. Carey I would let him know when the pups get big enough to go, and as he drove away, he kept smiling.

July 24, 1999

My dad called today. At first I held back with pleasantries and thank yous, but Daddy knows me too well to be fake, so eventually I just let it all out. I told him all about Judy Mathers and her big fake tits. I told him about my car breaking down, about the golf cart, about Randy, Carla, and Hazel, and how they are all helping me. I told him about Tad Holden and his mother and the visit from Mr. Carey. I told him about the puppies and the anoles and the money sent by Mama Jaspers. When I was done talking and crying, I settled myself down for some solid fatherly advice, but all I got was a few one-line questions that went something like this:

"How's the car running now?"

"Fine."

"Did Roman win the fight?"

"Yes."

"Any of those puppies die?"

"No."

"A grandma babysitter who makes good coffee, huh?"

"The best."

"Well, then I guess, Sissy, things could be a hell of a lot worse, couldn't they?"

"I guess so, Daddy."

"Okay then, call me if you need anything."

"Bye."

Not too sympathetic, by any means, but maybe he has a point.

July 25, 1999

I'm tired today. Not only do I get up every few hours with pups, but Carla, Randy, Hazel, and I have been playing cards every night. They all come over like they promised, after the campfire. Those three feed the dogs while I lay the kids down. Afterwards, we all play euchre. Randy and Carla are really good, while Hazel and I just laugh and have fun. It's actually been great, and I'm not missing Beau nearly as much.

July 28, 1999

I found out how to get some sleep. I let the puppies sleep with Roman and Henry. It works great. The two boys kind of make a circle with their bodies facing each other while they lay on Beau's sleeping bag on the floor. I place the puppies in the center of the circle, and they all kind of smash up together between both boys. It's really cute, and everybody is happy. At first I was worried about one of the boys lying on a puppy and smothering it in its sleep, but then I thought if a dog is smart enough to stay off her pups, then so are my boys. Yahoo, I was right. Sleep has never felt better.

July 30, 1999

I'm sick. I mean physically sick. How come every time things look to be going good, something terrible happens, and I'm flat on my ass again? I went to the bank today with Mama Jaspers' check, and after depositing $300.00 into my account, I asked for a statement, it read I had a mere $30.00. Not $300.00, but $30.00.

"You forgot a zero," I told the girl, which she argued was absolutely not the case. She then informed me that the reason I have no money was because of all my bounce fees. What bounce fees? I questioned. The blond, blue-eyed teller was obviously disappointed in me, because she spoke in a rather shaming voice. She told me that a letter had gone out to my home at the beginning of the week.

I hadn't opened much of my mail. It was sitting in a heap on my table. I had seen the bank letter. In fact, I used it as a dust pan and swept up some sand from the floor. I just assumed it was a statement that I could get to later. Later had not yet come.

I asked for a printout of my history. I read the sheets of paper, warm from the copy machine, as the blonde looked on in judgment and the people in line behind me impatiently tapped their feet. Beau had been using the ATM card. Four different times to be exact, each time drawing out $100.00. When I wrote the check for the doctor, I had insufficient funds and the check bounced, causing me to owe the bank the full amount plus a twenty-dollar bounce fee. I then wrote a check to the pharmacy, which also bounced, costing me twenty, and then the check I wrote to the grocery store, it bounced. That's another twenty, plus the two full amounts of both checks.

I know I looked crazy standing in that line reading those papers. I could feel my flesh burn with heat and my eyes sting with tears. I could feel my throat dry up and become sore while holding back a big lump. I left the bank with no further questions and no money.

Now I'm sick. Just when I thought I was beginning to heal, just when I had stopped missing him so damn much, just when I was beginning to feel good again, he hurt me from a distance. How could that son of a bitch take food, medicine, and care from his own children?

When he went into our account and took our money, he robbed his own children. Does he even know what he's doing? Does he know what pain we're in? Does he care?

I am numb. Everything seems surreal. My life is a nightmare. Beau is no longer the man I married. He is no longer the charming, blond country boy that wooed me into his heart. He is no longer the son of Mama and Pop Jaspers, salt-of-the-earth people. He is no longer the happy daddy of my babies, the man who adored his children, the man who taught his boys about the outdoors and how to make a decent fire, how to cast a rod or how to reel in a trout. The man who melted every time he looked at his baby girl. The man who could sleep for hours with a baby on his chest or could give mile-long shoulder rides through the woods or enjoy wrestling an eight-year-old. He is no longer my man, and he is no longer a man I want. I now know it's final. I am alone, and now I am scared.

August 1, 1999

I'm in a funk. I no longer write every night, because by the time Hazel, Randy, and Carla leave, I have only enough energy to cry myself to sleep. To add to my misery, it is August in Florida. I live and work in the overheated depths of Hell!

August 3, 1999

Daddy has a father's intuition. He sent me one thousand dollars. Again, all I can do is cry.

August 4, 1999

Hazel, the kids, and I went out today. I took a needed day off and thought I would just lie around. Wrong. Hazel insisted we get out and take the kids to the beach. Actually the day was wonderful. Roman seemed happy. Henry found more treasures on the beach than we have containers for, and Sabrina went along with it all, like the good-natured baby she is. The only downfall is the weather, but we stayed by the water's edge and kept cool.

Later in the afternoon, when we were all parched and starving, Hazel treated us to supper. I didn't want her to do it, but she insisted, and honestly, it would have hurt her feelings for me to refuse. We feasted on seafood and slushy virgin drinks with tiny umbrellas in them.

On our way back home, Hazel saw a photo studio and tried to talk me into getting a family portrait with just the kids and me. "No," I complained, "we're not dressed right."

Hazel was relentless, though. Finally we compromised and went into the studio to make an appointment. I go back with the kids on the seventh to have our family photo done. I think I will dress everybody in white.

August 7, 1999

Today is the day of my rebirth. Today I embraced my new self. I finally acknowledged that what is, is, and that I am a single parent now. My family consists of four: two little boys, a baby girl, and me. I know that I am my children's only caregiver. I know that I carry all the responsibility and all the burdens, along with all the joys and love. I finally have let in the fact that Beau is not coming back.

I have been so sad since going to the bank. I think I was as hurt by being left with no money as I was about being cheated on and even abandoned. It was as if the money sealed the deal. It was all the conclusion I needed. Now I am ready to move forward, with my children by my side. Surprisingly, I feel good. I actually feel liberated and free. I feel I can let go of my anxieties and pain and move through my days easier. I feel like I can make some plans for our future, plans that consist of my dreams and wants—my dreams, not Beau's.

It was the photo session that liberated me. My freedom bloomed during the process of being photographed as a lone parent, the idea that the kids and I could be captured during this time in our lives. With that photograph, the moment that we are now living in will remain frozen for eternity. It is such a defining moment, or rather refining, a moment that has changed us into who we are now, which is different from who we were three months ago. It is a moment that will mold us into who we are supposed to become, and now I'm giggling, because I love the kids and Hazel and me, and I'll be damned if she wasn't right.

The kids and I had a blast getting our pictures done. I won't be able to afford half of them, but we still had a blast. I dressed everybody in white, and we all looked clean, fresh, and new, much better than I ever could have known.

My initial idea for white was only because Sabrina has a beautiful white sundress that she had not yet worn. I retrieved the little cotton gown when I was only six months pregnant and happily married. I remember pulling the precious thing from the dryer, a lost item of clothing that brought me comfort. I laid the dress out neatly on the countertop and prayed that it would not be claimed. I patiently waited the three days before rescuing the sundress with the round collar. I can remember leaving the laundry room with the crisp white linen that smelled of dryer sheets and fresh air. I took the dress back to the trailer. Beau was out at other sites and had the boys with him. Carla was working the store, and the campground seemed amazingly quiet, so I used the time to lie down on our bed with the little dress laid out on my stomach and talk to my unborn child, which I knew was a girl.

To match Sabrina's dress, the boys wore white polo shirts and khaki shorts. They were also nice laundry finds, but not nearly as sentimental as the dress. I wore a simple white T-shirt and long white summer skirt. None of us wore shoes, a choice made because Sabrina has never owned a pair of shoes. I own only two pairs of cheap flip-flops, and the boys just have dirty sandals that need to be replaced; however, the barefoot look worked.

As soon as the kids and I walked into the photo studio dolled up in our summer whites, the photographer suggested we go out outside. In the back of the studio sits a beautiful lawn, and Kurt, our photographer, laid a white blanket on the green grass and told me to be natural and play with my kids, which I was able to do happily. The kids responded to me easily, and Kurt was ecstatic. He asked if I would sign a waiver so he could use our photos in his advertising. Of course I obliged. Kurt was adorable and fawned over the kids and me, making me feel like a beautiful model. I enjoyed the male attention as much as anything, another sign that I am healing.

August 8, 1999

It is so good to feel whole again. I was actually able to spend a day laughing. I laughed at Hazel, Henry, and those damn puppies. I laughed at Sabrina as she learns to walk. Once my little monkey stopped spending her days clinging to my back, she decided she could walk. I laughed at Roman, who can now do a back flip off the side of the pool. I laughed when Carla talked about sex with Randy and how he is even polite in bed. I laughed during the ice cream social that was way too hot to have and caused a huge melted, sticky mess. I laughed when parents, who didn't know how else to clean their children, instructed them to jump into the pool. The pool became white, cloudy, and unsuitable for swimming. I laughed at the campfire. I laughed at home surrounded by my kids and best friends, feeding puppies and then playing euchre. I laughed hardest when Hazel and I beat Carla and Randy for the first time.

August 10, 1999

My dad, honest to God, where do I begin? Yesterday in the mail I received another envelope from him. It immediately upset me, because just five days ago, he sent one thousand dollars. I thought there was no need and no way he could be sending me more money already.

I don't want to be given so much. It makes me feel like a failure. I may not have much more than pride, but I have my pride.

I opened the envelope anticipating fifties to fall out (my dad doesn't believe in banks). Instead I found a short, hand-scripted note and a photo of the Kitchen House that sits on the corner of Maple and Vine. The note simply read: "Yours."

I immediately picked up the phone. I can get a hold of him anytime I want. He doesn't own a home phone, just a cell that is constantly hooked to his jeans. My dad answered on the first ring, anticipating my call. When I asked him what in the hell the picture meant, he told me he had bought the house for me.

I have never really known my dad to show much emotion, but he actually sounded animated as he spoke of the Kitchen House and his intent.

The Kitchen House is the rumored haunted house of our town. It's a big white clapboard structure that sits directly in the center of town, across the street from the small post office and next to the one-room library. It is called the Kitchen House in memory of a family that once lived there and is believed to be haunted by them now.

Owen and Emma Kitchen and their two children, William and Sarah, lived in the house during the 1940s and 1950s. The Kitchens were a prominent couple. They were known to throw lavish parties and entertain writers, composers, and actors. I don't know how much of those rumors are true. If they were cultured at all, they would have been the only cultured people ever to live in Grace, West Virginia.

What I do know about the Kitchens is that they experienced a series of tragic events followed by tragic deaths. The Kitchens' son, William, died in a farming accident at the age of twelve. While the parents were in the midst of grieving for William, seven-year-old Sarah was stricken with scarlet fever and died. Two days after burying their second and last child, Owen and Emma Kitchen took their own lives in the most romantic of ways. The grief-stricken couple shared poisoned wine, wrapped themselves up in each other's embrace, and lay on their marriage bed, never to wake again. They were found in the morning by a visitor who had come to give his condolences for the loss of their children.

As kids we used to dare each other to walk past the house at night or on Halloween and call out the names of the Kitchen family. As a teenager I became obsessed with the Kitchens' story, since it is the only thing of real interest to come out of our town—that is if you don't count my mother's, along with her lover's, death. I researched old newspapers from the library about the Kitchen family and wrote a report on them for my English class. My teacher was so impressed that she shared it with the entire school and then made a copy to keep for herself.

The Kitchen home has had a slew of other owners. None of them have been from Grace or know the story. They have all been temporary, usually a young couple new to the area, a divorcee, or a wandering traveler. No one stays too long—two to five years max, and then the house goes on the market again.

I asked daddy to explain how he came to buy the house. He told me that he had actually bought it a few months back. The last owners had lost it to the bank in a nasty divorce. Daddy got it dirt cheap on auction. He and Charlie figured it was a moneymaker. They swooped in and fixed it all up with the intent of using it as rental property. When they heard about my situation, they both knew the real reason it fell into their laps was that it was meant for the kids and me.

This is where Daddy got truly excited. He told me that a brilliant idea came to him, after the night we talked. I had told him about Hazel, her coffee, the kids, and I, and how well we work together. Daddy swears that he had an epiphany that night, and that visions have been coming at him full force ever since. He says that when he shared his idea with Charlie, my brother called him a genius.

Daddy's voice came through as a bright light as he talked about his dreams for me, the house, the kids, and the makings of a lucrative business, a coffeehouse.

Daddy rambled on about how all the rich yuppies are all of a sudden into coffee, coffeehouses and Starbucks, which he mistakenly called Buckstars. All of it confused me at first, and I asked what yuppies and

Hollywood types had to do with Grace, West Virginia. Besides that, West Virginians have always drank coffee, Maxwell House in the big blue can, all day, every day.

"Exactly!" Daddy exclaimed "And wouldn't they like to drink their Maxwell House in a quaint coffeeshop like the sophisticated do? Especially if that Maxwell House had a little flare, like Hazel's coffee does." I have never heard my father more excited, and I giggled when he asked me to close my eyes and picture farmers and workers sharing a round table of coffee in my house. Or housewives holding book clubs and quilting parties in my coffeehouse. He said teenagers would come to pretend they're all grown up and fancy rich. Husbands would come to escape nagging wives, and women would come to gather and gossip.

He says that he and Charlie will rehab the kitchen and add a small bathroom for my business. The other parts of the house are for Hazel, the kids, and me to live in. When I reminded Daddy that the house is haunted, he exclaimed, "All the more charm, Sissy." The way he sees it, the rumors of the house being haunted may pull in other visitors. "Folks passing through will surely choose to have their rest and coffee in a haunted house. Who knows? People may come from all over to drink Hazel's comforting coffee in a haunted house."

I tried to tell Dad that I didn't know if Hazel would want to do this. I mean it's one thing for her to come up with the idea of babysitting my kids as her purpose and quite another to ask her to move to another state and go into business selling her coffee out of a haunted house. Still, I promised Dad that I would ask. I suppose that if Hazel says no, the house is still for the kids and me. Dad will come up with something else, for sure.

I have to hand it to Dad; he sure thought this one out. I never knew he could be so creative. I never knew he had dreams. When I asked him if he thought it would traumatize my kids to live in a notorious haunted house, he answered by saying, "Can't be no more traumatic than being raised in a campground." He had me on that one. We hung up in agreement that I would think it over, talk to Hazel, and call him back as soon as I decided something.

August 11, 1999

Since talking to Dad, I've been numb. One would think I would jump at the chance of going back home. I've wanted to be back in West Virginia since the day I arrived in Florida, but now, with the possibility right in front of me, I freeze up.

I worry about how the kids would do with a change right now. In all honesty, the kids are comfortable with their home environment. They are actually envied by other children and consider themselves lucky to be on permanent vacation. They are used to having a swimming pool out one side of their home and a miniature golf course out the other. They enjoy the rec room where they can go play ping-pong or billiards or pinball. They expect their nighttime ritual to consist of a campfire with marshmallows. Besides that, they love their school and do well with their teachers. Grace, West Virginia, doesn't have the advantages that my kids have here in Florida. Their education would not be as advanced. On the other hand, I graduated from Grace High, and I'm not stupid.

I also hate the thought of leaving Carla and Randy, who have proven to be such great and loyal friends. I fear the thought of something new. I fear failing. Mostly, I fear Beau coming home and our not being there. Stupid, I know. I tell myself that I have accepted the fact that Beau and I are over, that even if he came home, everything has changed and I could no longer be his wife. Even though I tell myself that, and even though I live it, there is still this little part—a tiny speck in my brain—that envisions Beau walking back in my door and us going on like nothing ever happened.

August 12, 1999

I'm going to talk to Hazel today. I have decided that if she likes the idea, we will go. It is stupid for me to stay here and live out Beau's dreams for him.

August 13, 1999

Hazel didn't know what to think or how to respond. First she laughed and then she cried and then she laughed again. She told me she would have to think about it, only to return five minutes later and tell me yes. She returned five minutes after that to tell me she would have to think it through a little further. I think I've sent the women into a tizzy.

August 14, 1999

I'm going to call Dad today and tell him that Hazel and I will be coming. What I thought was Hazel's apprehension was actually her disbelief in being included, not just her, but her coffee. After Hazel spent yesterday not talking much to anybody, she showed up at my door bright and early this morning, a huge pot of coffee in her hand, a new gleam in her eye, and stated proudly, "Let's do it Sissy. Let's do it." I threw my arms around Hazel and about knocked her over. She just laughed.

August 14, Later

Called Daddy and told him Hazel and I are coming. He said he knew and that he and Charlie have already been working on gutting the kitchen.

August 15, 1999

Talked to Carla about moving, and she's actually really excited for me. Like Charlie, she thinks Dad is a genius. She said to let her know when my grand opening will be, because she and Randy wouldn't miss it for the world. She asked what the name of my coffeehouse will be, and I automatically replied, "The Kitchen House." It's perfect.

August 16, 1999

Talked to Mr. Carey early this morning. It was actually harder than I thought it was going to be. He really is a very caring person. I wish I had known that sooner. He wished me luck and told me he thought I was an amazing woman. It felt awkward to be given such a compliment from such a successful man. What feels good now is that I know that he meant it. I also let him know that his puppy is about ready to be picked up.

August 16 (later that day)

Business is business. Amy, our part-timer, has already been given a full-time position, and my job is posted on the web site. I have to talk to the kids.

August 17, 1999

I sat the boys on the couch and started on my prepared speech, except the words didn't come out as easily as I had prepared, and they both kept interrupting me every few seconds, so they were only told in bits and pieces and then had the task of piecing it all together to make sense.

I left out the part about the house being haunted.

August 18, 1999 2:00am

Can't sleep. My head is turning with all that I have to do and the time I have to do it in. I would like the kids to start school in Grace, but that gives me only two weeks to pack up everything I own and haul it up to West Virginia. I don't know what to do with all of Beau's stuff, and I'll probably need to sell my car. I really need to buy a new car, because the Buick is not going to make the drive to West Virginia.

August 18, 1999

I picked up my photo of the kids and me. Hazel went along with me and talked me into buying my favorite print in the sixteen-by-twenty. I don't have any money, especially with the move, so I told Hazel no matter how good the pictures are, I'm buying only one. "Then make it big!" she said, so I did.

All the photos turned out great, and it was hard for me to choose, but I purchased the one that immediately drew me in. It was the simplest of the photographs taken and not necessarily the best, but it was the most honest. On a white blanket placed in front of a green garden, I sat poised looking straight on, with no real expression on my face. Sabrina sat on my lap, no smile, no frown, but pure contentment. Henry hung onto my left shoulder with a laughing smile. Roman stood behind me on the right. He had a peaceful look on his face with a slight grin, his head leaned up against mine in a sleepy way, his hand rested warmly on my shoulder. I could feel the love.

After we got home, Hazel presented me with a gift. It was beautiful thick white wooden frame, sixteen by twenty. No wonder she was pushing hard for that size. She had also gone back into the shop when I was putting kids in the car and bought me all the proofs. She's too beautiful for words.

August 19, 1999

1:30 a.m.

I woke a little while ago, to what I thought was the sound of whimpering puppies. I went to check on them only on second thought, just for reassurance that no pup was being innocently smothered. What I found, after peeling two layers of dogs off my child, was a whimpering boy.

Henry cried as I held him close to me. I believed him to be crying because of our move, his father's leaving, and all the confusion we are living, but as I soothed my child gently, he sobbed in gasps and said, "I don't want to give away my puppies!"

"Oh, Henry." I sighed, relieved, as I held his shaking body. Imagine, with all that we are going through, he's worried about puppies. Maybe I am a good mom.

Huge tears rolled down Henry's cheeks, and he used a floppy black puppy ear to wipe them away. Again I was blessed to glimpse that small angel living in my son.

"Henry, would you feel better if you could have one of these puppies?" I asked him. Sadly, he shook his head no.

Shit, I thought. *He's not going to make this easy*. I offered up two puppies, but Henry's downturned head continued to shake back and fourth. I breathed in and then out, closed my eyes, and then went for it. "Three puppies. What if I let you keep three puppies?"

"Three puppies!" Henry squealed and wrapped his arms around me in more of a headlock than a hug.

I had to hurry and explain the catch before his laughter woke up either sibling. I told Henry one puppy could come live with us in our new home. Another puppy could live with Grandpa and Charlie at their house, and one could go live with Mama and Pops Jaspers. All three dogs would belong to Henry, though, and he could see them all as much as he wanted.

Henry is too smart to fool, and he immediately went about trying to poke holes into my theory. Henry wanted to know, "What if Grandpa and Uncle Charlie or Mama and Pops Jaspers don't let a puppy live at their house?"

That's when I taught my son about manipulating. I told Henry to tell his grandparents and uncle how he rescued the litter of pups, how he fed them, slept with them, and kept them safe and alive. He could then tell them how he couldn't take losing another thing.

Henry wanted to know if he could name the pups. "Sure," I said.

"That's easy. You just tell them the puppy's name when you take it to their house to live." Henry was smiling when he asked me if our plan was going to work. I was honest when I told him yes. In fact, it is the one plan I have that I know will work.

August 19, 1999

Hazel, Carla, and Randy have been here most of the night. Tomorrow is Olympic Day at the campground, and we were making blue and red ribbons for this year's kids. Olympic Day is something Beau and I started a few years back. Every game and sport played involves water, because of the heat. There are refreshments set up in the rec room, and everybody receives a ribbon. It's always a great time, but this year it seems to be just another pain. Instead of packing my family up to move away and start a new life, I'm hosting Olympic Day for already overindulged youth.

Regardless, the night turned out to be my most productive. The ribbons we made are the best yet, thanks to Hazel's crafting abilities. The games are organized, the refreshments made, and most importantly, we spent all our time together talking about Hazel's and my future and our move. It's strange, but the more we got into it, the more things kept falling into place. It's as if this was all meant to be, and as irrational as it is, it seems to be the next logical step in my life.

Hazel and I will pack up her R.V. for our move. Randy is buying my Buick. I was worried about furnishing my new home, since all the stuff in the trailer belongs to the campground, but then Hazel reminded me that she owns a home and all its contents back in Indiana.

Hazel is going to call her neighbor of forty years tomorrow. He's been watching the house in her absence. Her plan is to give her neighbor an inventory of what is to be moved, basically all her big furniture, except for the kitchen and her master bedroom. The master bedroom has been untouched since Harry's death.

Next, Hazel will call professional movers to do the job. Mr. Davey, the neighbor, is to oversee that it is done properly. Later, after Hazel and I have the kids settled into school and I have Mama Jaspers to watch them, we will make a trip to Indiana to go through the rest of her belongings. Hazel says she thinks after that, she may want to rent out her home. If Mr. Davey is interested, he can be her property manager. He could collect the rent, pay himself, and send her the rest. I think it's a real good idea.

As for my things, most of it's toys belonging either to Beau or the kids. I can probably get rid of a lot of stuff just by donating it to the campground. I will take with me only what we need. I plan to start over in West Virginia.

August 20, 1999

I have already been living every day in a panic; however, today was the cherry on the top of my sundae.

Olympic Day games were going well. We started early, before it got too hot. Everyone met at the pool by 9:00 a.m. We had a huge turn-out. Carla and I had set out doughnuts, muffins, bagels, and cream cheese in the rec room for the participants and guests. We also served water, tea, orange juice, cranberry juice, and Hazel's coffee, which, by the way, received more compliments than sweet, humble Hazel could believe.

We divided kids into teams by colors, trying to be as fair as possible. Surprisingly, it worked. There were no poor sports. Everyone received ribbons and paper certificates that Carla had made. Even people without kids came over to watch.

When everything was kind of settling down, I noticed Nancy Kidwell's head darting around, looking for one of her children. That's not unusual, since the Kidwells have six kids, and they always seem to be looking for one of them. I noticed Nancy motion two of her older kids over and instructed them to go over to the campsite and see if they could find the missing sibling. It wasn't until the teens came back empty-handed and Nancy frantically called all her children together to go find Emily that I got nervous. When Nancy and her husband, Jack, and their five other kids started searching through the crowd in and out the laundry room, rec room, golf course, etc, I became frantic.

My first terrible thought caused me to grab Randy aside and whisper to him, "Get the golf cart and drive past every site. Make sure no one is packing up to leave or has left this morning without a check out." I could see Randy's mind catch up to mine, and he flew into action, immediately jumping into a cart and speeding away on a mission.

Carla gathered all the campers to form a search party, while I went over to talk with Nancy Kidwell. Nancy said she had last seen Emily by the pool, pouting. She said Emily didn't like competitive sports and refused to play this morning. The rest of the Kidwell children were involved in it all, and I guess Jack and Nancy got caught up in watching the other five play and forgot about nine-year-old Emily and her pout.

Nancy began to cry when fifteen minutes had gone by with still no sight of Emily. Thirty minutes into it, we had looked everywhere, shouting the child's name. Jack decided to call the police. As he dialed 911 on his cell phone, Nancy stood beside him crying. The entire park searched high and low for Emily, including Randy, who looked to have murder on his mind if he found anyone else to be involved.

I ran to my trailer to phone Mr. Carey. I thought that my worst nightmare had occurred. I have always feared a child or woman being snatched, a drowning, or rape, or even a murder at my campground. I was panicked inside while trying to appear calm. I swung open my front door and nearly tripped over the sleeping nine-year-old and the litter of pups that lay in my front room.

"Emily!" I gasped, reviving the sleepy child. Emily looked up at me in a Goldilocks stare and stated, "I just wanted to see the puppies. You're not mad at me, are you?" I laughed through my tears as I hugged the little girl, who had merely broken into my home and taken a nap.

"Nancy!" I screamed out my front door. "I found her!" The happiest words I have ever spoken.

Nancy and Jack and all the Kidwell kids came flying up to my house as a sleep-stunned Emily held a pup around its throat. The

Kidwells hugged Emily and then yelled at her and then embraced her again and yelled at each other.

The other camping children jumped and shouted, and Carla gave out leftover ribbons that she quickly scripted "Hero" on. We thanked them all for helping out and pulling together to look for Emily. The other adults hugged each other, thanked the Lord, and kept a closer eye on their kids. Randy deflated as he exhaled away his tension, but Hazel wasn't rejoicing, laughing, or hugging. She was sitting, looking winded or cloudy. "Hazel," I said, putting my hand on her shoulder.

"Sissy." She calmly replied, "Go get my nitro."

Nitro. Nitro? I instantly leapt back in panic mode as I hustled down the dirt road after Hazel's nitro.

It all turned out fine. I took the kids while Hazel napped all afternoon and woke up her jolly old self. Out of parental guilt, Emily got to take home the dog she had held in the choke hold, so I got rid of our first puppy. I realized I need to get out of this job before something bad does happen one day. It was my confirmation that I have made the right decision.

I'm just a little nervous now that I know Hazel has a heart condition, and I'm taking her to live in a haunted house.

August 23, 1999

Even with little furniture, no winter clothes, or collections of any type, moving is still an overwhelming task. I have donated six boxes of toys to the campground, not to mention all of Beau's belongings that I turned over to Randy's care. Beau's stuff mostly consists of enough camping gear to open a small store and an inappropriate amount of tackle and fishing poles. I'm taking only enough of Beau's belongings for Roman and Henry to be well-equipped Boy Scouts and fishing buddies of their grandpas. The rest of it can go in the community shed.

August 27, 1999

The puppies have slowly been finding their way into new homes. Henry cries every time one leaves, and I have to give him a pep talk. After Emily Kidwell took the first puppy, the couple camping next to them came down for one.

Carla and Randy both took a puppy today. I knew the pups they were both going to choose. Sweet, sensitive Randy, of course, scooped up the little runt, a tiny all-black female that I thought for sure would die. He named her Sable, and she hasn't left his side all day.

Carla, on the other hand, chose the biggest, fattest, sloppiest dog in the litter. When I prepare the puppy formula—that we once fed them through bottles—and put it into larger quantities in pie pans, it is Carla's greedy pup that will actually crawl into the pie pan of sloppy food. He will sprawl out his enormous puppy body in the muck and eat, causing the other pups to eat only what splashes out when he plops down. No doubt Carla's puppy will grow to be the size of a small horse. His paw covers my entire palm, and he snorts. Carla fell in love with this disgusting little beast, so she bought him a spiked collar, named him Bruno, and took him home.

The Olsens are leaving tomorrow, and they will be getting their puppy at check-out. That leaves Mr. Carey, who will be coming soon to get his. The remaining three will be leaving with us. I'm still in shock. In less than a week, the kids and I will be returning home. We will start a new life, without their dad, and in his place will be Hazel and three dogs.

August 28, 1999

Talked to Dad for about an hour today. It is the longest phone conversation we have ever had. Dad is pumped up about the house, Hazel, the kids, and me. His excitement carries through in his voice, and it is contagious. I am now excited.

Although the kitchen is completely gutted and the back wall has been torn down for expansion, we are welcome to come now. The rest of the hundred-year-old farmhouse is in good condition. When I asked him how I was supposed to live with three kids and no kitchen, he responded with, "Well hell, Sissy, you've been on a camping trip their whole lives." I honestly think Dad believes I've been living in a pop-up tent for the past ten years.

He said that as for the rest of the house, the wood floors have been worked over, the minor repairs have been made, and all the walls have been painted the colors of spring, designed by Charlie, of course. The living room is lilac, and the parlor off to the side of the living room is the color of honeydew. There are three bedrooms upstairs. Roman and Henry's room is sky blue. Sabrina's and my room is dusty rose, and Hazel's is coral. The huge bathroom with its claw tub is butter yellow. Charlie put oval braided rugs in each room that carry the same colors in them as the walls. Now all we need is Hazel's furniture. I can't believe I'm going to live in a real house!

On the front of the house is a covered L-shaped porch, which my father went on and on about. The L-shaped porch is soon to become a wraparound porch, C-shape, I guess. The porch will continue to the back of the house, which will be the entrance to the coffeehouse or my kitchen. Using white beams for reinforcement, Dad plans to hang twelve white porch swings on my wraparound porch, all facing different angles. He also plans to have twelve round tables inside the coffeehouse and a wood-burning fireplace.

When I mentioned how much the boys would miss their nightly campfires, Dad excitedly talked about building a fire pit in the back yard. He said we could have fires every night, if we wanted, and he would build me benches or chairs, another grand idea to bring in patrons. When I told him the kids will miss the recreation they have here, Dad instantly envisioned an enormous playground that he and Charlie would design and build. It will bring mothers to the coffeehouse so their children can play on my kids' playground equipment while the mothers sip their coffee in my back yard. There is no end to his ideas. He has given birth to a dream that continues to grow into a reality.

He is the leader in this journey, and we are his following tribe. We leave in two days. I sure hope the Kitchens don't mind the changes with the house. The last thing I want to do is piss off a family of ghosts.

August 29, 1999 early morn.

Today is the last day I will open this camp store. I will no longer be a fixture here. The regulars have been coming in all morning to tell me good-bye. For some unknown reason, this move is harder for me to make than I ever imagined.

August 29 - still

Mr. Carey came this afternoon and picked up his puppy. He chose the stocky male with a white blaze down its chest. Henry gave him a list of instructions, and he acted like he was paying attention. Before Mr. Carey left, he hugged me. I was startled at first by his embrace, and I stood stiff, but then I softened into his hug, and he talked to my back.

Mr. Carey said that he had never met another person like me. He actually said that I amazed him with all that I do and all that I am capable of. His words were beyond flattering. He brought me to tears when he said that I had "an unbelievable gentleness mixed with an unbelievable fire." I have never been given such compliments, and I don't know if I can believe them. I don't know how to respond to such praise, so I just cried as I hugged him.

Mr. Carey than gave me an envelope that contained what he called a "signing-off bonus." I almost fainted when I saw a month's salary and a note with a simple "Good Luck." After Mr. Carey left and I recovered from my shock, the kids and I sat outside and played with the remaining three puppies.

"Let's name this one Picasso," I suggested as I held up a pup. I explained to the kids that Picasso was a famous artist. The little puppy has a white tip on its tail, like it's been dipped in paint. It reminds me of a paintbrush.

"Can't," Henry told me.

"Why not?" I asked, a little offended.

Henry informed me that the puppy was already named Dr. Seuss. I tried to change Henry's mind by telling him that Dr. Seuss was a cat, but Henry is too smart, and he let me know that Dr. Seuss is not a cat. He is a man that writes about a cat. Just like Picasso is a man, except Henry likes Dr. Seuss better. Well, there you go. How can I argue with that?

The other two pups have also been named, and Henry has already decided their living arrangements. Buddy, named by Roman, is an adorable pup and may be my favorite. He has a white streak between his eyes and his hair is longer than all the other pups. He is the one that I want to keep, but it is decided that he will go live with Dad and Charlie. Lucky, the third pup, has much more white on her than the rest of the litter. Lucky is also smaller, shier, and more placid. Lucky will go to Ma and Pop Jaspers' house. We get Dr. Seuss.

August 29, 1999

Had a cookout dinner with Carla, Randy, Hazel, and the kids. Carla made a going-away cake that was awesome. She simply coated a store-bought angel food cake with Cool Whip and then covered it with kiwi, mandarin oranges, pineapple, and strawberries. I don't know if I have ever tasted anything so good. The boys swam and played while we sat eating and reminiscing. I can finally laugh at some of what I've been through, and we all cracked up while we talked about the golf cart and Mrs. Holden.

I will miss Carla and Randy. They have been my lifeline and touchstones through it all. They are the definition of true friends, and I know I will never be able to replace them with someone else.

Randy has done so much to help Hazel too. Thanks to Randy, we basically are set to go. We just need to pull her mobile home out of the cozy spot it's in and head on up the road, but first I must have my last campfire with this crowd. Randy is going to bring his guitar so we can all sing "Country Roads." My song!

August 30, 1999

It's been a roller coaster of a day. I'm preparing to leave the place I have called home for the last few years, the place where I made my family. The kids are excited and just as scared and nervous as I am. Our lives are completely different now from what they were when summer first arrived. It is hard for me to grasp the transformation. The campfire was the best and hardest part of the day.

Thank you, God, for Carla and her craziness, her loyalty, and her spunk. She reminds me that it's just life; don't take it so seriously, and whatever comes, you just deal with it.

Thank you, God, for Randy, for his sensitivity, his music, and the creative way he touches my heart. Randy is a man of true integrity, of country charm, and of pure goodness.

Thank you, God, for Hazel, my earth angel, my strength, my soul mother.

"Country roads, take me home
To the place I belong,
West Virginia, mountain momma,
Country roads, take me home."

August 31, 1999 after midnight

It happened. Beau always did have unbelievable timing. I had finally gotten the kids to settle down and fall asleep. I was packing up last-minute boxes and clearing out my food to pack a cooler and then give the rest to Carla. I was listening to soft country music and drinking my first beer in two years (Sabrina has stopped nursing). I was feeling good when the phone rang.

Beau's voice was almost a whisper when he said my name, and it shook me. My stomach immediately filled with knots and butterflies as my husband whispered my name three more times. Still, I could not respond. My voice had dried up and disappeared. As I held onto the phone in shock, Beau went on to tell me that he missed me and he missed the kids and he wanted to come back home. I said nothing, but my mind was spinning. *Is it that easy?* I thought. *Just leave your family for three months and then come back when you decide you miss them?*

Beau talked about Judy and how it's just not what he thought it would be.

I found my voice and managed to tell him I was leaving. "The kids and I are going back home tomorrow," I said.

Beau responded by telling me that I didn't have to go running home. He said that he would come back, and we could work everything out

Running home! What the hell did he know? I was angry at his callousness, hurt by his cruelty, and saddened by his self-centeredness. Who was this person who walked away from his wife, his children, his life? I no longer recognize Beau Jaspers. And I no longer love him.

As Beau spit out his pathetic apology, I silently raged. When I could take no more, I exploded. I spoke through my clenched teeth and with the emotions of anger, pain, and sorrow. I wanted to hurt him, to tell him what he did to us. I wanted to hold the son of a bitch accountable for everything.

I asked Beau if he realized it has been an entire summer since he left. In that time, he never called, and he stole our money. "But guess what, Beau," I said. "We survived without you. In fact, we thrived." I told Beau that when he left me, he did me the biggest favor ever. He forced me to realize that I didn't need him. Now I don't want him. I no longer love him.

"Come home," I said. "Your stuff is here, but your family won't be." I told Beau that he could talk to Mr. Carey about a job, but not to expect one. I told him that I was filing for divorce when I got settled back home in West Virginia. I hung up the phone before he could say good-bye.

Afterward, I sat on the floor hugging my legs and crying while three little puppies jumped up into my hair, trying to lick my tears. That's when Hazel came in. She was nervous about tomorrow and wanted to know how I was holding up. When she saw my tears, she was instantly by my side, and I know she was there for me to confide in. She was sent to mother me, except I didn't want to talk about it. I only wanted to know one thing: "What is it that makes your coffee so good?" I asked.

"Oh that, it's just plain ol' Maxwell House in the big blue can, except I like to sprinkle cinnamon in the grounds and put a splash of vanilla in the bottom of the pot."

I couldn't help smiling from ear to ear. I just love Hazel and her simple creativity. "Let's go make a new life," I said as I leaned into her loving embrace.

"Lets!"

EDEN

But a bird that stalks down his narrow cage
Can seldom see through his bars of rage
His wings are clipped and his feet are tied
So he opens his throat to sing.

The caged Bird sings with a fearful trill
Of things unknown but longed for still
And his tune is heard on the distant hill
For the caged bird sings of freedom

"I Know Why the Caged Bird Sings" by Maya Angelou

September 13, 1999

Dear Mr. Richard Whiteman, Attorney at Law:

Am I to believe that you do not wish to file my petition of clemency? I do not know what else to think. I have not seen you in months, and every attempt I have made to contact you has been unsuccessful. Are you avoiding me? If this is the case, I am quite surprised. After all, I did make you a star, with the hard-earned weeks you spent seated at the defense table next to me, the crazy lady. How many times was your picture in the paper? How many news interviews did you give? Oh, you did look handsome and distinguished, decked out in your conservative navy suit, heavily starched white shirt, and red designer tie.

Now tell me, Richard, or may I call you Dick? Did your wife miss you during the long hours you spent on my case? Did your mistress? That was thoughtful of one of them to let me borrow an assortment of dresses to wear to court every day. They must have belonged to the wife, not the girlfriend, as they made me look like an old virgin. Or maybe you picked them up at a thrift store. Maybe you have a closet full of clothes to dress your criminals. Do you really think that by changing our look you can change our outcome? Maybe you can. It is true that man looks at the outside of a person and could basically give two shits about the person's heart and soul.

If I sound angry, it is because I am. I realize my case is not one for the appeals court. I not only confessed to killing my boyfriend, but I also called the police on myself. I guess I could use the circus that the media caused as an appeals defense, but that would only prolong the parade, and like all parades, this one too is obnoxious. I guess my only recourse is to plead to our rich, white, Republican governor that I am not a threat to society or to myself, and that although I shot my lover in the head while making love to him, I am not crazy, sadistic, or evil.

What I am is poor and broken, and that may have something to do with the reason why you, Mr. Richard Whiteman, have not come to see me. I understand that defending me was a job for you and the means to how you survive in your suburban housing development. At the time of my arrest and trial, though, I somehow came across the idea that you actually cared, that you felt some small sort of empathy and that you believed that people like me were the reason you had become a defense attorney. At least that's what you said.

What exactly did you mean when you said "people like me?" Did you mean poor people, or the downtrodden? Did you mean the lost, better known as losers? Did you mean the forgotten or the abused, the castaways, the victims? Did you mean women of domestic violence or grown-up foster kids or the offspring of mentally ill mothers? Did you mean bastard children who grew up fatherless? Did you mean people who have never owned a home or a decent car, people who work long days at mentally and physically grueling jobs and have never made more than $7.00 an hour? Did you mean welfare people, white trash, or rednecks or just people who have been handed shit for most of their lives? Do underdogs make you feel like a champion? If they do and if that's what you meant, I am all that and more. What I am not is a cold, brutal murderer. What I am is a survivor.

I am mostly guilty of believing that I had a right to survive, to protect my life, to live free from harm, and to escape my abuser by any means.

"To kill or to be killed; that is the question."

I understand the attention my case drew, the curiosity, repulsiveness, shock, horror, disbelief, and fascination that erupted. The public is intrigued by me, attracted and then disturbed by their attraction. I shock as well as titillate them. The media ate me alive.

"Inquiring minds want to know."

They devoured what was left of my painful existence. They used me, just as everyone else has used me, to shine a light and make known brutality, hate, anger, pain, passion, sex, sin, life, and hell, and nobody could look away. They read my story in the paper; they watched me on TV and talked about me on the radio.

I saw a sketch someone had drawn of me. My body was naked, my muscles ripped (as if they know), and I was straddling a wounded man. I had given the artist an excuse to dabble in the porn he had been craving to draw. An artist should know his subject, and the truth should reveal itself in the work. That's why I see the sketch as more porn and less art. First, the artist should know that I am ripped from a life of fighting, hard labor, and loose bowels, and instead of eating, I have smoked a pack of Marlboro Lights every day since the age of fourteen. None of that showed in the sketch. Instead, he drew me pretty.

It makes me wonder, if I were an ugly girl or a fat girl, would my case have been different? Did I deserve to be abused by a man because I'm what society views as *sexy*? Am I sexy because I killed him during sex?

I guess it doesn't matter, because whether I'm seen as sexy or crazy or evil or sane, nobody truly knows me. You, Mr. Whiteman, do not know me. I will tell you what you know, what they know. I will confess again.

Yes, I killed my lover, blew his brains all over our already dirty bedspread and pillow. I shot him in the back of the head while I screwed him, naked and on top. I screwed him during his apology, just like always. I screwed him straight-faced and passionately, just like I was supposed to.

That was the game that Ricky liked to play. He enjoyed beating me close to death, scaring me, bruising me, making me bleed and cry. He enjoyed calling me a whore and pulling my hair, kicking me, threatening me, and when he was finished and I was a battered mess, he enjoyed whispering, "I love you" in my ear, wiping up my blood and tears, and kissing my bruised lips. Always he cried, big sobbing tears, shaking as he held me, making me promise not to leave. Suddenly he was the victim, unstable and scared, begging for reassurance, pleading for my body, my heart, my life, and my soul. He had to have me; he would die without me; he would kill for me. He may have to kill us both, homicide, suicide. Ricky loved the romantic notion of doing us both in.

Hours after the beatings and minutes after the confessions of suicidal and homicidal thoughts, Ricky would want me, all of me. He would want my ripped clothing stripped all the way off, my cold and stiff body lying upon him, my shaken legs and bruised arms opened and inviting. Although I was still nothing more than a puppet, following the orders of my master, a moment would occur when I would feel Ricky go weak underneath me, putty in my hands, so to speak.

It was then that his mouth would slowly gap open and he would let out a small, struggling moan, and I could watch his eyes roll back into his head and see his defenses slip to the other side of his brain, far out of reach. It was during this climaxing time that I was able to lean forward onto Ricky in a hugging embrace and slip my hand under our bed pillow. I had done this very same move many times before and many more times in my head.

I had often fantasized about killing Ricky while I screwed him; however, the scenario never really seemed possible. It was far-fetched, one might say. Usually my fantasies led to Ricky reading my mind and coming out of his ejaculating trance, grabbing my cold, bruised arms, and shaking me like a rag doll while laughing hysterically at my weak effort. Sometimes in my fantasy, when I reached for the small metallic piece that Ricky kept under his bed pillow, Ricky got to it first. There were times in my fantasy when during the attempt to kill Ricky, the bullet lodged in the pillow and Ricky beat me for my murderous intent. "*Thou shall not kill.*"

Mostly, though, my fantasy was a vision of me missing my target. In my mind's eye, I could see myself lean forward and allow my breasts to brush Ricky's skin, my stringy and dingy hair to fall in his face, my breath to suck him up, like a cat on an infant. It was then I would slip my hand under the pillow, finger the cold steel, and blindly shoot through a mass of fluff. I imagined that the speeding bullet would come straight through our bed pillow, whistling past Ricky's ear and land in the center of my own skull, creating a hole between my eyes. This fantasy seemed the most realistic to me and came to me often, in our angry bed.

Even so, there was always the slim chance that I could shoot Ricky. It was this hope that I clung to. Maybe, just maybe, I could survive this life, and if not, so be it. If it was to be my end, then it was my destiny. Who knows? I may have been created so Ricky Adkins could have something to destroy. Maybe I was supposed to die young, to be abused. For abuse to exist, somebody has to live it. Maybe I am some sacrificial lamb, and if I endure all my beatings and hardship, I will be let into heaven and be given a seat at the right hand of Jesus, never to be hurt again. Or maybe my escape from hell on earth was to kill my Satan, put him out of his misery and put me out of mine. The answer to this riddle was not going to be decided by me. I had given it to God, or rather God had given it to me, with the ending already decided. I knew what I had to do, pull the trigger and "*what is, IS.*"

I remember watching the pool of scarlet expand across the pillow from underneath Ricky's head. I remember letting go of the gun and slowly pulling my arms out from underneath Ricky, my hands red with his blood that had already seeped through. I remember the intense quiet and calm of the once-angry room, and then I remember sound coming back to me, one noise at a time. First, I heard a dog bark, and then the sound of voices outside enjoying the warm afternoon, next a car, and then a crying child. Soon the noises intertwined back into normalcy, but still I sat naked and numbed, Ricky still inside me.

I can remember looking toward the window with an overwhelming feeling of nothingness. I remember focusing on the window and noticing all the paint chips that sat on the cracked sill. I noticed the dirtiness of the glass pane and the ugliness of the metal frame. I'm not sure how long I was on top of Ricky, looking out the window. I do know that I have heard of people disassociating themselves in times of traumatic events, and I imagine that may be why I was thinking, "I bet those chips are lead paint. It's a good thing Ricky and I don't have any toddlers."

At some time I climbed off my dead boyfriend, put on a robe, and called the police. The officers who came to the house were the same officers that had been at the house earlier that day, after Ricky had shut me in the bathroom, leaned up against the door, and enjoyed my panic. The two intimidating men had been firm with Ricky, warning him against scaring his girlfriend, threatening kidnapping charges if they were to come out here again.

"You cannot hold her against her will," they said. "If she wants to leave, she can leave." Ricky assured them he was just teasing, I didn't want to leave, we were only playing a game, and he got a little carried away and scared me. He meant no harm; it wouldn't happen again. As he explained, I sat silent. I think I may have smiled once or twice, a hidden gesture begging them to take him, and maybe this time while he was in custody, I could run for good. Maybe this time he wouldn't find me when I left. Maybe this time I could think of a really good hiding place for myself and then maybe a cloud would burst open and money would drop into my lap and I could get really far away and start a new life.

Instead, though, the officers left. Ricky was really angry at me then, for getting him scolded like that by those two big assholes, so he beat me until he found me sexy and then apologized sweetly for both incidences and begged for my love. As soon as those pigs walked away and Ricky's fist hit my face, I knew this was my life. When I climbed, broken and sore, on top of his erection, I knew he would never let me leave him, and if I tried, he would indeed hunt me down and kill me, like he always promised.

The second time the cops came, everything was surreal. There were more people, many more. Different navy-colored uniforms marched past me as I sat silently in a chair smoking a cigarette. Some of the uniforms were not police officers but paramedics. Sirens blared out my window as cruisers and ambulances lined up in front of my home. I must have looked a mess, because all the people who passed by me had the look of horror and disbelief on their faces. I'm sure Ricky's blood had saturated my skin, and my earlier beating had caused much of my face to swell and turn purple. I do remember telling them that I shot Ricky. I remember my voice sounding flat, absent of emotion. Before the officer took me in, I remember putting on a pair of gray sweat pants and a black sweatshirt, and I remember being cold. I remember walking out of my home past the crowd of gawking neighbors, catching bits of words and the sentence, "I knew somebody was going to die in that house; I just always thought it was going to be her."

I lowered my head into the back of a cruiser and was taken to the county jail. I had stopped talking, after my one-sentence confession, and just took orders. My fingerprints were taken and then my picture, but since I was silent, they gave up trying to talk to me and just let me sleep. I slept black; that is the only description I have for my dreamless sleep. When I woke, I met you.

I apologize for the length of time it took for you to pull the events from me, and I realize that even now, I am revealing things that you have been unaware of. You spent months trying to investigate my stories of domestic violence and find a justification in my taking a life. I remember your talks on my defense in regard to battered-woman syndrome. You said it would be difficult for the jury to understand why I just didn't leave, considering that I was not married to Ricky and we had no children together. With little help from me, your client, the silent murderous vamp, as I was being referred to, you came up with "not guilty by reason of insanity." I guess it was the best you could do.

Insane? Was I insane? I had to be; I had just killed a man, my man. I thought I was only protecting myself. It was self-defense; however, we were having sex, and since self-defense means the victim can use only as much force as the abuser, I would have had to fuck him to death. No, insanity was the way to go, except for the fact that it had been my sanest moment in a very long time.

I couldn't have been sane when I fell in love with him. How could I fall in love with an abuser? That's a crazy thing to do, isn't it? I mean, it's probably more sane to kill someone you believe may one day kill you than it is to embrace someone you believe may one day kill you. Which makes me wonder why falling in love with Ricky was so much easier than killing him. Are we animals or not? How strong is our need to survive? Evidently not as strong as our need for love.

I could have killed Ricky when my mother wanted to. Oh, I bet I surprised you with that one—more evidence of a premeditated murder. It's another fact to be piled on the list of facts that proves I am evil. If life were only that easy, Counselor. If you could actually read people by the facts presented. The problem with that concept is the facts are fucking irrelevant.

Back to my mother. Yes, my mother wanted to kill Ricky. It was shortly after I began dating him, shortly after I had turned eighteen years old and graduated from high school and foster care. That's right, foster kids graduate. It is their rite of passage. Mind you, they are not given a ceremony or party, and they do not have pictures taken in fields of flowers and pass them out to old foster families. Their only diploma is tightly wound with black ribbon and attached to their soul. It bears their course of study and all that they have learned. With that diploma and a shout of "Good luck," they venture out to live as independent adults. I found my mother quite easily and tried to rebuild our state-demolished relationship.

It was after my first beating from Ricky that my mother talked of killing or injuring him. Ricky had given me a black eye for flirting with his friend, but it was okay, because after giving me my first black eye, he gave me my first orgasm, so of course I forgave him. An orgasm is a powerful thing, you know.

My mother saw my eye as I came in the back door of the apartment we shared, and she went fucking ballistic, shouting, "That no good son of bitch better never touch you again."

When I tried to calm her down by saying, "Ricky didn't mean it. He is sorry. He loves me. I know, because he cried delicious tears and we made beautiful love and he promised never to hurt me again."

With that, my mother became more furious. "He ought to have his penis cut off!" She screamed. "That's it!" she exclaimed with newfound excitement. "Let's do it, Eden. Let's cut off his dick and toss it to the wind. We need to pull a Lorena Bobbitt."

My mother loved Lorena Bobbitt. She admired her courage and spunk. In my mother's eyes, Lorena was a hero, a champion, a liberator for all women, the Gloria Steinem of rednecks.

"I don't want to cut off his penis," I admitted to my excited mother, but she didn't hear me, and she continued with her best-laid plans.

When it became clear to her that I did not want to cut off my boyfriend's dick, she got angry again and screamed at me, "You're not going to see that boy again! Not fucking ever! I know beatings, Eden. I was fucking raised on beatings, and once they begin, they never end."

Needless to say, I didn't listen to my mother. After all, she didn't care enough to raise me. For all she knew, I could have been receiving beatings all along by the numerous foster families that housed me over the years.

When I left my mother's house to shack up with Ricky, she vowed never to speak to me again, and she kept her promise until the day that I killed him. After that, I was her hero. I had done one better than Lorena. I had shot my lover's brains out while screwing him. How cool is that?

In the beginning of my relationship with Ricky, I couldn't have taken my mother's advice or anybody else's, for that matter. I was the only person who understood Ricky, who empathized with his rages and knew his fears. Ricky was a beautiful broken boy from an ugly broken home, and he had learned to hit from his mean, abusive father. Ricky was not his father, though, and I was not my mother, and we were going to live a nice life in a nice neighborhood and pay our bills and go camping and grow a garden and sleep naked wrapped around each other and not hit each other or yell or lose our children to foster care or take too many prescription pills. The only dream we ever achieved was to sleep naked.

Three months went by before Ricky hit me again, and I did leave him. I got my own apartment and settled into a job waiting tables at night. Ricky wouldn't leave me alone, though. He hung out at my work and would be sitting on my apartment stoop when I got home. He sent flowers and love notes and dedicated songs to me. Since he was drop-your-pants good looking, and all the other waitresses thought I was crazy for not accepting his advances, I slowly lost my anger and mistrust. Day by day, he charmed it away. When I finally did go back, it was because he convinced me that I truly and completely loved and needed him and that he truly and completely loved me. The idea of love seemed nice, because it was something I had never known before.

A year after we reunited, the beatings began again, and they all kind of run together. The police were called, reports were made, and sometimes Ricky even had to go to jail. Many times I ran and hid, usually with a friend or at a shelter. Once I went to my crazy aunt's house, and after two days there, I decided I'd rather be on the streets. Always, Ricky found me. Eventually, I stopped running. It was easier just to take the beating, the sickening sweet apologies that came after, and then the detached sex. I had become Ricky's marionette, his slave, his possession. Ricky owned me and controlled me. It was as if my soul had morphed into his being, and I no longer belonged to myself. We were one, and if I left him, he would surely die, as he often told me. Riveting in that crazy fear of his, he had made a promise to kill me, and I believed him. Ricky and I were together for seven years. It was my longest relationship.

My mother had me for the first two years of my life, just her and me. Peggy was young, just seventeen when I was born. She was much too pretty for the life she had been given. She left the house of her insane parents, which consisted of a sickly mother, who died sometime after I was born; a crazy stepfather (now there's a story I'll get to); and a sister, my Aunt Paula, whom my mother hates. Those three individuals are all I know of my mother's family. According to Peggy, I have no father.

My deceased grandmother, her nasty husband, and my mom's sister were extreme, fanatical, religious nuts and believed my poor mother was carrying demon spawn. How mean of Satan! Peggy Devine, my mother, was a little whore and needed to repent for her sins. Once Peggy confessed her pregnancy, she was severely beaten and then locked in a room by her deranged family, with strict instructions to repent. Instead of praying for forgiveness, she packed her clothes into a pillowcase, took all the money that Paula had hoarded throughout the years, and climbed out of her bedroom window. She stayed with friends until she found a dirty studio apartment for the two of us, which she rented from an equally dirty landlord who asked no questions, but needed weekly payments made in cash.

She got through her pregnancy okay with no medical care and showed up at the hospital emergency room once I decided to torture her with my birth. Although the nurses and doctor tried like hell to convince my mother to give up her baby girl for adoption, she resisted. She had already fallen in love with me, and since she had nobody else, she embraced my birth. Peggy's first task as a mother was to name me, which she did with deep thought and poetic contemplation, so I am Eden Christine Devine, a name that the media ate like sprinkles on a cake, which added much melodrama to my drama.

I know that in the beginning of my life, my mother did love me, and I know that her intentions were good. Since my mom was only seventeen, she had to lie about her age to work the strip bars that paid our bills. My mom made it clear when she told me this story that she never danced at that time. Her job was to check IDs at the door, although nobody had checked hers. Eventually she began bartending. It was working out great. I was a good baby, and all she needed to do was lay me down at night with a clean diaper, a full bottle, and an old radio on low, and I was more than happy to put myself to sleep, allowing her to go to work at night.

At 4:00 a.m. when my mother came in, she would pluck me out of bed, change my diaper, and lay me down with her for the rest of my sleep. If we were snuggled up close together, I would let her sleep in until 10:00 a.m. We would lazily play the rest of the morning and afternoon away, eating dry Cheerios out of the box, my favorite and sometimes her only food. At 3:00 p.m. every day—like clockwork, was how she described it—we curled back up together and took a two-hour nap, such a good baby. By 10:00 p.m., my mother put me down for the night after a warm bath and a warm bottle, and I was happy to let her go to work and be content in my hand-me-down crib. Content, that was, until the night I got sick with diarrhea and a really high fever. I screamed and cried until a neighbor called the police and I was found alone in my crib, hot and smelly.

What pissed my mom off most was the fact that I had shit straight through my diaper. It covered my sheets, and I had gotten it on my hands and the crib rails, and it made me look much more neglected than I actually was. "You never had diaper rash," my mother told me. "Not once. I always changed your fucking diaper, even if it cost me my smokes for the week. Stupid-ass Children's Services acted like I allowed you to live in your shit."

After three years of jumping through hoops, my mother got me back, only to lose me again four years later; however, that time it was not for leaving me alone, but rather for having me with her. Ironic, isn't it?

My mother's fear of Children's Services and anyone else who could take her child was extreme and intense, and she carted me in the back seat of the car everywhere she went. It was not very rational, since leaving a child in the back seat of a car for periods at a time is still leaving the child alone, except not in my mother's brain. Once again, I pleased her with being content enough just to sit.

To her credit, on the nights my mom worked, she tried like hell to find a babysitter. Usually some of the dancers' kids and I were entertained in the evenings by the same person; however, if she couldn't find someone, the car would be piled with toys, books, a pillow, and blanket. My mother would remind me to keep my head down low, and she would run out every hour to check on me, usually bringing me chips or chicken fingers.

There was only one time, in all the time spent alone in the car, that I ever had a problem, and I mostly blame myself. I never should have opened the door for that drunken, horny man that was peering in at me, but I must have been lonely and maybe didn't see or know the danger. I can remember that his breath smelled of beer and his body like cigarettes, but I was used to those smells and never knew them as unpleasant. His hands were smooth, his nails round and clean, and he was immaculately groomed, compared to all the other men I had ever seen. He spoke sweetly to me, and I let him play with my toys. We talked and played for quite a while before he began touching me. When he did, I knew it was wrong, and that if I could only open my mouth to ask him to stop, he would, but this little sinister part of me liked it, enjoyed the affection and the touch and the soft words he spoke, and I imagined he was my daddy. When he was finished and he had come on my stomach, I remember calmly asking him, "What's that?"

My words snapped his mind back to reality, because the once-silent child spoke her innocence. It was then that his hands began to shake and he began muttering and begging me to forgive him. I felt sorry for him, as big tears ran down his face and he tugged at his pants. Once they were up, he leapt from our car and ran crying into the parking lot. It was then all my energy stopped tending to my own emotions and went leaping after my molester.

"Dear unbelievable God, I have just been given a revelation.

Thank You, Saint John the Devine. I have been enlightened."

Dear Mr. Whiteman, do you see it? Do you see Ricky in my molester? Do you see my molester in Ricky? And how did my daddy get in there? But that's it; I'm sure of it. It is the nature of my attraction. Take from me, hurt me, strip me clean, degrade me, devour me, scare me, and then cry and apologize, and I will love you forever.

Sick, aren't I? Absolutely sick. But proud, proud of myself for figuring that one out. I don't think a therapist could have done a better job of recognition and analogy. I am just totally floored by my own reality. Now all I have to do is work through it. Ha- ha!

I never told my mother about the sexual encounter with the strange man. If I had, she would have hunted him down and killed him for sure. Instead I kept quiet, and she kept lugging me around with her. One night, after she had a few too many vodka and cranberry drinks and we were on our way home to cuddle up together so she could sleep it off, she turned the wrong way down one of the many one-way streets that made up our area and slammed into another car. Nobody was hurt, but my mother was charged with drunk driving and child endangerment, and I was taken back to Children's Services, where I still had an active file.

They never let my mother have me again, and after a while, she stopped fighting for me and started dancing. I'm sure dancing was less painful, because the man who owned the club made sure to give her just enough cocaine to numb her, and on her days off, she found another escape hidden within prescription pills. Instead of the constant worry of a burdensome child, she could twirl up against a pole, a dizzying game that I imagine could be fun to play, especially with the right tiny, tight outfit and hot lights on her bare skin and men with adoring eyes caught in her trance. It would be much easier to do than to fight the evil and vindictive warriors that make up the Children's Welfare Agency.

After my mother stopped fighting for me, Aunt Paula started, and for two and a half years, I was placed in her home. My mother had already informed the courts that her sister was crazy, but Paula had made a good enough impression and my mother had made a bad enough impression that the court allowed me to go live with Aunt Paula. They soon found out that my mother was right.

After winning custody, Aunt Paula and Uncle Sherman had to cleanse me. Since I was born a sinner from a sinner, they must have dunked my head ten times into that cold lake. They also spent countless hours trying to teach me Bible verses and songs. I could not learn the Bible. It was mostly the pronunciations that stumped me, with mixing of the letters, the way they stood next to each other, out of any common sequence. The made-up names were foreign and unpronounceable, and the stories didn't make sense either, or the numbers that were counted. Everything took so damn long, and everyone was so old, yet it only took seven days to create the world and everything God made in it. I could not grasp such a concept, and because of that, Uncle Sherman and Aunt Paula felt that I must be retarded. It made perfect sense to them, since my mother was such a horrible sinner and I was her curse.

My days at Aunt Paula's and Uncle Sherman's were spent working, praying, or reading, and if I was not being asked to do one of those, you could find me out in the barren yard, counting the dandelion heads that grew across the street. I used to think, *Why is it that the mean old neighbors got all the pretty little yellow buds to spread across their lawn, while we just have a dirt patch out our front door? Life really wasn't fair.*

There were no other books to read at Aunt Paula's except the

Bible. It killed me. I was nine years old and an early reader, and I had just discovered the joy of living inside books. The Bible is a very scary book to live in, so I began writing my own stories in spiral notebooks that I carried with me everywhere and hid at night. There was always the fear of Uncle Sherman taking my notebooks and destroying them, which he did twice, ripping the pages out and burning them one by one as he preached about damnation. I cried wicked tears of hate and silently cursed him. Uncle Sherman stopped when my third grade teacher, Mrs. Whitaker, called Aunt Paula in for a conference and told her she thought I was gifted and that it was important for my gift to be inspired and I should be encouraged to write and read. Aunt Paula took it as a sign from God and bought me a new notebook and a whole bag of Bic pens.

The things that were fun to read at Aunt Paula's and Uncle Sherman's were the bumper stickers that held their car together. Jesus Saves was in big blue letters on a white background; He Lives was on another one; Jesus is my Savior, God is Word was another, and my very favorite sticker was 1 Cross + 3 Nails = 4 Given. I tried to make up my own sayings and write them out in my new notebook. These writings or quotes I would share with my aunt and uncle, who would swallow my words like candy and then shit out a bumper sticker to sell for a dollar.

During the two years I lived with Sherman and Paula, I was given a new guardian ad litem. My prior one got pregnant, had a baby, and then decided that foster kids depressed her and she would rather block it all out and be a stay-at-home mother. That was okay, because my new guardian ad litem was actually a guardian angel who had come to rescue me from the Jesus nuts. Vanessa was her name, and she was beautiful and sweet. She dressed in flowing skirts with T-shirts and sandals. She had a rose tattoo on her ankle. Her curly blond hair was wild and bigger than her skinny waist and tiny frame. She was flat-chested without obnoxious boobs, and she hung beads from her neck. Vanessa drove a small blue car that was always messy on the inside, with paperwork, food wrappers, and lots of music tapes. With Vanessa I developed my first girl crush.

Vanessa came more often than my previous guardian. She studied us closer, our home, our lives. She asked more questions and seemed more intrigued, than anything else, by our dynamics. Vanessa had a hard time hiding her dislikes or displeasures. Many times her nose would wrinkle up or her brow would narrow at some remark, gesture, or story. Most always, her eyes held tears. Vanessa was much too sensitive for the job she had been given, or maybe she was just sensitive enough.

I could tell she didn't care much for Jesus, because every time he was mentioned, a little sound escaped her lips, like a tiny sigh or an almost silent gasp. Sometimes she involuntarily rubbed her forehead, like the word *Jesus* brought forth some throbbing ache to her temple. I could also tell that she didn't like Uncle Sherman, or maybe he just grossed her out. Vanessa watched Uncle Sherman as one might watch a spider crawl across the ceiling, too far away for vigilant action, so you just sit and observe, wishing only that it would fall, so you could smash it with your shoe.

Uncle Sherman knew Vanessa didn't trust him or his preaching, and in return he gave the mistrust back. "Don't tell that woman anything," he would say to Aunt Paula and me. "She is seated at the right hand of the devil. She wants nothing more than to break up our holy home."

I didn't believe Vanessa wanted to break up holy homes any more than I believed our home was holy, so against Uncle Sherman's advice, I told her everything. I told her about the nightly bedtime rituals of prayer and cleansing. We washed our bodies every evening with scalding hot water, Ivory soap, and scrub brushes. Sometimes at night I could hear Aunt Paula in the bathroom doing a second cleansing.

"Cleanliness is next to Godliness."

We kept our house clean, too. Floors and walls were wiped down daily with bleach water. Aunt Paula's hands were reflections of harsh abuse, and although everything was always cleansed, nothing was ever fixed. I scrubbed cabinets that had no handles and walls that were cracked. I swept floors and porches full of loose boards and raked a dirt lawn. We never planted grass or flowers. We never painted or used a screwdriver or hammer to fix the endless number of things that needed repaired.

I told Vanessa that Uncle Sherman had the gift of tongues and talked in gibberish while he scrubbed himself. I also told Vanessa that Uncle Sherman would get rid of or kill all of Aunt Paula's pets, which I didn't believe was very Christian-like. Aunt Paula was a collector of stray animals, some lost little creature whose bad luck led him into our barren yard and across our path, only to be scooped up by a sweet childlike Paula. Paula's voice had the same sing-song tone of an eight-year-old child. Aunt Paula was mentally young. She was naive, meek, and mild, and she thought like a young virgin, yet she had lots of loud, moaning, thank-you-Jesus sex with Uncle Sherman, after which they both needed to scrub.

Aunt Paula happened upon her assortment of strays like any other collector. She would find an injured kitten just as one might recognize a rare coin or spot a starved and abused puppy, like the discovery of a pretty stone. Paula also took in turtles and toads, and her specialty was flightless birds. She built them hospital beds from discarded boxes or coffee cans. She cooed them back to good health, snuggled and loved them. And anytime she and I were out, maybe to the store or a church evening with the ladies, an animal disappeared. Sick birds just happened to take miraculous flight. Contented dogs and cats suddenly decided to run from our home. Turtles, toads, and snakes escaped from their cages and went back into the wild. Sometimes we would come home and a healthy, happy pet had mysteriously died.

I always suspected that Uncle Sherman was the culprit, and I desperately tried to explain to poor, simple Aunt Paula that it was not her fault. She always took each incident as a personal injury. "Isn't it strange," I would say to Aunt Paula, "how the animals run away or die only when you and I are out together and Uncle Sherman is the only one home?"

Aunt Paula would just look past me, and in her little girlish voice, she would say, "It is in the plan of my Lord." Since there was no reasoning with Aunt Paula, I told Vanessa, and she agreed it was indeed a strange coincidence.

Vanessa always took lots of notes when she and I were alone and talking, and I loved to watch her write. Sometimes I would elaborate my stories, just so I could see her hands dance across the paper. A black river of words flowed onto the yellow tablet. It was a winding stream of script artfully drawn by beautiful hands.

Each of Vanessa's fingers was wrapped with a silver ring and her nails were bitten short and kept clean. My favorite was her pointer finger that sat proudly perched on the point of her pen. Her pointer finger was always being hugged by a ring of children, hand in hand, connected as one might cut out paper. To me, this circle of children that Vanessa wore on her finger was her crown, and Vanessa was the children's queen. She was our savior and not our guardian ad litem, but rather our guardian angel, and out of all the children she was called on to protect, I think she loved me best.

Vanessa always wanted to walk from our dirt yard and our sterile, broken house to the park that was three blocks away. At the park was a high metal slide that I called the snake. I would climb its steep steps into the clouds and carefully sit myself on the hot, shiny incline. The sun reflected off the high silver skin of the long serpent. The snake slide gradually absorbed the rays, selfishly soaking up the heat of the day, and then, so as not to burst into silver flame or melt into a metal pool of liquid, the serpent slide slowly released the heat back into the atmosphere by scorching the legs of the young riders. I was cleverer than the snake, and I knew to bend my knees and take the heat only through my thick bottom and tough feet. I would ride the slide over and over as Vanessa sat under the shade of a tree, watching.

After mastering the snake and its attempt to burn me, I would join Vanessa under the tree and share my writings with her. Vanessa loved my stories, and she sat as content and excited as a child, her knees crossed underneath her long skirt with her bare feet proudly showing, her sandals abandoned in the grass. In between the pages of bumper-sticker quotes, I wrote about a fantasy land, a story of fairies and elves with tulip homes and lily boats and transportation by dragonflies. I wrote innocently of beauty. I described flower tops and cattails seen from the eyes of a pixie. I wrote of bliss, peace, love, and the song of the wind and of dancing blades of grass. In every story, though, my beautiful utopia turned murderously scary.

A heavy rain could drown an elf in seconds and crush the homes of any survivors or flood and dirty a once-calm and mellow river and carry a loved one off downstream. A pixie could be eaten alive, bit by bit, by an angry tobacco-spitting grasshopper or be carried off by a bird. To a pixie or an elf, a trout was a shark, and a praying mantis, God forbid, was a Tyrannosaurus Rex. Vanessa delighted in my stories. She always clapped during a heroic save or hummed sweetly during a calm river bed ride in a leaf canoe. She giggled and smiled at the sound of my young voice trying desperately to speak as an artist, and always she cried at the end.

I could always tell that Vanessa was looking for something in my stories, something valid and significant, something she expected to hear and would be able to connect from my fantasy to my reality. I wasn't sure at the time what she was looking for; I just knew she was growing impatient in not having found it yet. Finally Vanessa began to ask me the questions that had kept her up at night. "Has Uncle Sherman ever touched you?"

"Yes," I told her, and then I explained with innocence that he touched me all the time. We were required as a family to join hands in a circle of prayer before each meal and at bedtime, but that was not the answer Vanessa was searching for, so she pressed on.

It finally occurred to my eleven-year-old brain that Vanessa wanted to know if Uncle Sherman was trying to have sex with me. It was then that I told Vanessa that Uncle Sherman had never tried that yet, but she shouldn't worry, because my mother had already informed me about Uncle Sherman and how he wouldn't come after me until I had grown breasts and hair between my legs. At the rate I was growing, I figured I had a few more years, but I would be ready when he did come for me. I would not give him sex, like my mother had to. I would fight him off. As I calmly explained this information to my lovely guardian angel, her face grimaced and contorted as it did when she was given alarming news. She rubbed her temple with her lovely ringed fingers as she tried to put jagged pieces together. Vanessa rubbed her throbbing head with her two perfect hands, and I knew I had to explain our twisted family tree.

Uncle Sherman had once married my grandmother, long before. She had met him at a tent revival, and he had saved her soul. My grandmother was also a sinner and whore, because she had two daughters and no husband. Uncle Sherman brought my grandmother to the Lord, and she followed him everywhere he preached, my mom and Aunt Paula in tow. After my grandmother and Uncle Sherman married, my grandmother became sick, and after years of sickness, she died. It was after my mother had left her home to have me, and after my grandmother had already died, that Uncle Sherman and Aunt Paula fell in love, and then they were married.

Vanessa stood in shock as I spoon-fed her the garbage she had been searching for. She grabbed my hands and immediately we trotted back to my house. All the while, she mumbled to herself as if she were rehearsing a part in a play. When we reached home, she asked me to go out to the back yard so she could talk to my aunt and uncle. It wasn't long before I heard the angered shouts of Uncle Sherman, and I trembled with fear, because I somehow knew I had let out our vile little secret.

How dare Vanessa question Uncle Sherman's integrity? He was not going to tolerate a non-Christian woman placing judgment on him and his wife. Uncle Sherman denied that he had committed an immorality, let alone a crime, by loving Paula. His wife, Marlene, had died a terrible death, and he had grieved a terrible loss. Paula had grieved the same loss for the same woman. In the process of grieving together, they had healed one another. They found a love given to them by God (with the sacrifice of Marlene, that is). Sherman explained that many people married again after the death of a spouse. Paula was not his blood child. She was Marlene's child who had grown into a woman by the time of Marlene's death. No crime was committed. "For God's sake," Sherman shouted, "look at Woody Allen. And his wife didn't even die." Uncle Sherman's rant was so loud and vociferous that I was able to creep into the back door and watch the drama unravel in the front room. "If you think, you're going to take my child away from me, lady, you got another thing coming."

"She's not your child," Vanessa retorted. "She's is your niece," and before she could finish her sentence, a moment of clarity billowed down and settled in her head. Vanessa looked past Uncle Sherman to me, a skinny, frail, eleven-year-old girl, trembling in our rundown but clean kitchen, and then in an angry and cold voice, she asked, "Or is she your child?"

A deafening silence filled our house, and it was broken only when Aunt Paula covered her face and cried out loud. Vanessa had made her discovery. She had found the lost piece to the jumbled jigsaw puzzle and had fit it all together to reveal an image far more disturbing than she had imagined.

Vanessa filed an emergency order to have me removed from Aunt Paula's and Uncle—I mean Grandpa's—I mean Daddy's—house. Vanessa tried but failed at having Sherman put in jail for the rape of my mother, who would not cooperate. Why should she? The same agency that wanted to protect me could not have cared less about my mother. Where was Children's Protective Services when she, as a child, lay underneath her crazy stepfather as he heatedly pumped himself into her tiny frame while mumbling in tongues? What had Children's Services ever done for her? That is, except steal her baby, her only loved one, and refuse to give her back. "Fuck you, Vanessa!" is what Peggy said to that blond bubble-headed, idealistic bitch. "Fuck you and fuck Children's Protective Services."

I thought that was okay, because if I could not live with my mother or Aunt Paula, the only women in my life, I knew I was going to live with Vanessa. Vanessa, my beautiful, sweet, artistic, loyal, guardian angel.

We both know that's not what happened, though. Vanessa could not have raised me anymore than she could have raised the moon. Our intimate connection existed only because it was her job. The understanding of those two facts hurt me more than the realization that I was the illegitimate offspring of an incestuous child abuser. By the time I entered the sixth grade, I had begun another stretch of foster homes.

Brenda and Brian McNabb were nice enough people, for foster parents, that is. In a way, Brenda reminded me of Aunt Paula. Her voice was light and somewhat whiny, and her looks were pleasant yet plain and simple. Brian was just a male version of Brenda. Neither Brenda nor Brian worked. Both were too sickly for full-time employment, but healthy enough to take on the emotional stress and physical demands of foster children. Although Brenda and Brian appeared to be physically healthy individuals, their dinnertime conversations consisted of a litany of ailments, symptoms, medications, and diagnoses. We kids would quietly pass the peas and carrots around the table while listening to the vulgar descriptions of words and phrases such as colonoscopy, Crohn's Disease, gout, hemorrhoids, irritable bowel syndrome, ulcers, headaches, constipation, diarrhea, GERDS, bulging discs, panic attacks, and fibromyalgia.

Brenda and Brian were not the only ones affected by poor health. The children who were kept close to them also exhibited signs of physical distress. Their own two kids, Mickey and Tara, suffered from asthma as well as allergies to everything. Then there were the three foster kids, me included, that came with our own assortment of baggage. Some of us were physical wrecks, others more mental. Of course, we all had ADD (attention deficit disorder), ODD (oppositional defiant disorder), and LD (learning disabled). Because of these labels, our poor health, and the fact that we were foster kids in the system, Brenda and Brian were loaded down with meetings and appointments. We traveled from school to doctor's office to shrink to counselor and home again on any ordinary day. You would think that all this running and stress would have been the death of the unhealthy McNabbs. On the contrary, they marveled at our acute symptoms, analyzed their core, and fought like mad for our treatment. I am convinced that Brenda and Brian McNabb were deeply in love with the constitution of institutions. The McNabbs always arrived ten minutes early for every appointment. They were dressed appropriately and carried with them a tablet, pen, and a crammed-down education from the night before. They were a well-equipped couple bearing thought-out answers and appropriate questions for each professional seated across from them. In fact, the worst part of life with the McNabbs was their attentiveness.

At a time when I just wanted to dissolve inside myself and feel nothing, I was being forced to know my body. As it turned out, I was a very sick bird. I started my menstrual cycle that year and soon realized that I had been cursed. This curse came with irregular bleeding as well as cramping, backaches, PMS, post PMS, PMDD, and endometriosis, all of which Brenda diagnosed, of course. Even on days when my flow was light and I felt fine, I was encouraged to place a pillow on my stomach and fold myself in half or place a heating pad on my back and miss school and eat Midol. After I lived a little more than a year in the McNabb household, my placement was changed, although I am unsure as to why. I do know that my health, mental capabilities, and menstrual cycle improved dramatically after that year.

My second placement was in the home of Tonya White, who was actually black. There was no Mr. White in the home or any men, just Tonya and all her kids. Deshawn, Tonya's son, was my age, thirteen. Her twin girls, Tierra and Sierra, who everybody called T.T. and C.C., were nine years old. Tonya was also the foster mother to Kianna, a fifteen-year-old black girl, and Jordan, Kianna's baby boy. Besides us, Tonya did emergency placement, which was when a child was abruptly ripped from a home and brought to Tonya's for a night or more. Between Tonya's kids, their friends, her foster kids and their friends, her neighbors, her church, and her family, Tonya White's house was always full, and I was usually the only white person in the White household.

I had always been a non-participant, wherever I was. At Tonya's house that role was magnified. Being a minority made me become quieter and more observant. I watched the hectic household disentangle every day. There was so much energy in Tonya's house, so much volume, so much life that it was vastly different from any home I had ever been in.

When I had lived with my mother, she and I were quiet and content in our still home. After sleepless nights apart, we spent our days wrapped around each other in a blanket, eating out of boxes and watching fuzzy TV. We existed like rabbits in a burrow.

Sherman and Paula's place was also quiet, except for the occasional rant on redemption and sin. Even the McNabbs, with a full house and a full agenda, seemed relatively quiet in comparison to Tonya's house. Tonya's home was booming. It was always filled to the maximum capacity. It was always lively; it was always loud. Everything seemed larger in Tonya's house. Conversations bounced off the walls in laughter and shouts, music vibrated the floorboards, meals were feasts, and get-togethers were parties. I never knew one person could have so many people fill his or her life and home.

The ladies, Tonya's sisters, some of them related and some of them just "sisters," usually hung out in the kitchen. That was the place to fix hair, paint nails, and gossip. Before being a foster mom, Tonya had been a full-time beautician. When I was there, she worked her gift out of her kitchen. Kids made up the rest of the house. Kianna had set up Jordan in the living room with a playpen, bouncy seat, and swing. From there she ruled the television, Jerry Springer being another loud thing in Tonya's house. T.T. and C.C. mostly hung out in their bedroom or back yard with their friends, learning the newest dances and making up songs. They were really good performers, and I enjoyed watching them. Deshawn and his buddies took over the front porch and front yard. There was usually a basketball game in the driveway and double Dutch in the street out front. I stayed out of the way. Like a chameleon, I could blend into my surroundings and watch. I became the most exquisite observer. Tonya allowed me this freedom, and I suppose, just as I thought that all black people were loud, she believed that all little white girls were shy and quiet.

After a while, I became accustomed to the noise, and later, I delighted in it. Slowly I began to participate. In Tonya White's house, I learned how to dance. I learned how to laugh and get a joke. I learned how to cook soul food and eat more than three bites without my stomach cramping. I learned to work through my menstrual cycle and smoke cigarettes and take the bus. I learned how to fight and stick up for myself and for others. I learned how to change a baby's diaper and argue without crying. I learned what a family was. I learned how to love.

I would have stayed with Tonya White forever. I would have made her happy and proud, showing her each report card with a glowing smile or fixing the beans while she did hair. I would have gladly helped Kianna with Jordan or the twins with their homework. I would have learned to double Dutch and to do nails and to tell jokes just for fun. But instead, I went and fucked it all up and had to move away.

Deshawn and I had spent years silently studying one another. We lived as young voyeurs with raging hormones. We had observed each other come of age. We watched the slow and graceful act of maturing, developing, and eventually ripening into a sweet, delicious piece of forbidden fruit. Just as my name is Eden, I had to have a taste.

Sex with Deshawn was secretive, tender, emotional, magical, passionate, and lustful, like all first loves should be. In the beginning we were careful not to be caught, and we were guilt ridden afterwards, avoiding each other for as long as we could hold out. We would then come together again and ignite in such a fury it was easy to be burned. Deshawn and I had been having sex for almost a year before Tonya found out, and when she did, I believe it broke her heart. It was not that she couldn't understand its happening, it was in the knowing that I would have to leave. Tonya was an ethical woman, and although she had come to care for me greatly, her own child's life was a priority, and I could not stay there, tempting him to come get me. I could not ruin his life with an unwanted pregnancy from a girl with no real family or future.

At seventeen I went to live in a group home, and I chose to stick out the rest of my time there, refusing to get close to another family and only wanting to go back to Deshawn and his beautiful home with its overflow of beautiful people. Before leaving Tonya's home, I gave away the possessions I had collected over the prior three and a half years. Kianna got most of my stuff. She was my first and only best friend. Although Kianna was over eighteen, she and Jordan were still living at Tonya's house, and I was stuck somewhere between jealousy and happiness. At least the system had worked for someone. To my final placement, I took the same blue suitcase I had carried since the age of nine, as well as the lessons I had learned along the way. I had been created by each and every family, person, home, and dynamic. They all had a part in etching out my being, and like a stone cut with a chisel, I had been carved.

From my mother came my primal instinct of survival and the touch of maternal love. With Sherman and Aunt Paula, I developed obedience, and also the creative ability it takes to escape into a story. Most importantly, I had learned the forgiveness of sin. Vanessa introduced me to compassion, idealism, dreams, and hope. Brenda and Brian taught me to know my body and health intuitively and how to conduct myself in front of a team of professionals. And from Tonya White, I learned what it was like to be different, to be wanted, to be loved, and to love back. I learned passion!

It was these characteristics that helped me survive my year in the group home, and these same characteristics that led me into the arms of Ricky Adkins, first as his friend, and then his lover turned victim turned murderer.

Well, Mr. Richard Whiteman, I look at what I have written, and what was meant to be a letter asking for your help has turned into my life story. It is not at all what I intended to write; however, I think I will send it just the same. At least that way, somebody will know.

It is up to you as to what you decide to do with my story. Of course, my hope is that you will use the information in a motion to defend my actions and free me from this hell. I can write with a clear conscience that I do not meet the criteria of a person who deserves a life behind steel bars and barbed wire fencing. But it is not what I know that matters; it is only as I am perceived.

Here again I stand before you, naked and raw, realizing that I have arrived at the same crossroads as when I pulled the trigger. I know that my future is to be decided by a force bigger than you and bigger than me, just as my past has been. Whatever happens, I know to recall a lesson taught to me with the extraordinary wise words of my ordinary, simple aunt:

"*It is the plan of my Lord.*"

Sincerely,
Eden Christine Devine

CLAIRE

O hushed October morning mild,
Begin the hours of this day slow.
Make the day seem to us less brief.
Hearts not averse to being beguiled,
Beguile us in the way you know.
Release one leaf at break of day;
At noon release another leaf;
One from our tree, one from far away.
Retard the sun with gentle mist;

"October" by Robert Frost

October 24, 1999

I cannot believe how my day has unraveled. I feel as if I am a terrible mother and wife. I did not intend to wake up this morning and forget my husband and children, yet that is exactly what I have done. Now I sit here trying to figure out when it was that my surreal day and its journey turned into an act of abandonment.

This Saturday morning started out no different from many others. My goal was to meet Adam and the girls at the soccer field safely and not be too late. The twins, Sophie and Grace, both play soccer on an All-Star Traveling Team. Adam couldn't be prouder. He relishes the fact that the twins are natural athletes. This weekend the girls are to play in a series of tournaments two hours from our home. Because the first game was to begin at 8:00 this morning, Adam and the girls left last night and stayed in a hotel close to the fields. I stayed back at the house and attempted to deliver the 300 boxes of Girl Scout cookies we sold. I started out this morning at 6:30. I knew that I was going to miss the first half of their early morning game, but I also knew that there would be many more games to watch over the next two days.

It was during my drive that I began my escape. At first it was only mental and brought on by the beauty of my surroundings. Somewhere along the road it became a physical escape. I had been driving only an hour when I had to stop to pee. Since the drive consisted of winding routes through one small town after another, my bathroom accommodations were limited. For my pee break, I chose a quaint country log-cabin restaurant that nestled beside a stream. The name of the restaurant was On the Riverbank, and I have never been more charmed by an eatery. I parked my silver Lexus SUV in between the many dirty pickup trucks that filled the parking lot and I hustled inside to find a restroom.

As soon as I swung open the lightweight door to the restaurant, a surreal longing overtook me, and I became absorbed in my surroundings. The outside of the restaurant was made of beautiful logs, and it was surrounded by trees with their autumn orange leaves. The rustic log cabin sat between a country road and a winding stream, but it was the inside of the restaurant that knocked me back to a place and time I had long forgotten. The restaurant smelled of my childhood and the memories of my grandmother's house. I walked briskly between the brown wooden chairs of my grandmother's home and the wooden tables that held the same olive green salt and pepper shakers of Grandma's house into a bathroom that contained a small bowl of little pink and blue soaps just like Grandma's and a sink that had a curtain skirt. I peed with my eyes closed, envisioning Grandma and Granddad, and then washed my hands with Ivory soap and dried them on a cloth dispenser.

Feeling too guilty to pee and run, I ordered a cup of coffee for the road. At least I thought it was going to be for the road, until the server poured it into a short white ceramic mug with an avocado green strip around its thick rim. It was an exact replica of my Granddad's coffee mug, and I eyed it silently, breathing deep enough to fill my lungs with its aroma. The waitress, who reminded me of Flo from the 1980s sitcom *Alice*, asked if she had made a mistake and if I had wanted coffee to go. Surprising myself, I told her that I was staying. I seated myself in one of Grandma's wooden chairs, and then I impulsively placed an order for a bowl of grits.

Time quickly slipped away from me at On the Riverbank, and before I knew it, I had spent an hour daydreaming about a lost childhood and had missed my own children's soccer game. I called Adam from my cell phone and made up an excuse about not feeling well and getting a late start. We agreed to meet at a Champps restaurant near the soccer fields at noon.

It was only 8:30 a.m. when I hung up the phone with Adam, and I was not more than an hour away from him and the girls, yet I had lied for some subconscious reason and had given myself a three-and-a-half-hour leeway. I decided to walk around to the back of the restaurant and take a look at the winding river and its ripples of water. I leaned far out over the edge of the wooden porch railing, and I watched the mallards float downstream and the small fish swim close to the surface of the shallow water. The river flowed in a dance, bending around the curve of earth that the restaurant sat upon. I love a river and the way it plays and splashes up over the large rocks and up the bank, like an excited traveler.

I reluctantly pulled away from On the Riverbank and drove down the road. I was soon out of the little town that had captured me for a stolen moment and back out on the vast stretch of pavement.

As I kept moving, I became more and more aware of my detaching from my family. Adam and the kids and soccer were no longer important to me, and I got caught up in the nature and the beauty all around me. It was as if in a whispered moment, my family had become distant ghosts, haunting only the very back of my mind. I had become completely captivated by an October day.

The beautiful and flat fields that lined my stretch of road were breathtaking. While driving past the peaceful acres of goldenrod, I felt a bliss that has been absent in my life for a long time. I smiled at the purple wildflowers that waved with the goldenrod. Beyond those fields and farms of wheat and hay were hills upon hills of vibrant towering trees with their fall foliage.

Autumn in Ohio is breathtakingly beautiful. The maples and oaks are vibrant shades of orange and red. There are trees of yellow and purple and many shades in between.

Americans on the whole don't give the Midwest much respect. So what if we don't have mountains, oceans, or white sand beaches? We do have autumn. Autumn in Ohio is bright sun, blue skies, and crisp air. It is Indian summer, Indian corn, kettle corn, and apple butter. It is pumpkin patches and odd-shaped colorful gourds. It is a harvest moon, flaming leaves, and full apple trees. It is the smell of cider, campfires, and pumpkin spice, and it is beautiful.

I have always felt a calm and curiosity while passing the homes of the Amish. I am humbled by their black buggies, usually loaded with small, quiet children who are dressed like pilgrims. I love their farms with the laundry waving on the line and the smell of bread in the air. Suddenly, without hesitation or thought, I stopped at an Amish roadside stand. The two girls who were selling produce were about the same age as Sophie and Grace. They were both a combination of plain and beautiful, and I could not help buying their pumpkins and corn and tasting their apples.

I must have been taken in by the sharp colors of the fall fruit and vegetables, because even though I was not the least bit hungry, I immediately began eating a sweet, unwashed, Macintosh apple as I headed back down the road. I could actually taste the sunshine and the rain that had helped produce the luscious piece of fruit, and I thanked God out loud for his gift.

When I finished my apple, I came into the next town and the next winding river. Through the gap in the trees, I noticed a few men fishing, and I smiled to myself as the thought of Granddad filled my mind. Soon I was at a corner gas station that was attached to a small store with a sign that read LIVE BAIT. Parking my car, I questioned myself with "What in the hell am I doing?" I walked into the gas station and store. I wandered down the aisles through the ball caps, candy bars, magazines, Hostess snack cakes, and lighters until I found the bait shop. I eyed the small assortment of cheap fishing poles. I chose a starter pole, not because I am a beginner, but because it came equipped with a line, a reel, and a small tackle box that contained a few hooks, some sinkers, bobbers, and a small pair of scissors. The entire package only cost me $20.00, and I felt overjoyed with my bargain. I bought a container of a dozen night crawlers and checked my diamond watch. I had about two hours to fish before I was supposed to meet Adam and the twins; surely that was enough time.

I drove up the road until I found a nice spot to pull the car over, and then I made my way down to the river. The bank was steep and the heels of my expensive, black leather boots kept sinking into the soft earth. I wished I had on old tennis shoes and a pair of worn jeans instead of the fake classic look I always tend to wear. I found a beautiful flat spot under the branches of a tree, and I placed my folded canvas camping chair (used for soccer games) on the bank. I was proud of myself when I plucked a big, fat, juicy worm from its container and threaded it onto my hook. The black soil dug in under my red manicured nails, and I had to use the scissors to clean it out. My first cast was a bit of a joke, falling quickly down in front of me, not even out a foot. I reeled back in to try again. Next I got stuck in the branches of a tree. For a moment, I thought I was going to have to cut my line, but it unhitched itself. I prayed: third time's the charm. Surprisingly enough, I was right, and my line landed straight out before me, in the middle of the river.

As I fished, I sat under a honey-colored tree and listened to the silent world, which was not so silent. The river and the wind breathed deeply together. The birds sang, animals talked, and insects hummed. In the silent forest there were noises everywhere. The bright colors hung in the air, a hue of magic, where every living thing was wrapped in a vivid aura and glowing brightly. The longer I sat in stillness, the more I became connected to my surroundings and self and disconnected from my life. The thought of interrupting the process for a soccer game and my family left me devastated and frozen.

My bobber bounced with the ripples of the water, and I thought about Granddad and how he took me fishing. Into the woods behind his home we would walk, arm in arm, carrying a bucket of worms that we had dug up the night before. The lake was about a mile away, and it was a lovely walk. I loved fishing with Granddad. At home with Grandma, my siblings, mom, and me, Grandad's silent nature seemed awkward and out of place, but when you're fishing, it's okay to be a quiet person; in fact it's expected. It was with fishing that Granddad could meet his and everyone else's expectations. By day, Granddad worked at a plastics factory. At night he worked at home on anything he could find to fix. Granddad could not remain still, yet he almost always remained quiet. The silent worker, Granddad, taught me to fish. Mostly he showed me technique without much explaining. He taught my brother and sister, too, except they both found it to be dreadfully boring and completely uncultured.

Not me. I found it to be lovely. I could watch the rise and fall of the brook and of my bobber as one might watch a ballet. Like Granddad, I saw fishing as graceful, and I delighted in the spiritual pleasure of fishing—that was until high school. Then Granddad and fishing were no longer cool, and I came out of his shadow and began clicking along at the heels of my older and more sophisticated sister. I followed her path, and it led me to popularity, cheerleading, student counsel, high school parties, boyfriends, and then a move away from Grandma and Grandad, off to college.

Lost in my thoughts, I was brought back to the surface of my reality when my red and white bobber was tugged swiftly under the water. I squealed in delight and broke the universal silence as I jumped to my feet and began reeling in my catch. My wrist fought back and forth and my heels sank deeper into the mud. I couldn't help giggling as I fought my prize. I was as invigorated as I've ever been. It was a feeling of pure and genuine pleasure, out on the river. My large-mouth bass did not want to be caught, and I felt his strength as we struggled with one another. He came up out of the water thrashing his body about, caught on my cheap pole. I could barely get him under control as he swung his body around aggressively. Tired and hopeless, he stopped and dangled in beauty as he tried to breathe. How scary it must be, to be caught. I spoke gently as I grabbed his body. There was more flapping and fighting, and I almost dropped my pole. Soon his cold, wet, dark body was in my hands, and I tried to unhook the creature from the end of my line. I realized he had swallowed the hook. Not wanting to hurt him anymore than I already had, I reached for the tiny scissors in my tackle box. I took the squirming fish into my hands and snipped the line. I bent down to the water's edge and released him back into the stream. Watching him swim off with such speed after such an injury made me feel better about what I had just done.

After I lost my hook, I sat down on my canvas chair and began concentrating on the task at hand. I once knew how to string a fishing rod and tie on a hook and sinker. I focused completely, and when the pole was ready, I pulled another long worm from the white plastic container and punctured its middle as I wrapped it around my hook. My cast was good and sailed through the air with a slight whistle and landed in the shady spot of water I was aiming for. Granddad always said the fish like the shady spots.

I fished for three hours, unaware of the passing of time. I was brought back to reality when my cell phone rang. It was Adam wondering where I was. I lied and told him that I wasn't feeling well. He asked why I hadn't answered our home phone, and I told him that I had turned off the ringer to get some sleep. I told Adam I thought I should stay home this weekend. I felt too bad and could use the time to rest. As I said those things, I felt horrible for lying. Still, I continued to ramble on with untruths. Before hanging up, Adam gave the phone to the girls and they took turns talking on top of one another. They complained about how the ref made some bad calls and how the other team was elbowing and shoving. I listened patiently, but was completely annoyed and bothered by my family. How dare they break the beautiful silence that had swallowed me with accusations about a ref and a group of preteen girls!

"You'll do great," I assured my daughters before asking to speak to their dad, even though I wanted nothing more than to hang up on all them and get back to fishing. I swear I had gone mad. After a few more fibs, I hung up with a new appreciation for the cell phone. How easy it is to say you're one place and be another. I suppose lying to your spouse has probably never been this simple.

Moments after slipping my cell phone back into the pocket of my fitted blazer, I heard the voices of kids. They came in the form of shouts of slang and swear words followed by laughter, the echoes of young boys. I listened to them call each other "fag" and "sissy" and then talk of who could skip a rock the farthest. As their voices neared, I began to clean up my area, wiping my hands down the sides of my pressed designer jeans and then folding up my camping chair.

The boys came running from the side of the bank. The two older boys carried cane poles in their grubby hands and a coffee can full of worms. The smallest boy had no pole and ran five paces behind the other two. "Go home!" his older brother shouted back at him. "You're always following us."

"No!" cried out the little one. "Mom said you had to let me come."

"Well you're not using my pole," ordered his older brother.

"So I'll just watch," called back the little one.

I watched as the two big boys huddled over the blue can of worms, while the younger one stood off to the side and kicked the dirt.

I walked over to the younger boy with my pole, bait, and tackle box. "Here you go," I said. "I'm finished."

"You was fishing?" he asked, gazing up at me with the look of Opie Taylor.

"I was," I proudly answered.

He wanted to know if I caught anything, and when I told him I did, with a smile on my face, he smiled back at me, a gap-toothed grin. "You don't want your pole now?" he asked, clearly puzzled by me and what I was doing.

"No, I want you to have it," I said.

By then the two older boys were over at his side checking out both me and the fishing gear. I felt a dislike for the older boys, I suppose because of the way they had bullied dirty little Opie. Even though I know firsthand about sibling rivalry, and it was not my business, I added a stipulation. "One restriction," I said. "I don't want you to let your brothers use it."

"All right!" the young child exploded as I placed the pole into his small hands.

"I mean it," I said, sticking my intimidating finger into the face of the older brother. I then picked up my blue camping chair and started up the hill to my car.

I couldn't believe what I had just done. Oh my God, I am a mother. Never have I encouraged children to fight or not to share. I make my own daughters share everything. How could I stick my finger in the face of another woman's child? How could I give a gift with restrictions on not sharing? Why did it feel so good?

I put the camping chair in the back of my Lexus and grabbed the hand sanitizer and tissues from the center console. My manicured hands were a mess. With the tissues, after cleaning myself up some, I tried wiping off the heels of my Von Maur boots. I pulled my Nordstrom blazer from my body and laid it in the back seat. The day had turned warm, with a bright sun in a clear-blue sky.

Where to go now? I wondered. *I'm closer to my family than I am to my home, and yet I have lied and told them I'm in bed.* I pulled away from the side of the road just after I caught a glimpse of the young child happily casting out the fishing line.

I felt free, relaxed, and slightly hungry as I started out on my drive. I had no destination or any idea of what to do next, so I just drove with my windows down, head cocked into the wind, and the radio station on classical music that Adam and the girls never let me listen to. I had driven for about twenty minutes when I noticed the dark brown road signs, an indication of a state park. I followed the signs to the left and then right, past corn fields and into nowhere. I figured the parks had nice, safe hiking trails, and if my boots were up to it, so was I. The brown signs that led me to the park pointed me in numerous directions. I could go to the Visitors Center, lodge, cabins, picnic area, marina, golf course, primitive camping, or beach. I chose the picnic area to find a nice trail.

I took a two-mile hike down a graveled path. I hadn't hiked by myself since I was a kid. Adam and I like to take the girls hiking at the little metro parks near our home, but I often feel sorry for the people on the trail who are hiking alone. Boy, have I been way off. That lone hike through the amber trees was about as close to heaven as I have ever been. I hiked behind couples hand in hand and running kids, daddies giving shoulder rides, and crying babies. When I wanted to stop, I did, and I stayed on a bench for as long as I wanted. I thought on my walk, but not about my children or my husband. I thought about myself. When had I become this woman, this voided, blank, uninteresting woman, and why? I am so very different from what I thought I would ever be.

I cried on the last stretch of my walk. I cried because I have been unhappy for so long, and I cried because I wanted to blame Adam and the twins for my sadness. I began losing the best parts of myself, starting with the girls' conception.

I have always believed that it was twice as hard for me to have both children at once than it was for my sister, to have her two singleton births. I know I was twice as sick, twice as hungry, twice as constipated, twice as big, and twice as hormonal. When the kids came and there were two of them, I know I felt twice as scared, twice as overwhelmed, twice as sleepy, and twice as incompetent, and I had a double dose of the baby blues.

I knew immediately after the girls' births that I could never, ever become pregnant again. I could not endure another terrible pregnancy or another horrific C-section, sliced open and gutted. Neither did I want another tiny, helpless, needy infant draining all my energy and time. I know my words are horrible. They are difficult even to write, but it is true. Motherhood has not been easy for me. I was often overwhelmed by my babies, unhappy and tearful. I shared these feelings with no one. How could I? I had to be a horrible mother to endure and conquer a high-risk pregnancy for twins and not be grateful for my gift.

Breast-feeding drained me. I cried myself to sleep at night while nursing a baby, only to be awakened seconds later by another child wanting to nurse. I went to a meeting of the La Leche League in hopes that those extraordinary mothers would inspire me. Instead they grossed me out. Finally, after months of hiding my indescribable sadness, I made an appointment with my doctor, and I confessed. She diagnosed me with postpartum depression and put me on antidepressants. What troubles me now is that the girls are twelve years old, and I still take a Zoloft every day.

I ended my nature walk back near my car, having made a lovely little loop. I was feeling extremely hungry and still a little sad, even though I had come to an acceptance of my maternal nature long ago.

I hopped back into my SUV and drove slowly and respectfully over the colorful dipping hills of the state park, toward the lodge. I had never been to that particular state lodge before, but I knew, like all state lodges, that it would be beautiful. I walked into the large front door and into the lobby with wooden furniture and mounted animal heads. To the right of the long front desk was the gift shop, and beside that, the formal dining area. In the gift shop I peeked into books of nature and looked at stuffed black bears and turtles.

I came upon this leather-bound journal, and on an impulse, I bought it. I have always wanted a leather journal, and this thick brown one with an oak tree carved in its front was perfect. At the front counter where I purchased my journal were jeweled colored pens. I bought one in ruby red.

Next I went into the formal dining room and chose to sit at a small table next to a large window that looked out onto the lake. This is where I sit now, filling pages of my journal with my private thoughts. I have ordered the pecan encrusted salmon over a bed of rice with mixed vegetables and a glass of white Zinfandel. I feel content and confused at the same time. I feel as if I am on the verge of a discovery and maybe some resolutions. After I eat my meal, I plan to sit in one of the big wooden rocking chairs around the fireplace and continue my process. I suppose I will also get a room for the night. Oddly, I have reached a destination.

My meal was delicious. I am now in front of the fire. I booked a room on my credit card. I look through this journal now and see that I have written so much and said so little. I suppose the work starts here. This weekend has switched my intentions. It is no longer about my kids, husband, and my free time spent with their activities. It is about me, my life, my emptiness, my happiness, my sadness, and what I think is my mid-life crisis. I suppose now what I must do is retrace my adult path. When was it that I allowed myself to go astray, or rather vanish?

I left my grandparents' home and went off to college, because it was expected of me, and I was following the path of expectations. My mother believed that college was a must for all three of her children, but not all for the same reasons. My brother was supposed to get his B.S. degree in business and become a financial success. My sister and I were going to go to college to get our "Mrs. degree" by marrying a man from school who would become a financial success.

My mother has always believed in the sanctity of marriage and believes even stronger in marrying well. In her own quest for Mr. Right, she managed to produce three illegitimate children by three different fathers and raise them all rather poorly in the home of her parents. Eventually my mother did find her millionaire, and just as he decided not to bring his wife into their union, Mom decided to leave her kids out. My mother and Burton Winningham were married when I was fourteen years old. They went to live in a mansion and take long vacations, while Elizabeth, Luke, and I stayed with our grandmother and grandfather. Even though my mother went with her husband and left us behind, she did not completely abandon us, and she lived with a great amount of guilt. She saw us almost every Sunday, when not traveling, and she paid my grandparents an enormous amount for childcare. She also made sure we had money for college and a goal for our future.

My sister and brother obeyed our mother's wishes. Luke obtained a degree in international finance, and although he claims to hate capitalism, he is an extremely rich businessman. My sister Elizabeth married a doctor, had two kids, and built a mansion, trumping my mother's dream of dreams.

I, on the other hand, rebelled. I dropped out of a four-year university to go to culinary arts school. Just as Granddad had instilled in me the love for fishing, Grandma taught me to cook. Grandma was a wonderful cook, and she filled my life with scents and tastes that I called love. I worked as a chef in a French restaurant for ten years before my girls were born. I loved my work.

It is in the kitchen that I am an artist, just like I am a poet on the river. Sadly, I was convinced that I had to give up my career. The late nights, weekends, and holidays I worked were not conducive to raising babies.

Ironic now, but falling in love with Adam was also an act of rebelliousness. Adam was not known as a man who would obtain great financial success. In my mother's eyes, Adam could not hold a candle to Greg, my sister's husband. Greg was a med student, wanting to specialize as a surgeon. Adam was a laborer, a contractor in construction, building pre-fab homes and wearing steel-toed boots. My mother was heart-stricken. I fell in love with Adam because of his work and his humbleness.

No, he couldn't heal people or make scientific conclusions, but he could take a piece of wood and sand it into something beautiful or pound two by fours into a structure of strength, where a family would live. To me that was the most romantic notion.

Adam and I would spend hours lying together after sex, talking of homes and creating plans. We were going to rebuild a house together. Neither of us desired a new home that would be the exact replica of its neighbor. We both thought that idea was boring and common. We wanted an older home, one that had history, a life, and a personality. We wanted a home that had already held a family and had been worn out by love and life. We would rehab the home together and give it a facelift and a new beginning. We wanted a Victorian style house made of all brick with numerous fireplaces and a slender staircase. Adam would build me a beautiful kitchen, and together we would create gourmet meals, using fresh vegetables from our small garden, and we would drink wine created from our own grapes.

We spent our weekend looking at homes, entering ancient houses in ancient neighborhoods and redesigning them in our minds. "We will take down this banister and refinish it," Adam would exclaim in excitement. "I'm sure we could pull out its natural beauty again. Isn't it gorgeous, Claire?" I miss that Adam so much.

After we married, Adam and I moved into a small two-bedroom ranch that we refinished and then sold. From that home, we moved into a larger three-bedroom ranch and did the same thing. Flipping homes can be fun, and we had a blast. We kept looking for the Victorian dream home, while flipping ranches. After three years of marriage, I became pregnant.

It was during my pregnancy that Adam hit his success. The city was changing, and everybody was moving out. Suburban growth was booming, and what was once the country was being developed into city. Four-lane streets started replacing country roads, and large, beautiful housing developments began popping up everywhere. Adam was contracting and building enormous subdivisions, one right after the other.

During that time, I was pregnant with twins and miserable. Adam was never home. I worked up until my seventh month. By that time I could not touch the pans on the counter, because my belly was too big and my arms too short. I also could not bend down or turn around, and I constantly had to pee. I left work reluctantly and have never gone back.

Soon I was a new mommy and Adam still worked. I got little sleep, little help, and little support. It wasn't fair. Adam loved the girls. He carried them around and cooed with them all the hours he was home. The problem was that he wasn't home much. Life for Adam was exciting and blessed. His work was great. The homes he was building were beautiful and plentiful. His babies were healthy and his wife was a good cook.

We stopped looking at Victorian houses. We stopped talking about English Tudors, Japanese flowerbeds, and homemade wine. One day Adam came home and proudly announced that he was building our house, a surprise to me. I didn't know we wanted to build. I had thought we were going to buy an old home in the city and refinish it. That was before kids, Adam informed me. Now, with the girls, there was the school system to think about. Adam wanted the girls to go to a nice suburban school in a nice new building with new textbooks and young teachers.

I had never really thought about the school system before and assumed the girls would attend public school in the city, like Adam and I had. Once it was brought forth as an issue, I was forced to look at how the city had changed in the years since I had been there. I took a closer look at schools and at their individual philosophy of teaching. I fell in love with the idea of Montessori and found a Montessori elementary close to the heart of downtown. When I ecstatically shared this news with my husband, he practically shamed me.

"What were you thinking? How could you possibly want our girls to attend that old decrepit building that sits in an area wrought with violence and drugs, especially when we are just about to begin building a luxurious home that will be within walking distance of a new school? Are you completely and totally insane?"

Soon I was doubting myself. What was wrong with me? Didn't every white middle-class heterosexual want what I was about to achieve?

Adam broke ground on our lot on the twins' first birthday. He was a king that day, building a palace for his princess daughters. He was happy, excited, and confident. He was a family man who had worked hard and exceeded even his own dreams.

Why wasn't I happy? My girls were at an adorable age and just learning how to walk. They took two-hour naps and slept through the night. They were cute, smart, and received loads of attention everywhere we went. My husband was successful. He was making excellent money and enjoying his work and was even going to take part in the constructing of his own home. Life couldn't be better, and I was still depressed.

Adam brought me paint samples, countertop samples, and floor samples to go into our new home; however, I always let him choose which one it would be. There was only a choice of three or four possibilities, according to the builder's regulations, and we could not veer from the pattern. Adam knew what colors looked best, which floor had the nicest finish, and which countertop was the most striking. He had been building those homes for a couple of years by then, and he knew all the secrets for making ours the finest. It is true; our home stands out on our cul-de-sac. The other homes in our area are beige with colonial blue or mauve shutters. Then there are the colonial blue homes with beige shutters. We are the only family that chose a mauve house with colonial blue shutters, which also makes our house the *only* home that does not contain the color beige on its front. What radicals we've become!

We moved into our beautiful mauve house with its brand-new sod and *no* trees. It was during that transition that I felt the rest of myself—the parts I had been clinging to—slipping away. There was one day in particular when I woke up incredibly sad. My sister was coming over to help me put the girls' rooms together. They had been sleeping in a playpen in our room.

I cried tears of good-bye to my Victorian home as I sorted through their abundance of plush animals and board books. I managed to stop my tears and clean myself up about an hour before my sister's arrival, but I still could not shake my somber feeling.

My sister acted as one should in a newly built home. She whizzed through my house in a euphoric frenzy. She held up pictures to the walls, trying to figure out where to hang our small assortment of art. She moved around my plants and gave me decorating advice. She moved from room to room in a quick flow. Each room delighted her and brought forth more ideas and excitement. As I watched her energy and jubilation, I could feel my own weight. I actually felt heavy, like weights were bearing down on my shoulders.

Elizabeth and I were in the twins' room, putting together their heavy, wooden Pottery Barn cribs, when she finally asked, "What is wrong with you, Claire?"

My tears began to fall, I looked up to my big sister for comfort, and I cried, "I'm never going to live in an old Victorian House."

A look of utter amazement passed across my sister's face. She dropped the screwdriver to her side and looked around our delightful lilac nursery with its vaulted ceilings and skylights, and she said, "Are you fucking kidding me?"

It was the same reaction I had received from Adam when I had mentioned Montessori Schools. It was at that moment that I knew I could never complain about the big, beautiful house, the house that Adam built.

Elizabeth confirmed it; I was nuts. I needed to get over myself, look at my life for what it was, and it was good. I had nothing at all to complain about, so I shouldn't. That night when I went to bed I prayed good-bye to my Victorian home. Good-bye to my big, old, brick house that sits on an old brick street. Good-bye to my homes' many gables and odd-shaped rooms. Good-bye to its claw bathtub, Victorian fireplaces, and old wooden floors. Good-bye to my dusty wine cellar, to my wrought iron fence, to my downtown markets and mature trees. Good-bye to my neighbors, who were going to be eccentric and intelligent. Good-bye to the old Claire.

I was spent after writing about the house, the babies and my own struggles with depression. I had been sitting in that chair in front of the fire for nearly two hours, spilling my heart into this journal. When I finally looked up from my pages, I saw there were people all around me, in and out of the restaurant, bar, gift shop, and at the front desk. A feeling of vulnerability and a little embarrassment overtook me, and I closed my journal and retreated to my room.

First I called Adam and the twins to see how their day had gone. They all were excited and happy and seemed to be having the time of their lives. The girls fought over the phone, each telling me her own version of how they won two out of the three soccer games they had played that day. Their team was in the running for the championship game, and they believed they had it in the bag. Adam was having a good time too. He loves watching the girls in sports, plus he said he had a couple of beers and a great meal with the other parents at dinner. That is all Adam needs to feel content: sports, beer, and food. I wish I were that easy to please.

Adam asked me to turn the ringer back on the phone. He had been trying to reach me a couple of times today. I should have told Adam that I was not at home and that I was only about twenty minutes from where they are. I should have told him that instead of watching my girls play a championship soccer game, I had chosen to check myself into a lodge and be alone. I should have told him, but I did not, and he did not ask.

After I hung up the phone, I had an argument with myself. I felt quite conflicted. One part of me—I'm not sure which is head talking and which is my heart—believed and still believes that I should go to my family and surprise them and forget about this venture into self. That same part of me thinks that I am a terrible person, a self-absorbed, spoiled person who has abandoned her family.

The other part of me says that everything is okay. I have been gone from my family for only two days. Men, in fact, do this all the time. Besides, my family is doing fine without me. It is also self-centered to think that they need me in each and every one of their experiences. This part of me decided to go swimming.

I had packed a bathing suit, because when we go to those faraway soccer games, we always try to stay in a hotel with a pool. I was pleasantly surprised that when I got to the pool, nobody was there. I am a great swimmer and have always loved the water. It is the one thing about myself that I have not had to give up. I wonder if it's because my zodiac sign is Pisces. Usually in the water I swim laps, fast, furious things from my swim-team days, but not tonight. Tonight I floated and glided. My legs did not kick rapidly like fins, but rather scissored in and out slowly like a frog on dope. I watched my fingers push through the water and was amazed by the concept of water and how it takes your form. Water outlines any solid form that decides to plop into it. It clings to it. It carries it. It doesn't matter what it is, a person, an old tire, an ice cube. Water envelops any object. It then occurred to me that the reason my love for water has never left me is because I have become water.

I am water! I seem to take the form of anything that plops into me. My family, friends, community, church, and school are solids, and I am only water. At that realization, I cried a pool of water that was dropping into the pool of water that I, water, was in. The others then showed up. It must have been some sort of reunion, because it seemed to be three or four different families with children of varying ages, and they all appeared to be related or very close friends. I left the pool and retreated to my room.

I was not ready to write all this stuff down, and I could not sleep or concentrate to watch TV, so I went to the bar to have a drink. After two cosmopolitans and a nice chat with an elderly gentleman, where I mostly listened, I went up to my room and was able to sleep soundly for exactly four hours. It's now 4:00 a.m. I do not plan to lie down any longer. I must be home today, way before my family. In the meantime, I need to figure out how I can reach a center of contentment. I do not think that I will be completely content and whole by the end of the day, but I hope I will have formulated a plan and a means to find myself.

It is now 6:00 a.m., and I am enjoying a lovely continental breakfast while I look out a large window and view a pristine lake that is surrounded by golden trees and weeping willows. I had planned to take a nature hike today, a crisp walk on a wooded path, while I contemplate my existence. Maybe I will still take one, but mostly I plan to be out on the lake. Since I have decided that I am only water, I think I need to be out on the water to find myself. If I had decided I was a tree, a walk in the woods would fit perfectly, but being water means I am going to have to rent a canoe.

It is now 2:00 p.m., and I have so much to write, but no time to write. I ate a beautiful lunch, packed my car, and checked out of my room. I will be home at 4:00. I have talked to my family, and they should be home by 7:00 p.m. It will be during that three-hour stretch of time that I plan to fill these pages with my thoughts and ideas.

I have no regrets about this weekend. I fully accept and embrace every lie that I told my husband and kids. I accept every selfish act and mean thought. I accept and embrace my depression, my lack of fulfillment, and my discontentment. I have recognized it all, claimed it, examined it, accepted it, embraced it, and then surrendered it up to God.

It's 5:30 p.m., October 25, 1999

I am home. I have changed into comfortable sweats and one of Adam's flannel shirts. I stopped at the market and bought fresh meat, fresh flowers, imported wine, rosemary crackers, and a beautiful cheese with a thick rind. I plan to create a special meal for my family. The pumpkins I purchased from the silent Amish girls are on the porch waiting to be carved. The corn is husked and the tomatoes cut. The apples are in a white ceramic bowl sitting on my butcher-block kitchen table looking pretty enough to paint. Adam called and said they should be home by 7:30 p.m., and yahoo, they won the championship! Adam said, "You missed it, Claire. You missed the twins winning a state championship."

I simply apologized, and after we hung up, I had to reread my no regrets on the page before. I then pulled out the flour and decided I will bake a cake in honor of the girls.

A lot of things came together for me out on the lake, and more came together on the drive home. At least now I have some sort of plan. As I paddled through lily pads and cattails, my mind cleared. I had emptied most of my nasty thoughts into this book, and in doing, left room for some new and positive ideas to develop. I decided that a major part of myself that I had given up was my work, and though I no longer desire the late nights and weekends that make up the hours of a chef, I do miss being considered an artist in the kitchen.

It occurred to me that I would be a great teacher. With my passion and love for French cuisine, I could easily hold cooking classes for my elite neighbors and friends. I could hold another class for everyone else. I could teach simple yet elegant cooking for the fast-paced family or, for the lovers, the creation of a true romantic meal, one that flows with lustrous ingredients and leads to sex. I could hold classes in wine tasting and appreciation and classes on appetizers, or maybe desserts. I could break up the classes in an endless number of ways.

I could teach classes out of my home or at a community or rec center, and what I am truly hoping for is The Center for Cultural Arts. Being there would put me back into the downtown element that I miss. It would place me around arty people who are not afraid of the inner city. I would love to work in that old brick building not far from the Montessori school that I fell in love with and just a few blocks from the art museum and the little galleries and ethnic restaurants downtown. I could teach classes in the day while the girls are at school and give some evening classes that would not interfere with my family. I am excited about my new idea. I feel hopeful, and more importantly, I feel a piece of Claire returning. I am emerging slowly from the deep blue, and I am breaking the surface.

I will write my proposal, along with a résumé, and I will pitch the idea to my husband, who will support me, and then I will contact The Center for Cultural Arts. If the directors do not see a need at this time, I will look elsewhere. I have such a good feeling about this plan that I am sure it is meant to happen. I will make it work.

First, though, I need to lay down this beautiful journal that has carried me through my weekend and my first baby steps into finding my happiness, and I must go cook a gourmet meal for my champion twins and their father, my husband. Bye for now.

JESSIE

"The sound of a kiss is not so loud as that of a cannon, but its echo lasts a great deal longer."

Oliver Wendell Holmes

November 23, 1999

My dearest diary, I am no longer who I was this morning. I have switched to the opposing team, traded shirts for skins, and uncovered my soul. I have crossed the bridge that extends the river of all that is natural and true. I have been transformed, lifted onto a new plane. I have been altered. I have had a change of heart, all because she kissed me, a kiss as light and gentle as the morning dew that rests on the petals of pale pink flowers.

Her kiss tasted like tears. It grew within me like the passion flower, large and pleasing. We were sitting on the couch, a couch so overstuffed and soft it surrendered under our weight and gradually descended, settling on its bottom. Submerged within the mocha-brown fabric and fluff, she kissed me, a long, throaty kiss followed by gentle wisps of soft and sweet fluttering kisses around my mouth.

We were watching a chick flick, some trendy movie that stars Julia Roberts. We were eating yellow-white, greasy, Butter Lover's popcorn, straight out of the microwave bag it had been popped in. We were drinking Bartles & Jaymes original coolers from their silver-labeled green bottles. I could feel the way I was gradually becoming loose. The crisp cooler was not only giving refreshment to my mind, but also to my body—four silvery-green bottles, two for Shelly and two for me.

Shelly's legs were curled up under her body, her knees poking out through a hole in the denim. Her T-shirt was bright orange, the color of tangerines. Her shirt fit tight and rose up at the midriff, exposing her hard stomach and the gold ring that pierced her navel. She smelled strong, like eucalyptus and mint tea.

I was wearing a long, cotton skirt, black in color, my favorite skirt, a skirt I can wrap around myself like a blanket. With my skirt I wore a black sweater. This outfit is too dark for my white skin, causing me to look transparent. I glow milky white with a blue tinge. My mother hates this outfit. She calls me "Dark Jessie" when I wear it.

(Note to Mother) "*Sorry, Mother, it's not a Liz Claiborne or an Anne Taylor. It's not tailored or expensive or even flattering. It is the color of rich soil. You see me in mourning in this outfit, gloomy and depressed. I see myself as the opposite of white. The opposite of you."*

My mom wears white a lot. White wool sweaters, white camel-hair coats, long white sundresses, white, white, white!

(N.T.M) *"Don't you see, Mom? We are the complement of each other, or maybe the antithesis. You, in white, reflect all light, and I, in my soil-black outfit, absorb all the light. It's easy, once you think about it. In my Dark Jessie outfit, a girl kissed me."*

Jenna walked in shortly after the kiss, her arms loaded with various shopping bags. She had just competed in a marathon at the Sunny Village Mall, a contest of strength and endurance, exclusive to the day after Thanksgiving. The runners wake at 4:00 a.m. in jubilation, ready for a day of long lines and blue-tag sales.

Jenna set her shopping bags in front of her and immediately began to pull item after item from her sacks. She had bought lovely gifts for Christmas as well as many items for herself. She had materials in bright blues and purples, silks, and heavy wool sweaters woven to perfection. She showed us each piece of merchandise as if showing us the seven wonders of the world. She was so consumed with her own reflection that she did not notice the glow to my face. She could not see the echo of our kiss still lingering in my eyes. Just moments before Jenna's entrance, Shelly and I sat mouth to mouth. Our lips matched perfectly, our tongues flicking silent secrets to one another. Nobody knew our tasty little secret. It made me want to shout, "WE JUST KISSED!" I wanted to tell my sister. I wanted to rub it in her face. I wanted to know her reaction. Would she gasp in horror or exhale a captured breath? Would I suddenly make sense to her, like I suddenly make sense to myself? What would Jenna say?

Jenna is my beautiful older sister and my only sibling. First came Jennalee Anastasia Kingston. Eighteen months later came me, Jessalyn Analiese Kingston. I was the completion of the perfect family. Jenna and Jessie, the daughters of Jack and Eva. We were called two little princesses, two rays of sunshine, two peas in a pod, two girls in a room.

Jenna and I have been roommates since my birth. First we shared a little pink-and-white bedroom. Our walls were papered with tiny rows of pale pink flowers with mint-green leaves. We slept in matching canopy beds with white tops after we had slept in white canopy cribs with pink tops. Each of our beds contained four decorative pillows trimmed in lace. Two pillows were pink and two were white. We were not to play with or sleep on those pillows. One white end table stood between our beds. On the table sat a brass lamp with a pink shade; a small, white alarm clock; and a small vase that held tiny pink-and-white silk tea roses. There were other bedrooms in our large home. One bedroom was a guest room; one was our playroom. When I became older and wanted to claim one of these rooms for my own, strangely, our mother wouldn't allow it.

Now Jenna and I share an apartment with our mocha couch and butcher block tables. We have decorated mostly with candles of all colors, sizes, shapes, and scents. We burn them every day and replace them weekly. We have a small kitchen with white appliances. Our bathroom is decorated with Betty-Boop memorabilia: its colors are red, black, and white. We finally have separate rooms. Jenna's bedroom is lilac, and mine is green.

As Jenna showed Shelly and me her purchases, I was silently shouting. My body said, "Listen to me, sister, I am shouting now!" My eyes were glossy and shouting. My ears were red hot and shouting. The little hairs on the back of my neck were shouting. Jenna could not hear it, but Shelly could. Shelly took hold of my hand and squeezed. Jenna was oblivious.

"How's Mom?" I asked Jenna as Shelly stroked my palm.

"She's great, as always. She bought you this," Jenna said as she flung a black scarf toward me.

Shelly caught it. "God, this is great! Your mom has great taste."

"Exquisite," Jenna mocked, using her Eva voice.

Mom didn't come up, though. She and Dad are going to some stuffy fundraiser tonight.

"Oh God, Jess! You should see what she's wearing." Jenna stood up so Shelly and I could get a more dramatic effect. She motioned her hands along her body in a sultry, seductive way as she described my mother's attire, a long and fitted solid white dress with NO BACK. "The ladies are going to talk for sure." Jenna laughed.

"Their husbands too," I reminded her. I visualized Eva in her backless, silky, shimmering, white dress skimming her well-kept body. I envisioned a goddess. Leave it to my mother to wear backless white in November. Eva doesn't keep to fashion rules, not unless she made them. My mother is certainly uncommon, a woman who intimidates other women and all men. Eva is my protagonist. She is my antagonist. She is my hero. She is my enemy. She is my mother.

(Note to Mother:) "*MOM, I KISSED SHELLY! And it felt so right. More right than I have ever felt before. She tasted delicious, Mom. She makes my mouth water and ache. I want to kiss her all over and stroke her hair. I want to sniff up her whole body and wrap my limbs around her. Do I scare you? I scare myself.*"

I walked Shelly out into the hall of our apartment building. I wondered if anyone was watching. Shelly cupped my face in her hands, and she kissed my forehead. Chills ran up my arms, and my knees buckled. Shelly kissed my cheeks. Her dark skin was cool. It felt like glass. Shelly kissed my mouth softly and slowly, one peck at a time. No tongue, no aggression, just soft, silent whisper kisses. My breath blended with her breath. "See ya tomorrow," she said when she gently let go of my face.

"See ya," I responded, blushing like a child.

When I walked back into the apartment, Jenna asked how Shelly was doing. I told her fine, but then she questioned me as to why we were holding hands, and why I walked her out. I didn't know how to respond to my sister, so I told her that Shelly and I are becoming close. Jenna was pissed, I could tell. She's jealous by nature. We both know that Shelly is actually Jen's friend, and Jenna has always kept score of our friends. To escape Jenna's mood, I went into my room.

First thing I did when I was alone was look into the mirror. I wanted to see if my change was as visually apparent as it felt. Could I see the effects of my emotions or be able to perceive with my eyes the awesome sensations and desires that surged through my body?

My hollow cheeks were definitely tinged with red. Could that be because I was still on fire? My eyes looked glossier; my lips still felt moist. I suppose these could be consequences from the wine coolers; however, I hate to give them any credit. I want this beautifully woozy, delirious felicity to be the result of the kiss.

I lay on my bed and shut my eyes. Never had a boy made me feel as right. Not ever had my hunger for someone been so raw. My sexual appetite and compassion felt uncontainable. I have kissed boys. I have gone through the motions without emotion. I have had boyfriends and prom dates. I have rounded the bases of sex at keg parties and in back seats. I have made out on a picnic blanket, and I have walked hand in hand down a wooded path, but I have never known this pure craving before.

Once Jenna and I dated identical twin brothers, and I ended up tongue kissing both of them, because I never could tell them apart. Jenna swears that she only kissed her boyfriend and not mine, but I seriously doubt it. Those boys were two manipulating, shrewd opportunists. I'm sure they found a way to kiss us both. I'm just thankful that I never screwed either one of them.

I realize now that never, in all my experiences, have I felt such a stirring. Shelly's kiss has aroused me from my slumber. I am now awake. I am inspired. I am whole. I have been tapped on the soul and woken up to my natural essence.

While I lay on my bed fantasizing, Jenna opened my door abruptly to let me know that Shelly was on the phone. Turns out my territorial sister had called Shelly to see what was going on. Shelly told her everything was just fine and then asked to speak to me. Jenna was boiling inside. I felt bad for her. It's not that we don't share the same friends. We do; we always have. We have always shared everything, and that is why our understanding of each other is so important. We both know exactly what belongs to Jen and what belongs to me. Jenna has dibs, as she puts it, on all that she brings into our lives, and I have dibs on all of my own contributions. Shelly was brought into our circle by Jenna. Jenna would naturally expect Shelly to be closer to her. I nodded to my sister as I picked up the phone. She nodded back as she slammed my door. I know she's hurt, but I can no longer hold onto the responsibility of Jenna's rivalry or her emotions.

"Thank you" were the first words I spoke to Shelly.

"Are you okay?" were the words she spoke to me.

I was touched that she was worried about me. Didn't she know that she had just figured me out, a chore that I have been trying to accomplish my whole life? I am okay. I have always been okay. It just took Shelly to help me realize it.

Shelly and I stayed on the phone for hours. She said she couldn't understand how I didn't know that I was gay. She said she knew since our first meeting. How could that be? How could someone else know me so well, when I don't even know myself?

I admitted to Shelly that I once felt that it could be possible, but I had pushed those feelings so far down into the pit of my stomach that they had been absorbed. It's true. Whenever I search inside myself, I have always found a quiet nothingness. I have been empty of my own senses. I explained to Shelly that I had always played the role my mother had scripted for me. Although I played it badly, I still felt that it was a necessary part of my life and was the only significant connection existing between Eva and me.

Shelly understood. She told me that she believes her mother suspects that she is gay and that Shelly has acknowledged her suspicions. In return, Shelly has been considerate enough to keep her mouth shut, to stay in the closet, so to speak. Shelly's father, however, who is divorced from her mother, has absolutely no idea. He is the type of man who believes the world exists just as he thinks it should, and he would not believe Shelly if she told him herself.

Shelly told me her first sexual experience was with a butch on her junior varsity baseball team. She was in high school, and word got around. The pain it caused her was indescribable. Since moving away from home and starting college, she has kept her friends and her lovers separate.

I don't believe that Shelly would suffer the same pain now as she did when she was sixteen. Being gay is in style now, and her family is miles away. I told her there was no reason that she should hide her true self.

Shelly explained that she does not see herself as being dishonest. She is who she is, and her life is no more complicated than anybody else's. Shelly chooses not to talk about her sex life because she is private, not because she is gay. She said that if she were heterosexual, her relationships would still be private. Further, she said that if she is perceived as being straight, because she wears her hair long and her skirts short, it is only because the presumption was made within a narrow mind and not because she is a fraud. Shelly and I made a date for tomorrow night before hanging up.

Shelly is much healthier than I am. Who am I to give advice on being honest with yourself? I have lived a lie. I am the master of anonymity. I have kept my emotions silent for so long they became extinct. I don't want to hide anymore. Comparable to a fairy tale, I was woken with a kiss. Once silent and still, I now burn with vulnerability. A fire has been lit inside of me. I am a tigress, and I wish to roam free from boundaries.

I wonder how my family will react to my coming of age. What would they do if I became honest with them, if I showed my soul, if I let them in?

Jennalee, my sister, my best friend, will love me unconditionally in the end. This I can count on. It is simple; we are sisters. Our attachment is too great to be broken. In our relationship, judgment does not exist. We are different from one another, but we are the same. We have been bonded since birth. Before knowing her, I had slept in the womb that she had kept warm for me. Before knowing me, she kissed our mother's belly and chanted the word "Baby."

Jenna is much like our mother, but only on the surface. Their deeper waters contain different animals. Jennalee may be the Eva of a younger generation. Jenna is much less pretentious. She is more authentic, and she is nicer. Jenna will be shocked with me for a while. She will probably be more shocked that Shelly is gay. In time, she will come around. She may say terrible things to me, but no doubt she will defend me like a mad woman to anyone else who dares. That is the nature of sisters.

My father, Federal Judge Jackson A. Kingston, will be kind, because it is the quality of his character. A lot of his outward reaction will depend on Eva. He may have to hold back his emotion for my mother's sake. She always has had a way of keeping Jack in check. My father, a man of great influence, insight, and authority, falls powerless under her spell. Jackson's life is consecrated to Eva. He loves to watch her with entirety. She is his queen. He still watches my mother like a lovesick boy. He stares longingly as she drinks her coffee or brushes her hair. He is devout with passion. Eva still impresses Jackson. It's in the way she moves into a room and takes it over. He indulges in her beauty and strength. He soaks her up. He is intoxicated with her. She is his long, cold drink.

I can hear my father exhale to my news. "Daddy, I kissed a girl, and I want to do it again."

I can see him wait for my mother's reaction. If Eva responds approvingly to my sexual exploration, Jackson will sigh. He will pat my head as if I am still six years old. "I just want happiness for you, princess." That has been Jackson's response to many of my "identity-crisis" moments, from the time I cut my own hair at the age of three to my becoming a vegetarian at twenty and everything in between.

Eva, my mother, is our matriarch. She is unpredictable. There are many different ways her towering stature may fall. She may stand proudly among her social circle and pronounce, "My daughter Jessalyn is a lesbian." Eva always strives to be vogue. This may be all she needs to be considered alternative as well as classic. Eva is a leader. She may very well lead her fellow socialites on a field trip to un-conventionalism, or Eva may hush me. She may even bind and gag me and then ship me off to the Island of Lesbos to live. Or worse, she may ignore me, simply choose not to recognize me. Eva is a true believer in pretense. Simulate it never happened, and you can make it go away. I love my mother. I hate my mother. Everyone does.

Why do I sit at 3:00 a.m. scripting my family's reaction? Why do I contemplate? Why do I care? Am I fucked up? Is my need to shock too strong? That is what Eva said when I pierced my nose. I wear a tiny diamond chip on my left nostril. She said it again when I tattooed the small of my back. She said it when I stopped eating meat and when I wear my Dark Jessie outfit. "Jessalyn has always felt the need to shock. She adores negative attention." That has always been my mother's description of her youngest child. I suppose it rings true. Truer than she yet realizes.

It is true I liked the sharp and lovely pain when the piercing gun punctured my left nostril, but that was not nearly as nice as the brutally poetic pain I felt when the artist persistently pricked a purple-blue iris into my pigmentation. Still, that was not as good as the beautiful pain that showed itself on Eva's face after both of these occurrences. I thoroughly enjoyed all three pains. Is that a sad or mean statement to write? Does that make me a masochist? Does that make Eva's perception of me true? Do I yearn for only negativity?

NO! No, No, No!

I define myself differently than my mother does. Expounding, I have lived numb! I have played my part in life without feeling. I have been numb for so long that I have taught my brain to be aroused only when my feelings have a degree of severity. I have lived an emotional indifference; depriving myself of truth has caused my subjective unresponsiveness.

The kiss was severe. Severely divine. I want that feeling again and again and again. I will not sleep. I will not dream a life of happiness. I will live a life of happiness. If it is kissing Shelly that makes me happy, I will kiss her over and over and over, for as long as she will allow.

One kiss, one brush of my lips, one caress, one touch, one taste, and I have grasped the hidden truth. Regardless of all logic and all consequences, I have finally found my beauty within.

MAGGIE

"Chains do not hold a marriage together. It is threads, hundreds of tiny threads, which sew people together through the years.
That's what makes a marriage last...more than passion or even sex."

Simone Signoret

December 15,1999

Happy Holidays to all our family and friends.

Can you believe twelve months have already passed and 2000 is upon us? It seems like only yesterday I was typing out last year's Christmas letter. I am looking forward to a new year. I always see it as a fresh beginning, full of hope, promise, and resolution. This year Daniel and I have not only made resolutions for ourselves, but we have also made quite a list for our children.

This past year has been a very busy one for our family. It was full of hurry, but packed with fun. We claim that we would like to go slower, but I honestly believe that we are just hyper people.

Erin, our oldest, is now a junior at St. Mary's. I realize in a blink of time I will be sending her off on her own, so it's very important that I not blink. Erin has loved St. Mary's, and we are proud that she was able to find a niche and be happy in high school (sometimes a daunting task). Erin plays the clarinet and is very musical. Daniel and I have no idea where this talent came from.

Ryan is now in second grade at St. Peter's Elementary. He claims to love recess and gym class. He hates his uniform, spelling tests, and fish on Fridays. Ryan is also playing hockey, which he loves, and I love watching him.

Molly, our baby, is now three years old. Molly is attending preschool at St. Catherine's twice a week. It was an adjustment at first, but now *I'm* doing fine. It's been good for Molly too.

As you can see from our photo, we have added a new member to the family. Bailey, our Irish setter, is eight months old and already sixty pounds. She is a very happy, hyper, energetic, yet sweet puppy who makes sure I get my exercise.

As for Daniel and me, he is still practicing law with Simon, Ussing, Clemmons, and Kline. We joke that the initials are "SUCK." Daniel also enjoys helping coach Ryan's hockey team. I have been busy volunteering my services at all three schools. I thought I was going to have much more time on my hands once preschool started. How wrong I was! The sisters are very good at finding lots to do for stay-at-home moms.

In all, our family is truly blessed and is looking forward to a Merry Christmas and Happy Millennium.

Season's Greetings,
The Clemmons
Daniel, Maggie, Erin, Ryan, and Molly

What a load of shit! After writing that stupid letter, I felt like I could puke. People can't honestly enjoy getting these holiday greetings. Just once I would like to receive a Christmas letter with a little substance behind it, not the self-absorbed, unrealistic, boasting proclamation that I write and receive every year. How refreshing it would feel to tell the blatant truth, to be real!

Wouldn't Daniel just shit his pants if I vented in our holiday letter? What if I unveiled the naked truths that we have covered with fashionable clothes and smiles? What if I wrote the ugly crap that we have been living these past eleven months, the crap that truly matters and makes or breaks our days and nights.

I can do this. I can print it out on light green stationary with a holly border. I can place it in a foil envelope and seal it with a gold sticker. I can use the Michelangelo angel stamps. I'll even include a different photo of our happy family. I know, the vacation picture taken on the beach in Tampa. Daniel is so sunburned in that photo that you can't tell where his red hair stops and his red face begins. Erin is wearing a skimpy bikini and is pouting, because we won't let her walk the beach alone. Ryan has his tongue out and his eyes crossed, and Molly is pulling my hair. I am the only one smiling at the camera. Actually, I'm clenching my teeth through the painful hair pull, but I still look the best. Wouldn't Daniel just shit?

The Clemmons Family's First Annual *Honest* Christmas Letter
The truth shall set me free!

December 15, 1999

Hey All,

I hope you all are having the commercial, pretentious, and shallow Christmas that you are striving for. Guess what? I've decided to be real this year.

First let me start this letter with a note of apology to all who will be offended. I mean no harm; however, I found the Y2K bug. It is up my ass.

Since this letter is meant to be real, I will be the first to admit that this year has sucked for my family, and unfortunately, it doesn't show any signs of getting better anytime soon.

For starters, we adopted a puppy this year. Not just any puppy, a gigantic Irish setter named Bailey. Getting a dog was not my decision. In fact, I was against the idea from the start. I eventually caved in, because of the loud whining of my family. I mean really, what a bitch I would be if I didn't allow my children a dog, right? Right! So now we have a dog, a big, red dog, like Clifford, except not as bright. I have heard many people say that Irish setters are very smart animals. These people are wrong, or as luck would have it, we have the only retarded Irish setter ever produced.

Bailey seems to be as untrainable as our children. She does everything a puppy does, plus a few more stupid things. Bailey loves to jump on people when they enter my home, and she likes to sniff up their crotches. She loves to howl and disturb our neighbors, especially when we put her out to potty late at night or in the wee hours of the morning. She does not potty at that time, No, that is her barking time. She pees once we bring her back into the house.

Bailey loves to chew. She has devoured things like my shoes, my underwear, the remote control, the gas grill cover, toilet paper, three school books, several pencils, and the molding around our home. She has also chewed on Ryan's baseball mitt, numerous toys, all the Barbie doll heads, my couch, and the bottom of our kitchen table. The list could go on forever, but I would like to end this letter sometime soon, and I'm sure you want me to also. Bailey's favorite delicacy is shit.

That's right, she eats her own shit; that is, if she hasn't rolled in it first, which she also loves to do.

The only good news is big dogs don't live as long as smaller dogs.

Now onto motherhood. Let me be honest in saying motherhood is a chore, or rather a test, and I'm failing. As for being a wife, I'm not happy with that either, but that is mostly Daniel's fault, because he has not been much of a husband. Sorry, Mother Clemmons, but your son has it coming.

My children seem to be spoiled brats, and my house is never completely clean. In all honesty - since honesty is what this Christmas letter is about - I am dreading this holiday season, and here are just a few reasons why. The pine needles from our real tree have already broken my vacuum cleaner. We can't get the hanging lights above the garage to work, and as always, we have spent far too much money on commercialism.

These are family traditions that have always helped make the season unbearable. There are many more traditions that my family partakes in. Each one helps make me slightly more insane.

Tradition 1, Daniel's favorite, is cutting down a real tree. We spent last weekend doing it, and every year, with each growing child, it gets worse. Erin did nothing but bitch all day about having to be with her family—as if! Ryan relentlessly bugged the shit out of both his sisters, and Molly cried, yet each year we continue to do it, just as each year we hang lights, we decorate, and we shop. And each year these activities are associated with being cold, hearing complaints that others are cold, fighting, frustration, hunger pangs, cursing, and sometimes real physical pain or even a trip to the E.R. They are never associated with the birth of the Christ child. What have we done?

Another joyous tradition is choosing extended family to spend time with. This task always causes some stepping on toes and hurt feelings, which seems to work out okay in the end, as long as you remember the green bean casserole and gifts.

This year we will be spending our Christmas Eve with Daniel's family at the home of Mother Clemmons. This is never much fun for me, because after eighteen years of marriage to Daniel, I am still made to feel unworthy of the honor. I know I will spend hours picking the perfect gifts for Daniel's family members, only to have them snubbed. I will spend half the morning preparing the most special and colorful recipe I could find, only to be outdone by Daniel's mother.

As bad as that seems, Christmas Day with my family should be far worse, only because I have been elected host. What host actually means is that I will have to scrub my home from top to bottom to keep my anal-retentive brother-in-law (that would be you, John) from talking behind my back. It also means we have to make a great fuss over Great Aunt Delaney's famous annual Christmas dressing. Let me be the first to say it: I hate that stuffing! (Auntie Delaney, you put far too much sage in the recipe, and not everyone loves mushrooms, namely me. Neither should you mix mushrooms with raisins and nuts. Do one or the other, Aunt Delaney, not both.)

But hey, family is family, right? I need to shake off my resentment and get my ass in gear. Christmas is coming and the goose is getting fat (so are you, Colleen). Now it's time to unfold my holiday apron, a gift from Daniel's sister Kate, two years ago (You have always been a cheap-ass, Kate). Regardless of everything, I will get into the season, even if it kills me. And it may. It is the least I can do for my children. Speaking of children, let me info-tain you with all the little tidbits of our life with kids. Erin has turned into a full-blown teenager, which in actuality is just a sexual misfit. Our musician Erin has not only been blowing her clarinet, but also I actually got the chance to walk in on my beautiful daughter doing the same thing to her boyfriend. The experience was extremely painful for all three of us, and we should probably look into group therapy. I have put our cute little girl on birth control, yet I have not told her father. Oh, the secrets that we keep! Further, this child I live to protect hates me. In her words, I am a bitch, or at least that's what she tells her friends when she is on our phone during all hours of the night. Of course, I'm not supposed to know that she calls me a bitch. It is only by listening on the other end that I have become aware. I have also read her diary and snooped through her room.

These are things that I very seriously swore I would not do as a parent, but I guess if everyone else in this house can break their vows, so can I. As a result of my snooping, I also discovered that Erin smokes, Virginia Slims Menthol Lights 120, to be exact. She has also tried marijuana and has been drunk. You should all be interested in this, because so have your children. My Erin is not partying alone.

As you all know, Erin is beautiful, talented, and popular. What you are learning is that she is a terrible decision maker, she is setting herself up for a broken heart, and she has abandoned her mother's friendship. The teen years are not only difficult on the parents; they are hell for the teen, too.

Ryan, our middle child, is all boy. He is constantly getting into mischief, which has caused many fights between Ryan's second grade teacher and me. This birdbrain lady (that would be Mrs. Carol Howard) has decided that my son is ADHD and is insisting that I put him on Ritalin. The next paragraph is for all you teachers out there who secretly hate children.

What in God's name gives you the right to label my son, or any child, for that matter? To label a child is to take away his or her identity. You are stripping young minds of their creative freedom. You are stunting personal growth and sending out the message that these children are not unique individuals.

First, I do not believe that Ryan has attention deficit or is hyperactive, nor do I believe that my son has a disorder of any kind. He is, however, a seven-year-old active boy, full of zest and life, which is something his uptight, narrow-minded teacher wouldn't know a thing about.

Second, for anyone to recommend that I actually drug my child is completely lewd, crude, and inappropriate.

Third, I would like to know when Mrs. Howard had the time to get her degree in medicine as well as mental health. (I suppose it's possible, since she seems to have no life.)

Because my son Ryan is a rough and tumble, wild little boy who is not medicated, he spends most of his school days sitting in the reflective seat, a time-out chair covered in aluminum foil. I receive daily phone calls from his teacher. Ryan has been put on a daily check sheet that I must sign nightly, and he must turn it into the teacher the following day. From this check sheet, I am supposed to know when to reward my child for good behavior and when to punish him for bad. I have a wild little boy. I say learn to deal with it, Mrs. Howard. He is not the first wild little boy you've had to teach, and he sure as hell won't be the last.

As you can all tell, I am very frustrated with the situation. I have gone to the principal to have Ryan's room changed, which is a useless battle. I vent; he listens; nothing changes. The man has actually gone so far as to defend the birdbrain teacher. I feel as if I am Ryan's only voice. Daniel is no help. He thinks that Ryan will get through this year, and next year will be different. Daniel recalls how much we both loved Erin's third grade teacher. He is convinced Ryan will get the same one, and everything will work out, just the type of rationale that pisses me off. It also confirms how truly different Daniel and I think. The fact that one kid has a good experience with a teacher does not seal the fate for a totally different child. Erin has always been an honor student, able to play the game of school. Ryan, on the other hand, has no idea a game exists.

My fear is that if we allow our child to sit every day of second grade either in a shiny chair or in the principal's office, his self-esteem will be greatly affected, not to mention how far behind he will become. My child's school foundation is being laid now. The mold is being set.

This paragraph is for anyone who disagrees with my opinion of Ryan and who thinks it would be best if we looked into medication. I prefer that you keep your opinions to yourself, thank you very much.

I feel the need to rescue my little boy. My solution is to teach him at home. I want to lead him into his future. I want us to write mathematical equations together, read together, spell together, and discover outer space. Ryan is so inquisitive that he should be an honor to teach. Daniel says home schooling is out of the question. It is also out of the question to switch schools. Daniel is being a prick. He is too much of a traditionalist. As far as he is concerned, all three of our children will follow in our footsteps. They will attend St. Peter's K through 8 and then go on to St. Mary's High School, and if dreams do come true, off to Notre Dame. I say to hell with tradition! What is so great about tradition, if it slowly destroys your child? If things continue as they are, Ryan will be lucky to make it through St. Peter's, let alone St. Mary's and Notre Dame.

Now I move on to tell you all about our third child, beautiful baby Molly. Molly is angelic looking, with sparkling green eyes and a crown of red ringlets. To see her is to look at an angel. To spend a day with her is pure hell. The child is as spoiled and strong-willed as they come. She definitely has a mind of her own and a true Irish temper to go with it.

Molly may be our smartest child yet; however, she absolutely refuses to use the potty—that is, at home. At school she goes potty, and at the playground and swimming pool. In fact, Molly loves to potty at the grocery store, mall, and restaurants. I am praying that she does not have a public-restroom fetish, but at home, Molly prefers to pee and poop in her pretty panties and have me wash them out in the toilet.

Molly also takes the gold in tantrum throwing. She will throw her head back and howl as if she is in pain, if things don't go her way. She is able to drop to the floor in an instant, like a limp noodle. Trying to move the petite little person in this state is damn near impossible. Molly's favorite places to throw these tantrums are the grocery store, restaurants, doctor's offices, shopping malls, libraries, the post office, and banks. Basically, I can't take the child out in public; neither can I complain about her at home.

Molly is the apple of Daniel's eye. She is daddy's little princess. Molly has her father wrapped so tightly around her finger that she will never want for anything. Like I said, she is smart. Even when Molly was found to be the culprit in what I call "The Case of the Mad Cutter," Daniel could only laugh.

Yes, mothers who were unaware, it was Molly who was giving the haircuts. (My apologies to the parents of each victim.) I was unaware that my precious angel had been carrying safety scissors around in her "Hello Kitty" backpack. That was, until the children in Molly's preschool class, dance class, and park near our home had already been scalped. It took approximately three weeks and at least a dozen haircuts before the facts came together and I became aware that my child was the guilty cutter. Big clue: she is also the only one who still has decent hair. (All other suspected children are now off the hook.) I have retrieved the scissors and hidden them. Needless to say, Molly has been restricted from the cutting corner at preschool.

That leaves me with Daniel. Would you like to know how Prince Daniel has been this past year? Daniel has been a lying and cheating bastard. That's right, my husband has been having an affair. Merry Christmas! I have admitted it. I have written it. It is true. (Father O'Leary, did you already hear about this in confession? If you did, please tell Daniel I've got his penance right here!)

I have suspected the affair for months. I have known for weeks. I have only admitted it now. I do not know who the other woman is, so if you receive this holiday letter, you hussy, know that I am on to you.

The woman that my husband has been sleeping with bathes herself in Bath & Body Works products. I can smell the fruity scents on Daniel's clothes and on his skin, and it makes me sick. My husband smells like our oldest daughter. His hussy also leaves secret messages on his cell phone and pager. She buys him Hallmark cards and writes him letters about their great sex (I found one). She made him a CD of love songs (it is in his car). She must prefer boxers to briefs, because Daniel has switched to boxers. I have been snooping not only through Erin's belongings. Daniel's has proven to be more shock worthy.

Of course you're asking yourself, "Why is she so shocked?" Some of you will remember that this is not Daniel's first affair.

Erin was five years old, our only child at the time. Daniel and I had been married seven years (the seven-year itch). The memory is fresh in my mind. Daniel came home to find me packing Erin's and my clothing. How he cried! He fell to his knees and begged me to stay. It felt good to see him in such a pathetic state. I was strong then. I shook him free from my leg like the dog that he was. I loaded our things into the nicer of the two cars, and I drove away without looking back.

Erin and I spent two nights in a hotel enjoying room service and the swimming pool before going to my mother's. There we stayed longer, six months longer. All the while, Daniel courted me like a schoolboy. For two straight months he pleaded and begged. He left flowers and letters, messages, and cards, not only for me, but also for Erin and my mother. He was on a mission to win us back. Erin and Mom were the first to forgive. After all, Daniel does have a way with the ladies.

For four months we dated. I dated my husband! We went to movies and ball games. We spent afternoons in the park with Erin and evenings at restaurants. Daniel was sorry and quite convincing. He told me that he could only love Erin and me. We were his world, and he had to have us in his life. He admitted to not being as strong as me. He regretted his mistake, a stupid, weak, mistake; one that he could never take back and would always regret. Daniel asked, "Could you really let a mistake come between us?" In the end I couldn't.

Daniel and I have known each other our whole lives. We grew up in the same Irish Catholic neighborhood. We went to all the same schools. Our families worshipped at the same parish. Daniel and I went through confirmation class together. We graduated from high school together and went off to college together. Daniel was my first kiss; he was my first sex, and he has been my only love.

Daniel and I made it through the affair. We both grew and learned from the experience. More difficult, I had to learn to trust him again. That took time, lots of time. Daniel was patient. By the time Ryan was out of diapers, Daniel was once again my hero.

This time I have been sucker punched. I am no longer young. I am settled. I have no desire to rip up my three children and take off. I do not have the energy to fight.

Maybe some of you think the affair is my fault. It is no secret that I have never lost the baby weight after Molly was born. I suppose such things happen when you have your third child at age forty. I am telling you this: it should not matter!

It is completely irrelevant that I could stand to lose twenty or more pounds. It is also irrelevant that I now keep my hair short for practical reasons and that my wardrobe is functional and not fashionable. It should not matter that I can see my youth slowly slipping away. I watch my daughter Erin. She is beautiful. Her body is that of a model; her skin is flawless. She is me twenty-five years ago. I feel envious and then I feel guilty. My age, my weight, and looks should not matter. It is not my fault that Daniel is a cheat! Daniel too has aged. His belly hangs over his belt, he picks tiny hairs from his ears, and he farts in his sleep. I can't believe another woman wants this man. We live in a double-standard society!

Do any of you think that I no longer satisfy my husband? Is that what he feels? Many of you have voiced your opinions about our sharing our bed with our children. Some of our family members, friends, and the pediatrician believe that it is a bad habit. I completely disagree with all of you. In some countries they sleep six to a bed. We live in a spoiled society among narrow minds.

I have always loved going to bed as a family. It seems as soon as Ryan started sleeping in his own bed, Molly came along to fill the space. I love watching Daniel stroke Molly's hair as we lay nestled together. I love whispering to each other about our days as the baby lies in the middle. This is what a family is made of! And guess what. Daniel has never been denied sex because we sleep with our children. There are ways around that, if you're wondering. We simply wait until the baby has drifted off and then we tiptoe into her room and ravish each other on the floor or in a toddler bed. Why is this wrong? It feels right.

Maybe some of you are wondering if I want a divorce. No, I do not. There is not an ounce of me that wishes to be alone. I do not glamorize divorce, as some of my friends do. (That would be you, Deb, Linda, and Sue.)

My three best friends are very happily divorced. They love dating. They especially love shared parenting with weekends to themselves, which gives them time to feel young and free again. My friend Sue actually told me that nothing makes a woman hornier than getting a divorce. (You're turning into a real slut, Sue).

I choose comfort over horny any day of the week. Honestly, I like sex with Daniel. He is comfortable; he is my home. It doesn't really matter if it takes two minutes or ten or an hour. Daniel knows where to touch me. I know where he likes to be touched. I am used to his hands, and I am used to his mouth. I know his body and he knows mine. Our bodies have no secrets. We can actually fall asleep while Daniel is still inside of me. He spoons around my back, and we stay connected. (Are you blushing, Mother Clemmons?)

I choose comfort over horny. You may think this is not just my choice. What does Daniel want? Like I said, Daniel likes tradition. Unfortunately he also likes to have his cake and eat it too, so where does that leave me? Sitting here, spitefully venting out a holiday letter that will hurt my husband and others.

I suppose all of you think I should talk to Daniel about his love affair. I suppose you also think we should go to counseling. You may even think I should get my hair done, go on a shopping spree, join Weight Watchers, and start exercising. Maybe you are exactly right, except I don't give a rat's ass what any of you think about my life!

Tomorrow I'll wake up early. I'll brew a full pot of strong coffee, but only drink two cups. The remainder is simply for aroma. I'll make a big pot of vegetable stew and allow it to simmer all day long in a slow cooker, which will fill my house and mind with comfort. I will take Bailey for a walk in the park. I will carry a poop sack and have my arm pulled out of its socket. I will wash Erin's new jeans (hip-hugger bell bottoms, like I used to wear) and Ryan's favorite Batman shirt (once on him, he'll jump off the back of my couch). I may argue with Erin about going out, but I'll try not to. I will brush Molly's hair. She will scream the entire time. I will grocery shop for Christmas cookie ingredients. Molly will throw a temper tantrum. Yes, I will make a hair appointment, and I will have my carpets cleaned, but those things will be for me, not Daniel or the kids. I will pick Daniel's clothes up from the cleaners (or for spite, I won't). I will meet again with Ryan's teacher. This time I will get my point across.

This is my life. It is what I do. It is what I know. I am not that different from all of you. I know in my heart that eventually Daniel and I will work everything out. I know my kids will grow up and I will miss them being young. I know someday my house will be clean and I will have time on my hands.

The only thing you can count on in life is change.

Until next year, Happy Holidays,
Maggie Clemmons

CPSIA information can be obtained
at www.ICGtesting.com
Printed in the USA
BVHW070541130122
626117BV00002B/22